Not Until Now

- A Hope Springs Novel -

Valerie M. Bodden

Not Until Now © 2021 by Valerie M. Bodden.

Cover design: Ideal Book Covers

Valerie M. Bodden
Visit me at www.valeriembodden.com

Hope Springs Series

Not Until Christmas
Not Until Forever
Not Until This Moment
Not Until You
Not Until Us
Not Until Christmas Morning
Not Until This Day
Not Until Someday
Not Until Now
Not Until Then
Not Until The End

River Falls Series

Pieces of Forever
Songs of Home
Memories of the Heart
Whispers of Truth

Contents

A Gift for You . . .

Members of my Reader's Club get a FREE book, available exclusively to my subscribers. When you sign up, you'll also be the first to know about new releases, book deals, and giveaways.

Visit www.valeriembodden.com/gift to join!

Need a refresher of who's who in the Hope Springs series?

If you love the whole gang in Hope Springs but need a refresher of who's who and how everyone is connected, check out the handy character map at https://www.valeriembodden.com/hscharacters.

Two are better than one, because they have a good return for their labor: If either of them falls down, one can help the other up.

                               —ECCLESIASTES 4:9–10

Chapter 1

"Now what, Lord?" Kayla whispered the words into the silence of her car, an unfamiliar restlessness gathering in her soul as she eased the hand accelerator toward the steering wheel to pick up speed on the highway.

She'd always believed God opened and closed doors in a person's life for a reason—but she was struggling to understand the reason he'd literally closed the doors of the camp for disabled children that she'd worked at for the past decade. The place that had gotten her through the hardest time in her life. That had given her a purpose again. That had helped her find him again.

Even so, she trusted he would open another door eventually. "It'd be nice if you'd let me know what kind of door to look for," she muttered, although she knew that wasn't how God tended to work. More likely, she'd walk through the door without realizing it, not seeing it until she had the benefit of hindsight.

In the meantime, she'd focus on enjoying this visit with her brother and sister-in-law in Hope Springs. The small tourist town on the shores of Lake Michigan always eased her spirit. And with Vi's baby due in a little over a month, she could be there to help out. Her heart filled with joy once again that after years of worrying it would never happen, Vi and Nate's dream of starting a family was at last coming true. And that she was going to be an aunt. She had every intention of spoiling her niece or nephew rotten.

Her own biological clock gave a tiny twinge, but she ignored it. The doctors had reassured her after the accident that she'd still be able to have children. But in order to have children, she'd have to marry, and in order to marry, she'd have to date—and in order to date, she'd have to give up some of her independence. An independence she'd worked too hard to regain after her spinal cord injury to give it up for any man.

She settled back into her seat, letting herself pour out her hopes and fears and joys and disappointments to the Lord as the miles passed. By the time she neared Hope Springs, the sun was setting, but her soul felt like new life had been breathed into it. Whatever happened next was in God's hands.

She turned onto the road that would take her the last ten miles into the town, lowering the car's visor as the angle of the setting sun directed its beams directly into her eyes. The car in front of her was driving slower than the speed limit, but she didn't mind. She opened her window a crack, inhaling deeply even as she shivered in the frigid November wind that whistled into the car. The scent of pine and cold tickled her nose, and she smiled. She would enjoy Thanksgiving and Christmas with Nate and Vi, then figure out her next step from there.

"See, Lord, I can be pa—" She gasped as the car in front of her swerved once, then veered off the road and into the ditch, where it traveled a good fifty yards before coming to a stop.

Shoving the hand control forward to slow her own car, Kayla jerked the wheel toward the shoulder. Jamming the car into park, she grabbed her phone and punched in 911. As soon as it started to ring, she hit speaker and tossed the phone into the center console, then opened her door. Reaching toward the passenger seat, she gripped her wheelchair frame and flipped it over herself and out the open door. With her other hand, she shoved a wheel onto the frame. Then, balancing the chair against the door, she yanked the other wheel across the seat and rammed it on before she shoved her seat cushion into place.

"911. What's your emergency?" The voice came from the phone she'd stashed in the console.

"There's been an accident on Highway 10." Thank goodness she'd driven this way enough that the roads had become familiar to her. "A car went in the ditch."

Kayla barely heard the woman's reply that a squad car was on the way as she braced her hands on the seat to scoot her bottom as close to the edge of the car as possible. Bracing her left hand on her wheelchair and gripping the steering wheel with her right, she shifted her body into the chair. Quickly, she lifted one leg at a time onto the chair's footrest, then backed away from her car. She scanned the scene but could see no indication of what had caused the accident. The road was deserted, and though it was cold, there was no ice.

She eyed the shallow ditch, then with a quick decisiveness leaned back and gave a tug on her wheels to pull her chair into a wheelie. With her hands firm on the hand rims, she guided the chair in a controlled roll down the small hill and through the dried grass toward the car.

When she reached the car, she let her front wheels drop. Through the driver's window, she could see a woman's form slumped over the steering wheel, and her breath caught. "Please, Lord, no."

"Please help." The faint sound of a child's voice yanked Kayla's attention to the back seat. A little girl with tear-streaked cheeks gazed at her with wide eyes.

Kayla turned her wheelchair so she could open the girl's door. "Help is coming. Are you okay?"

"Mommy!" The girl bolted out of the car and tugged open the driver's door, clutching her mom's arm and shaking it.

Kayla reached gently for the girl. "Help is coming," she repeated. "They'll help your mommy." *Please, Lord, let that be true.* "Can you tell me what happened?"

The girl blinked at her, and Kayla wasn't sure she'd understood the question. But just as she was about to ask again, the girl said, "We were coming home from riding lessons, and I asked Mommy if we could get ice cream, and she said no, and I said, 'pretty please with a cherry on top,' and she said, 'Ruby Jane.' And then she took both hands off the steering wheel and grabbed her head and didn't say anything else. And then we went off the road. I didn't mean to make her mad." The girl's eyes filled with tears again.

Kayla reached for her hand and held it tight. "I'm sure she wasn't mad. Your name is Ruby Jane?"

"Just Ruby. Mommy only calls me Ruby Jane when I'm sassy."

"Okay, Ruby. My name is Kayla."

In the distance, the sound of sirens cut through the sharp air. "Here comes the ambulance. Let's get out of their way." She and Ruby moved away from the car as an ambulance pulled onto the shoulder and paramedics scrambled out.

"Kayla?" One of the paramedics did a double take. Nate and Vi's friend Jared. "Are you all right?"

She nodded. "I was following their car when it went off the road."

"Did you see what caused it?"

Kayla shook her head. "Nothing that I noticed. But Ruby said her mom grabbed her head before driving off the road."

Jared nodded, giving her a grim look. His eyes went past her to Ruby. "And you're Ruby? I think I've seen you at church."

The girl nodded.

"Are you hurt?"

The girl nodded again, and Kayla's stomach dropped. How could she not have thought to check the girl for injuries?

"Where does it hurt?" Jared moved closer and squatted in front of Ruby.

She held up her hand, revealing a band-aid on her finger. A relieved laugh escaped Kayla.

"Anywhere else?"

Ruby shook her head.

"Good." Jared straightened. "Can you tell me your mom's name?"

"Bethany Moore." Ruby's voice was timid but proud.

"All right, good job, sweetie. Why don't you go with Kayla and wait over there? We're going to help your mom." He jogged toward the car, where another paramedic had already begun working on Bethany.

"Come on." Kayla led Ruby toward her own car. It was too cold for the little girl to stand out here without a jacket.

"What are they doing to her?" The girl's eyes went straight back to the car in the ditch the moment Kayla had gotten her settled into the back seat.

Kayla glanced over her shoulder, to where the paramedics were lifting Bethany onto a stretcher. "That's my friend Jared, and he's really good at helping people who are hurt, so you don't have to be scared. He's going to help your mom." She sent up a quick prayer for God to guide Jared's hands.

"Where are they taking her?"

Kayla bit her lip. "They're going to bring her to the hospital to get her more help."

"What about me?" The girl sounded so lost that Kayla wanted to sweep her into her arms. But she didn't want to scare her more. The truth was, she had no idea what would happen to the girl now.

"Can you stay with her?" Jared called as they reached the shoulder with the stretcher. "Ethan's on his way in another rig. He's going to want to check the girl. And the police are going to need your statement." They slid the stretcher into the ambulance.

"Of course." The words were barely out of her mouth before Jared climbed into the ambulance, pulling the door closed behind him seconds before the ambulance roared off, its sirens shrieking and lights flashing in the gathering dusk.

"Mommy." Ruby's voice cracked, and this time Kayla leaned over to pull her into a hug.

"It will be okay. We'll go see her in a few minutes." She didn't know where the *we* had come from. But she *did* know she wasn't leaving this little girl until she knew Ruby wouldn't be alone.

A police car and a second ambulance rolled to a stop, and Nate and Violet's friend Ethan jumped out of the ambulance and jogged toward them, a police officer close behind.

"Hi, Kayla." He squatted next to her wheelchair and looked at the girl in Kayla's arms. "Who's your friend?"

"This is Ruby." Kayla shifted so Ethan could get a better view of the girl.

"Hi, Ruby. How old are you? Wait—" He held up a finger. "Don't tell me. Twenty."

"I'm seven." The girl giggled, and Kayla could have hugged Ethan. She supposed knowing how to comfort kids came with the territory, since he was a dad.

"Seven?" Ethan feigned shock. "You're way too brave to be seven. Does anything hurt?"

The girl shook her head, and Ethan pulled out a pen light and shined it into her eyes, then unwound the stethoscope from around his neck. After listening to her heart and checking her pulse, he felt her arms, legs, and head. "Well, it looks like you're as healthy as a horse."

The girl giggled again.

Instead of getting up, Ethan settled onto the gravel, as if he were going to stay for a chat. The police officer, who had been examining the crashed car, came up behind him. "Can you tell me what happened?"

"Mommy was driving me home from riding lessons, and I was asking for ice cream." Guilt flooded the girl's face again, and Kayla rubbed her back. "And she said my name, and then she grabbed her head like this—" Ruby lifted her hands to her temples and squeezed her head. "And then she drove off the road."

"Did she say anything else after that?" Ethan asked.

Ruby shook her head. "I kept calling for her, but she wouldn't answer me. I prayed that God would send someone to help us. And he did."

Kayla let out a shaky breath. *Is that why you brought me here right now, Lord?*

"He sure did." Ethan glanced at Kayla with a quick smile, but his eyes were somber. She wanted to ask what he was thinking but didn't want to scare the girl. Ethan hopped up from the ground and held out a hand to Ruby. "Want to take a ride in my ambulance?"

Ruby looked to Kayla. "Can you come with me?"

"Of course." She had no idea if that was allowed or not, but one way or another, she was sticking with this girl.

"Actually, I need you to stay and give your statement," the officer chimed in.

"I don't want to go without Kayla." Tears splattered onto the little girl's cheeks.

Kayla turned to Ethan. "Can you wait a few minutes?"

Ethan nodded. "For my friend Ruby? Of course."

"Let's go over here." The officer gestured toward his car, and Kayla followed, making sure to give Ruby a reassuring thumbs-up over her shoulder.

After she'd recounted how the car had gone off the road, the officer lowered his voice, asking, "And was the driving erratic before the incident? Crossing the center line, changing speed abruptly . . ."

Kayla bit her lip. "The car was going a little slowly, but nothing erratic that I noticed."

The officer gave a knowing nod. "Probably drunk," he muttered.

Kayla's heart sank. She had only too much experience of the cost of drunk driving. But she didn't want to believe that any mother would drive drunk with her child in the back seat.

An overwhelming desire to protect the girl overcame her. "What will happen to Ruby?"

The officer shrugged. "We'll notify family. I found the mother's phone, but she doesn't have any emergency contacts listed. Hopefully, the little girl knows her dad's name. Otherwise, it could take a bit to track someone down."

They made their way back to Ethan and Ruby, who had Ethan's stethoscope tucked into her ears and was holding it to her own heart. She pulled it off and looked up as Kayla and the officer reached them. "Can we go see Mommy now?"

"Yes. But I need to call your dad to have him meet you at the hospital," the officer said. "Do you know his name?"

Ruby shook her head. "I don't have a daddy."

The officer nodded, as if he'd suspected as much. "What about your grandma and grandpa?"

"My grandma and grandpa are in heaven."

Kayla's heart melted a little more for the poor girl. "How about an aunt or uncle or—"

The girl brightened. "I have an uncle!"

"Yeah?" Kayla reached to squeeze her hand. "That's good. What's his name?"

"Uncle Cam." Pride filled the girl's voice. Cam must be some uncle.

"Do you know where he lives? Close to here?"

"Far away, Mommy said. That's why he doesn't come to visit."

The radio on the officer's shoulder crackled to life, and a voice spewed out some codes Kayla didn't understand. The officer closed his eyes for a second, shaking his head. "I need to get to that. Take her to the hospital and have them contact child services to start processing her. We'll try to track down the uncle, but we don't have much to go on . . ."

"Wait." Kayla pointed to the phone in his hand. "Ruby, does your mom have your uncle's phone number?"

Ruby shrugged. "I think so."

"It's locked," the officer said, before speaking into his radio to say he was en route to the next emergency. He passed the phone to Ethan. "Have them give it to CPS. Maybe they can get someone to unlock it and track down the uncle." With that, he dashed for his car, taking off in a spray of gravel a second later.

"All right. Ready for that super cool ambulance ride?" Ethan turned to Ruby, who gave Kayla an uncertain look.

"Will you come with me?"

"I can't leave my car here, but I'll be right behind you, okay?"

As Ruby nodded, Kayla's eyes fell on the phone in Ethan's hand. "Ruby, do you know your birthday?"

Ruby gave a proud nod. "Yep. April 10."

Kayla held out her hand for the phone, then quickly tapped 0410 on the lock screen, letting out a sound of triumph as the phone unlocked. She held it up to show Ethan, then quickly scrolled through the contacts until she came to the name Cam.

She glanced at Ethan. "I'll make the call, then meet you at the hospital." She had a feeling this wasn't the kind of conversation a little girl should overhear.

"You're sure you want to make the call? We have people who can—"

Kayla shook her head. She didn't know why she felt it was important that she be the one to call, but she did. It was like the moment she'd opened Ruby's car door, she'd forged a connection with her. She felt responsible for whatever happened to her next.

Ethan studied her for a moment, then nodded and led Ruby to the ambulance.

Kayla waited until it pulled onto the road, then drew in a breath and tapped the number.

Hopefully in the next three seconds she'd receive some divine insight into how to tell a complete stranger that his sister had been in an accident.

Chapter 2

*W*hat was wrong with him? Tonight was a big night. Cameron should be content, if not ecstatic.

He took in the spacious living room of his boss's mansion—big enough to fit three of the houses he grew up in.

The place was packed with mingling and laughing people, all of them here to congratulate Cameron on the multi-million dollar merger he'd just brokered.

The truth was, he would have preferred a small celebration to this over-the-top soiree. But George Holt had a flair for the dramatic. And putting up with the party was a small price to appease George. If Cameron played his cards right and continued to oversee deals like this, the law firm of Holt, Barrow, and Wright would someday be Holt, Barrow, Wright, and Moore. Maybe sooner, if tonight went well.

"Are you ready?" His girlfriend Danielle leaned over him, her hand coming to his pocket, where she knew very well the little ring box was, given that she'd put it there herself.

He nudged her hand away. "I'm ready." He blew out a breath, trying to figure out why he felt sicker and sicker the closer they came to this moment.

It was the next logical step. The key to his future: perfect job, perfect promotion, perfect life.

He only felt sick because they were doing this so publicly. If he had his way, he'd ask Danielle at a small, intimate meal, with candles on the table and soft music playing in the background. But like her father, Danielle preferred drama and attention.

He swallowed down the agitation in his stomach and touched the box in his pocket.

"You're sure you don't want to use my mother's ring?" He knew better than to ask again, but he had to try one more time.

Danielle made a face. "We've had this conversation a thousand times, Cameron. The diamond in that ring is barely visible."

"It was all my dad could afford at the time," he muttered. "It has sentimental value."

Danielle laughed. "Not to me. I never met your parents, remember?"

Cameron bit his tongue before he could lash at her that that was because they were *dead*.

"Lucky for me—" She batted her fingertip against his nose. "*You* can afford more. Anyway, you already bought this one. Let me see it again."

With a sigh, he pulled it out of his pocket and discreetly opened it to reveal the three-carat round cut ring she had picked out.

She smiled, then whispered for him to put it away before he ruined the big moment.

As he tucked the ring back into his pocket, it hit him—he was about to tie himself to this woman forever. And suddenly he knew he couldn't do it.

It wasn't so much that he was afraid of commitment. But he *was* afraid of committing to the wrong person. And right now, he was afraid that might be Danielle.

He swallowed hard, then leaned closer to her. "Danielle, I think we need to—"

"Excuse me, everyone." George's voice boomed from the top of the high balcony that overlooked the living room, and Danielle gripped Cameron's arm.

"This is it," she whispered, her breath too hot in his ear.

"But I need to talk—"

She hushed him with a wave of her hand.

"Thank you all so much for coming tonight to celebrate my protege, Cameron Moore," George was saying from the balcony.

Hearty applause broke out across the room, and Cameron lifted a hand in thanks. He needed a way out. Right. Now.

"When my daughter first brought Cameron home, I thought he was going to be some young punk who didn't stand a chance—at the firm or with my daughter." Laughter echoed off the marble staircase. "But with this deal, Cameron has more than proved he deserves his place in the firm." He cut off as a ringtone blared into the room. It took Cameron a moment to realize it was coming from his own pocket.

"Sorry." He fumbled in the pocket of his suit coat for the phone, not managing to get his hands on it until it had blasted its brassy beat into the room two more times. He nabbed the button to dismiss the call and tucked the phone as discreetly as possible back into his pocket.

Danielle gave him a withering look, but her father laughed. "On the clock even now, eh, Cameron? This guy would do anything short of sell his soul to get a deal done." A smattering of laughter rippled across the room.

The blare sounded from Cameron's pocket again.

Oh, for Pete's sake.

This time he managed to snatch it out of his pocket on the first attempt.

"Silence it," Danielle hissed from next to him.

He nodded, scrolling to the volume settings and setting it to vibrate instead. As he did, he gave a cursory glance at the number of the missed calls.

Bethany.

His stomach turned. He hadn't realized he still had his sister's number in his phone. He hadn't spoken to her in ten years or more. And he'd gone through at least half a dozen phones in that time. Apparently, her number had followed him from one to the next.

"What do you say we get the man of the hour up here?" George called. "I believe he has an announcement of his own that might make us closer . . . But I'd better stop talking before I steal his thunder."

Danielle squeezed Cameron's arm tighter. "This is going to be amazing," she whispered, nudging him toward the stairway and putting on a bland look so she could pretend to be surprised when he pulled out the ring.

"I really think we should talk—"

But Danielle shoved him harder. "Don't embarrass me, Cameron." She managed to get the words out without moving a muscle of the smile plastered to her lips.

He swallowed dryly. He could do this. Danielle was the right woman for him. He just had a momentary case of cold feet. Perfectly normal.

As he stood, his phone jangled against his chest, a muffled vibrating sound coming from under his coat.

Danielle's eyes shot fire. "I told you to silence it." Again, her lips didn't move even a fraction.

"I did," he whispered back, pulling the phone out. His sister's number again.

Three calls in a row after a decade of no contact. A rock settled in his stomach. Something was wrong, that much he was certain of.

And as much as he didn't owe her a single thing—not even a simple phone call—he couldn't ignore it.

"So, without further ado, I give you Cameron Moore." George's voice was muted as Cameron's heart pounded in his ears.

"I'm sorry." Cameron whispered the words to Danielle. "I have to take this." He slipped past her and out the massive front door, vaguely aware that George was calling after him.

The LA night was cool, but a prickly sweat broke out on his forehead as he answered.

"Bethany." He made his voice hard, unyielding, even as a tiny part of him—the part that had worshiped his big sister as a child—let off the tiniest glimmer of hope. "This had better be important. I swear, if you need—"

"I'm sorry." A woman's voice, tentative but calm and sounding nothing like Bethany, came through the phone. "Is this Cam Moore?"

Cameron dropped onto the sprawling stairway, leaning his head against the wrought-iron railing. He'd always known this day was coming. Ever since the first time he'd caught Bethany sticking a needle in her arm. Thought sometimes that she deserved it, actually. But that didn't mean he was ready for it.

"This is Cameron, yes. Who is this? Where's Bethany?" The questions came out oddly croaky.

"This is Kayla Benson. I'm sorry to have to tell you this, but your sister was in an accident."

He couldn't pull in air. Couldn't exhale what was already in his lungs. So he just sat there, lungs burning.

"Um. Are you still there?" The voice on the other end of the phone was overly gentle.

"Is she dead?" They were the first words he could think of.

"The doctors are working on her now. They don't know if . . ."

"They don't know if she'll make it." He nodded, his heart suddenly turning to stone. He'd always figured that one day Bethany would take things too far, that she'd end up costing herself her own life. The same way she'd cost their father and mother their lives. "Was she high?"

The woman made a strange sound, and Cameron couldn't tell whether it was a denial or an affirmation. Not that it mattered.

"I can stay with your niece until you get here."

"My niece? What niece?" Cameron tried to process the word. If he had a niece, then that meant Bethany had . . . a daughter? Was that even possible?

"Yes. Ruby. I said I'd stay with her until you could get here."

"Get there?" Why did he feel suddenly like a parrot, unable to form his own sentences?

"Yes. How long do you think that will be?"

Cameron's head cleared suddenly. Bethany had brought this all on herself. It was too bad she'd decided to bring a little girl into it too, but that wasn't his problem. He had his own life. And it had nothing to do with Bethany. "Look, I'm kind of in the middle of something here. I need to go."

"What about Ruby?"

He rubbed his face, remembering suddenly that Ruby had been the name of the doll he'd bought at a garage sale and given to Bethany for her tenth birthday. He'd only been five at the time and hadn't realized until years later that Bethany had no longer played with dolls by then—but even so, she'd kept it in her bed long enough that her friends had teased her about it. To which she'd always answer that it was special.

But just because his sister had named her daughter after a doll didn't obligate him to care. "I don't know. What about the kid's dad?"

"She doesn't have one."

Cameron curled a lip. What did he expect? But that still didn't make the kid his problem.

"You'll have to find someone else, then. Thanks for the call." He pulled the phone away from his ear.

"Wait. No." The woman's shout was loud enough for him to hear even with the phone three feet away.

He lifted it again. "I can send some money. Would that help?"

"Money?" Disgust dripped off the woman's words. "The girl's mother is in the hospital, she has nowhere to go, and you think money is going to fix it?"

In his experience, money fixed most things. Which was why he worked so hard to earn it. "You can hire someone to watch her. Or you can watch her—use the money for whatever you need."

"Me?" The woman sounded incredulous. "She doesn't even know me. I just happened to witness the accident. She needs *family*. And as far as I can tell, that's you."

Family. He almost snorted. His sister had never understood the meaning of that word.

Anyway, he was no more family to this girl than this Kayla person was.

"Look, Cam, I know I don't know you or your situation," the woman was saying now. "But I have to believe you know the right thing to do is to be here for your niece."

"You're right." He pushed to his feet. "You don't know my situation. And you have no right to expect me to— I didn't ask you to call me."

"She's a little girl, Cam." Kayla's voice was equally heated. "She didn't ask for this either. And she doesn't get a say in what happens next. Unlike you."

Something hit Cameron in the gut. He'd felt helpless like that once. Like all these things were happening around him that he had no control over. And even if that had been Bethany's fault, was he going to take it out on a little girl?

He did some mental calculations. He could move a few meetings, maybe get George to cover for him for a few days. "I can be there on Monday."

"Monday? That's three days away." He couldn't tell if that was disgust or amazement in her voice. "Where's she going to go until then?"

"I don't know. What do you want me to do, just drop everything?"

"That's exactly what I want you to do. Your niece needs you *now*."

He let out a sharp breath. Something about the idea of being needed did him in. He shook his head even as the words came out of his mouth. "Yeah. Okay." He dropped his chin to his chest. "Where is she?"

"At the hospital in Hope Springs."

"*Where?*" He'd never heard of the place.

"Hope Springs." She repeated the name louder, as if maybe he hadn't heard her the first time.

"What state is that in?"

"Wisconsin. You really don't know where your sister lives?"

The door behind Cameron opened, and he turned to find Danielle barreling down on him, fire flaring from her eyes. He made what he hoped was an apologetic face and held up a finger, turning his back on her as he spoke into the phone again. "I'll catch the next flight I can, but I probably won't get there until early morning. Can you stay with her until then?"

"I'll stay with her." Kayla's voice was gentle. "You're doing the right thing."

He shook his head. He highly doubted that anyone else would see it that way.

Least of all himself.

Or Danielle, judging by the anger pulsing across her face the moment he hung up.

She crossed her arms in front of her. "We'll skip over the part where I was totally humiliated for a moment. Where exactly are you going?"

"My sister was in an accident, and I have to go to Wisconsin to take care of my niece." Cameron reached for her, but she jerked away. He sighed. He wasn't necessarily a hugger, but right now he felt so mixed up that a little bit of comfort would go a long way.

"What are you talking about? You don't have any family."

No family that he cared to acknowledge anyway. "My sister and I haven't talked in years. I didn't know I had a niece until just now." That part still didn't seem real. None of this did.

"So why do you have to go then?" Danielle pursed her full lips. "They obviously don't mean very much to you if you've never even met your niece."

"No. I know. But they're still my family. I feel like I have to go." He couldn't explain even to himself why he felt that way. Bethany had never brought him anything but heartbreak, so why he felt any obligation whatsoever was beyond him. All he knew was that he couldn't shake what Kayla had said about his niece needing family.

He'd known that need more than once in his life.

"This is just something I have to do. I'll be back before you know it. I'll go, get things sorted out, find someone who can take care of the girl, and then I'll be back."

"And we'll have an even bigger party and do this." She raised an eyebrow and wiggled her ring finger.

The slither of doubt from earlier went through him again, but he pushed it aside. Maybe some time away was what he needed. A chance to put things in perspective. To realize he just had cold feet.

Absence made the heart grow fonder, wasn't that what they always said?

He leaned to kiss her cheek, but she turned away at the last second.

He shrugged. He didn't have time for her drama. "I'll be back before you know it. Tell your father I'll manage everything remotely. I'll call Mary to set it up." His secretary was a whiz at things like that.

He turned and marched down the steps, toward what, he didn't even know.

Family, he supposed.

Chapter 3

*S*o this was where his sister had ended up.

Cameron scrubbed at his face, glancing at the clock on the dashboard of the budget line sedan he'd picked up at the airport. Not his usual wheels, but apparently it was the best they could do on short notice in this backwater.

Four a.m.

In the dark, the little town was completely still, except for the rhythmic in and out of the waves along the shore of what his phone's GPS told him was Lake Michigan. He wouldn't have figured the sleepy town as Bethany's kind of place. How had she even found it, let alone come to live here?

He followed his phone's directions to the hospital, where he pulled into a parking spot, then just sat. Exhaustion had set in on the plane, but he hadn't been able to sleep, his thoughts swirling between Danielle, Bethany, his parents, the woman on the phone—and even the niece he'd never met. He hadn't even thought to ask how old she was.

Well, sitting here wasn't going to get this over with any faster. He shoved his door open and stepped into the morning dark, a shiver immediately working its way up his spine as a sharp wind cut through the dress shirt he hadn't bothered to change out of before rushing to the airport. He ducked back into the car and grabbed his suit coat. At least it helped cut the wind a tad. If he was going to be here more than a day or two, he'd have to invest in a winter jacket.

But hopefully it wouldn't come to that.

He'd find his niece and make arrangements for her, then get back to his normal life.

With Danielle?

Of course with Danielle.

He'd realized on the plane that cold feet were only a feeling. And he well knew that feelings couldn't be trusted.

Logic could.

And his relationship with Danielle was nothing if not logical. She was as ambitious and as dedicated to the firm as he was. She understood the long hours and the constant interruptions. And, like him, she didn't want a family. Their relationship made sense.

See? Already the trip had given him some perspective. That was all he'd needed. Now he could get things figured out here and go home and continue to live his life as he'd planned.

He pushed through the hospital's revolving door, and a wave of memories assaulted him—powerful enough to stop him in his tracks for a moment. Dad. The ambulance. The sirens. The doctors shaking their heads. Mom's desperate cry. And Bethany nowhere to be found.

He shook the thoughts off and made his way to the front desk, where a much too bubbly receptionist directed him to the ICU. A minute later, he stepped off the elevator and strode past the empty counter toward the open waiting room door. A dark-haired woman sat on a worn-looking couch on the far side of the room. His eyes went to the young girl—maybe three or four years old, though he had no experience guessing children's ages—lying on the couch next to her. With blonde hair framing her face and a pert upturned nose, the kid was the spitting image of a young Bethany. At least he knew he was in the right place.

"You must be Kayla."

"Shh. She just fell asleep." The woman shot him a dirty look, her whisper scolding. "She's exhausted."

"All right." He lowered his voice. "I'll take her off your hands."

Kayla gave him a doubtful look. What did she want—identification?

"Bethany is out of surgery, but she's in a coma." Her voice was laced with sympathy. "I can stay with Ruby while you talk to the doctor."

"I don't see any doctors around, do you?"

"If you wait a minute, I'm sure they'll—"

He gave an impatient shake of his head. He wasn't ready to deal with whatever had happened. Or with what would happen next. "I'll call later and talk to someone."

He closed the distance to the couch but stopped abruptly as he reached them. How was he supposed to wake the girl up? Shake her? Shout at her? Turn on his phone alarm and let it blare in her ear?

"Can you wake her up, please?" He didn't know why he was still whispering if he wanted the girl to wake up.

Kayla looked at him as if he were crazy. "Don't wake her up. She's been through a lot."

"How am I supposed to get her to my car then?"

"Carry her." She said it like it was the most obvious answer in the world.

He sighed, studied Ruby's still form, then slid his hands under her and lifted. She was heavier than he'd expected, and he grunted.

The girl curled into him, her head coming to rest on his arm. For some reason, the movement made all of this way too real, and Cam nearly staggered with the fact that he was suddenly responsible for keeping another human being alive. He drew in a slow, quiet breath. If he could finesse deals with multi-million dollar companies, surely he could manage one little girl for a few days.

"Where am I going?" he asked Kayla.

29

"Oh, uh." Kayla pulled out her phone and tapped a few times. "I asked Ruby for her address before. It's 301 Southridge Court."

He gave her a blank look.

"I'm headed that direction anyway. Why don't you follow me, and I'll lead you to the house?"

He could only stare at her, baffled by why this complete stranger who had already given up her entire night was now offering to do more. But his niece wasn't getting any lighter in his arms. And all he really wanted right now was to find a bed and crash. "All right. Thanks."

She nodded, and he turned toward the door, angling his body so he wouldn't bash Ruby's legs—or her head—on the doorframe. He was all the way to the elevator when he realized Kayla wasn't behind him. He considered getting on it without her, but after all she'd done, that seemed too rude. Besides the fact that he hadn't written that address down.

Readjusting his grip on Ruby, he tromped back to the waiting room, stopping in the door as his eyes fell on Kayla using her arms to push her body up and off the couch and into a wheelchair that he'd only vaguely registered before. When she was seated, she lifted first one foot then the other and placed them on the chair's footrest. Her hands went to the rims of the wheels, and she spun the chair toward him.

"Ready?" Her voice was still hushed, her smile calm, as if she hadn't done anything out of the ordinary.

He nodded mutely and stepped back from the door to let her through.

But as he followed her onto the elevator, he couldn't help but wonder. Who *was* this Kayla woman?

The elevator lurched to a stop, and Kayla rolled out, glancing over her shoulder to make sure Cam was following. Ruby's head lolled against his arm—they'd make a cute picture if it weren't for the fact that Cam looked as if he'd rather be anywhere but here. Since the moment he'd walked into the waiting room upstairs, looking like a slightly rumpled version of a guy straight from the pages of *Forbes* or *GQ*, Kayla had been questioning her decision to call him. Everything from his suit to his stance to his surly expression exuded power. He was the kind of man who was used to getting his way. The kind of man who would run right over you if he had to.

Show a little grace, she scolded herself. She didn't even know the man.

As they exited the hospital into the dark of the early morning, weariness pulled on Kayla's eyelids, and she suddenly realized how tired she was. All she wanted was to get to Nate and Vi's and plop onto their guest bed—but not until she saw Ruby safely settled in.

"I'm parked over here." She gestured to the handicapped spots near the doors.

She waited for the usual, surprised, "You drive?" but Cam simply nodded.

"I'm over there." He bobbed his head toward the next row. "I'll pull up behind you."

"Okay." Kayla moved toward her car. "Make sure you put her in the back seat. And put a seat belt on her."

Cam stopped, looking as if he was about to say something, then shook his head and strode off, his back still rigid.

Ten minutes later, Kayla pulled up to the address Ruby had given her. The house was small but cute—at least from what she could tell in the dim streetlights. As Cam's car pulled in next to hers, she grabbed her wheelchair and assembled it, then transferred into it. By the time she was done, Cam had extracted the still-sleeping Ruby from his car.

"How do we get in?" His half-whisper cut through the dark.

Kayla held up the keys the police had pulled out of Bethany's car. Thankfully, there were only two on the key chain, so they wouldn't have to spend all morning figuring out which one it was.

Cam readjusted Ruby to hold out a hand for the keys, and Kayla started to pass them to him, then hesitated. What would the little girl think when she woke up with a strange man in her house? Would that add to the trauma she'd already experienced?

"Maybe I should come in with you. Just until Ruby wakes up. So she won't be scared when she sees you."

She thought she heard a low chuckle in the dark, but it could have been a bird. "Am I that scary?"

Maybe. But Kayla didn't let the word slip off her tongue. "She's been through a lot today. Waking up to a strange man in her house probably isn't going to help."

"Suit yourself. Can we just get inside? It's freezing out here. And she's not exactly a feather."

Kayla snorted. She highly doubted the broad man was having any trouble carrying his tiny niece. But she wheeled toward the front door. Fortunately, the doorway was at ground level, and she didn't have to worry about getting onto a porch in the dark. She slid the key into the lock and turned, grateful when it opened on the first try. She rolled back, gesturing for Cam to pass through with Ruby.

Kayla followed, popping up over the low doorframe with ease and nudging the door closed behind her.

"I can't see a thing," Cam muttered.

Kayla felt along the wall for a light switch. When her fingers fell on it, she flicked it tentatively. A weak light that didn't quite fill the space revealed that they had walked into a small, cozy living room.

"Do you want to put her on the couch for now?" Kayla whispered, pointing to the worn sofa along the far wall.

Cam didn't answer but moved toward the couch and lowered Ruby onto it.

Then he strode out of the room, into what Kayla assumed must be the kitchen. She stared after him for a moment, then let her eyes rove the living room. There wasn't much furniture: just a couch, a large, cushy armchair, a single side table with a small lamp on it—the only source of light in the room as far as Kayla could tell—and a small TV.

Kayla's gaze fell on a blanket crumpled next to a dollhouse made from a cardboard box, and she wheeled toward it, reaching down occasionally to scoot a toy out of her way.

She picked up the blanket and brought it to the couch, draping it over the girl and brushing her hair off her face. Something raw and maternal stirred in her middle, but Kayla pushed it away. It wasn't that she wanted her own child—it was just that she knew the challenges this girl was in for in the days ahead.

Please let her mother live, Lord. She'd been saying the prayer all night, but it had an extra urgency now that she'd met Ruby's uncle. Clearly he wasn't an ideal candidate to raise her.

A low clunking came from the kitchen, and Kayla lifted her head, listening. After a second, there was another clunk. And then another. It almost sounded as if someone was opening and closing cupboards. She supposed Cameron might be looking for some food. Her own stomach was rumbling as well.

She gave Ruby's hair one last stroke, then wheeled toward the kitchen.

Sure enough, Cam was opening cupboard doors, rummaging through the contents, then closing the doors again.

When he'd opened the third cupboard, Kayla spoke up. "You're going to wake Ruby. What are you searching for?"

Cam threw her a dark look and opened the next cupboard. "Bethany's stash."

"Stash of what?"

"Drugs." He lifted out a stack of plates and ran his hand along the back of the cupboard.

"Her tox screen was negative. It was a brain aneurysm." Which he'd know if he'd bothered to talk to the doctors.

Though she knew an aneurysm was life threatening, Kayla had been beyond relieved to learn that Ruby's mother hadn't been driving drunk.

Cam stilled with his hand on a cupboard door. Though his back was to her, she noticed the way his shoulders dipped.

But then his back stiffened again. "That doesn't mean she doesn't have a stash." He opened the last cupboard, shoved the glasses aside, then closed it.

"Didn't find anything?" Kayla didn't know why she felt vindicated. It wasn't like she knew Bethany. But the way her brother seemed so dead set on believing the worst of her made Kayla want to stick up for her.

"She must keep them somewhere else." Cam turned his back on her and stalked into the hallway, which she assumed led to the bedrooms and bathroom.

Kayla watched his retreating form for a moment, then shrugged and made her way back to the living room. He could go on his witch hunt all he wanted. All she cared about was that Ruby wasn't alone and scared when she woke up.

In the living room, Kayla gave the couch a longing look. She ached to lie down and go to sleep herself. But there really wasn't room for her on there with Ruby already sprawled across it.

She shifted in her wheelchair, making herself as comfortable as possible, then tucked her chin to her chest and let herself close her eyes.

Chapter 4

The house was a shoebox, and Cameron had prowled every last inch of it. Still, he hadn't found his sister's stash.

Which meant either Bethany had gotten better at hiding it or—

Or she was clean.

He didn't know why that thought left him unnerved. Maybe because it was too late.

The damage was already done.

As he crept back to the living room, his eyes fell on the window. Outside, streaks of peach and lavender had just started their slow crawl across the sky. Cameron rubbed at his aching temples. He needed sleep. Badly.

But there was nowhere to lie down, unless he wanted to use his sister's bed. His eyes traveled to the ratty old couch, where Ruby was still asleep, a blanket now draped over her—courtesy of Kayla, he supposed. Which only went to prove that she'd be a much better caregiver for Ruby than he was.

His gaze flicked to Kayla in her wheelchair. Her head was tucked into her shoulder, and her eyes were closed, but he couldn't tell if she was sleeping or just resting. He wondered again what she was doing here. Why she was helping them. Why he was letting her.

Maybe because he had no earthly idea how to take care of a kid. He supposed he had to feed it and water it, but beyond that, what was he supposed to do?

Bethany had better recover quickly so he didn't have to worry about it.

What if she doesn't recover? The nagging voice had been tugging at his brain since Kayla had said the word aneurysm. He was no doctor, but an aneurysm was a pretty big deal, as far as he knew. *What if she died?*

He shoved the thought away. More than once over the years, he'd thought about how much better his family's life would have been if that had happened long ago—before she'd cost them everything. But he'd never really meant it.

And if she died now, he'd be saddled with a kid he didn't want.

With a ragged sigh, he rubbed at his cheek—Danielle would hate how scruffy it was—and fell into the oversized armchair, which nearly swallowed him. He was so tired it didn't matter.

It felt like two minutes later when a sound jolted his eyes open. Something warm weighted his legs down, and he glanced at his lap to find a white cat curled on his black pants. He gave it a hard shove, and it flew off his lap with a protesting meow.

"Mommy." The voice was small and plaintive, and it took Cameron a minute to remember where he was, to figure out that it must be his niece talking.

"It's okay, Ruby. You're at home now." Kayla's voice was low and soothing. "I came with you. And your Uncle Cam is here too."

"Uncle Cam?" Ruby turned her wide eyes on him, and he realized with a start that in place of Bethany's dark eyes she had his silvery-blue eye color.

"Cameron." The correction came out automatically. Danielle hated the nickname, so he'd stopped using it.

Kayla's eyes darted to his, filled with disapproval. Well, what? It was his name—he had a right to be called what he wanted.

"Where's Mommy?" The little girl's lip trembled, but she didn't cry.

"She's still at the hospital, sweetie." Kayla reached for the girl's hand. "The doctors are still helping her."

"When will they be done?" The girl's hair stood up in funny tufts, and for a moment, Cameron had a flash of Bethany at that age, all fun and innocence. He missed that girl sometimes.

Kayla tugged the girl closer to her, throwing a desperate look at Cameron.

He shrugged at her. It wasn't like he knew what to do.

"Do you want some breakfast?" Kayla asked the girl.

"Then can we go see Mommy?"

"Of course," Kayla started, but Cameron cut in with a flat, "No."

Ruby broke into tears, and Kayla sent her to the kitchen, promising to be there in a moment, then turned to regard him.

"What?" He crossed his arms. Why did he feel like he had to be on the defensive? She was the one intruding in his life, which until last night had been perfectly ordered.

"You're not going to take her to see her mom?" Her voice was quiet but seething.

"I've got a lot to do." Namely finding Ruby's father so he could take responsibility for his kid and Cameron could go home.

"Are you at least going to go over there yourself? I could stay with Ruby if you want—"

But he cut her off. "I'll call the doctor later."

"She's your sister." Kayla bit her lip as if she hadn't meant to say the words. "Sorry. It's none of my business."

He nodded. That was the truth.

"Do you want me to stay to help with breakfast?" Her voice was less forceful now, but he could see the effort it cost her.

Yes, actually. He wanted her to stay and do all of it. But he really had no desire to spend more time with her. He shook his head, skirting her wheelchair and making his way to the front door. He pulled it open. "Thanks again. I've got it."

She pressed her lips together as she watched him, as if trying to decide whether he could be trusted to care for the girl. But after a moment she called, "Ruby, I need to go. I'll see you soon."

He raised an eyebrow. He had no plans to make Kayla a regular visitor here.

"Bye, Kayla." Ruby came charging into the room and threw her arms around Kayla, who squeezed her back as if Ruby were her own niece.

Then Kayla rolled silently past him and did a quick wheelie over the doorframe.

He closed the door behind her, then blew out a long breath.

Now what?

"I mean, he acted like it was all one big inconvenience that he couldn't be bothered with." Kayla blew a piece of hair off her forehead as she helped unbox a set of Victorian silhouettes for Vi's antique shop. "And the way he treated Ruby—I don't think he said a word to her. Oh wait— I take that back. He corrected her when she called him Cam. Apparently he goes by Cameron." She rolled her eyes. Because clearly his name was the most important thing right now.

"Maybe he's not around kids much," Vi offered, rubbing a hand over her own adorably rounded belly.

"Yeah, maybe," Kayla mumbled. She should try to assume the best of him, she knew that. But something about him made that nearly impossible.

"And he acted like he didn't even care that his sister is in a coma. He doesn't plan to visit her. Or to take Ruby." So much for assuming the best of him. But she couldn't help it. Circumstances had prevented Nate from seeing her when she was in the hospital, but she knew he would have given anything to be at her side.

"Everyone deals with trauma in their own way," Vi said calmly.

Kayla blew out a breath. She knew Vi was right. Kayla had reacted to her own accident with anger in the early years, while Vi had dealt with the death of her first husband by refusing to move on for a long time.

"You're right," she murmured, turning her attention back to the silhouettes. She came across one of a mother pushing a baby carriage. "You should hang this in the baby's room."

Vi took it from her with a smile. "I can't believe this is finally happening." It was true, apparently, what they said about a pregnant woman's glow, as Vi's cheeks were practically radiant.

Kayla reached to squeeze her hand. "You two are going to be the best parents. And I'm going to spoil your kid rotten."

"He or she will be like you then." Nate strode into the store from the back room, and she stuck her tongue out at him. Laughing, he crossed the room and bent to give her a hug. "Sorry I missed you this morning. We had an early rehearsal. And as far as spoiling our kid, don't forget that turnabout is fair play."

"Good luck with that." He knew very well that she had no intention of having kids of her own. "Maybe I'll get a hamster someday and you can spoil that."

Nate and Vi exchanged a look, and she knew she was about to get the whole "never say never" lecture.

Fortunately, Vi's phone rang, cutting them off. As Vi answered it, Kayla took the opportunity to escape to the back room with the empty box. After she'd broken it down, she pulled out her phone. She'd put Cam's number in it last night, in case she needed to reach him while he was on the way. Maybe she should call him now and make sure he'd at least remembered to feed Ruby lunch.

Her finger was hovering over his name when Vi stepped into the room. "That was Jade."

Kayla tucked her phone discreetly back into her pocket.

"I told her about Bethany's accident. I guess Dan already knew. He went to visit Bethany this morning. And he said he'd check on Ruby tomorrow after church. So you can stop worrying."

"Oh, that's great." Knowing the pastor was going to check on Ruby took a weight off Kayla's mind.

But—

"What is it?" Vi eyed her, and Kayla had to laugh. Though she and her sister-in-law had only known each other for seven years, Vi knew her better than probably anyone else.

"I just hate the thought of Bethany being in the hospital alone, you know? Do you think it'd be weird if I went to visit her, considering she's a complete stranger?"

"Yes." Nate popped into the room. "But when have you ever let that stop you?"

"Hey." Kayla wheeled across the room to slug her brother's arm. But she knew without a doubt that if she ever needed anything, Nate—and all his friends—would be there for her. It was too bad Bethany didn't seem to have a family like that.

Well, then we'll have to be her family. She pictured Cam's sour look when he'd said he didn't need any more help. *Whether Cam likes it or not.*

Chapter 5

"I'm bored."

Cameron ground his teeth as he looked up from the ratty old box he'd brought up from the basement. It was the three hundredth time Ruby had uttered those two words today. Somehow, they'd survived their first day together yesterday, mostly because he'd plunked her in front of the TV and told her not to bother him while he worked.

"Can we play checkers?"

Apparently TV only worked as a babysitter for one day.

"I'm busy."

"But Mommy says it's your favorite game."

Cameron set down the stack of useless papers, mildly surprised that Bethany had ever mentioned him. What else had she told the kid about their past? Had she mentioned that checkers had been her favorite too, until getting high had become more important than spending time with her little brother?

"It was my favorite when I was a kid. Not anymore."

The cat jumped on the table, and Cameron shoved it off with a snarl.

"What's your favorite now?"

"Working."

The cat jumped up again, and he shoved it harder this time.

"That's silly." Ruby came farther into the room. "What are you working on?"

Cameron eyed the papers in the box. When he'd called the hospital yesterday, the doctor had made it clear that the bleeding in Bethany's brain had been severe enough that there was a chance she'd never wake up—and even if she did, she might never be the same—which was why he'd been searching through paperwork since dawn. He needed to find Ruby's birth certificate or Bethany's will or . . . or *something* that would lead him to a better guardian for his niece. And allow him to get back to his life.

So far, he'd found nothing useful.

"Did your mom ever tell you anything about your dad?"

Ruby shook her head, her blonde hair flying. "I don't have a daddy."

Cameron tried to hold back his exasperation. "Of course you have a dad. Everyone has a dad." Even him—even if his dad had died way too young, thanks to Bethany.

"Not me," Ruby said proudly. "The stork brought me."

Cameron rolled his eyes. *Way to teach the girl how the world works, Bethany.*

"What year were you born?" Maybe he could do some digging through public records.

The girl shrugged.

Was talking to little kids always this frustrating? "All right. How old are you?"

She gave a proud grin, revealing two missing bottom teeth. "I'm seven."

"Seven? Really?" Wow. He needed to work on his skill in judging ages. Then again, he didn't suppose he'd ever need it again.

"When can we visit Mommy?" Her grin fell away, replaced by pleading eyes.

Cameron nearly pulled his hair out. If she wasn't complaining she was bored, she was asking to visit Bethany. She couldn't seem to get it through her head that he had no plans to see his sister—at all.

"I don't know." He pushed the words out through gritted teeth. "Go watch TV."

"You're not as cool as Mommy said." Ruby flounced toward the living room.

Cameron snorted. Yeah, well, his sister wasn't as cool as he'd once thought either.

A light weight landed in his lap, and he looked down to find the stupid cat curling into a ball. The moment he shoved it off, it jumped back up.

"You really don't know when you're not wanted, do you?" But it wasn't worth the fight. He left it curled there as he pulled out his phone and scrolled through his calls from yesterday. Danielle had called three times, but he hadn't had the energy to call her back. He hit her number and waited, trying to figure out how to break it to her that he'd be here a few more days at least. But there was no answer. He hung up, wondering vaguely if she was still angry that he'd left. But what choice had he had?

He girded himself to dig into the paperwork again, but the doorbell rang. Rubbing a hand over his unshaven face, he pushed to his feet, sending the cat flying, and strode around Ruby's scattered toys to the front door. He'd have to have her clean those up later. He opened the door to find a man who was probably in his early thirties—about Cameron's own age.

"You must be Cam." The man held out his hand, but Cameron regarded him coolly. He had no interest in meeting his sister's latest supplier-boyfriend. That was the way it had always been with her. Though this guy didn't look the part, in his dress shirt and jeans, clean-cut hair, and clean-shaven face.

"I'm Cameron, yes."

The man withdrew his hand when Cameron didn't shake it. "I'm—"

"Pastor Dan!" Ruby shot straight past Cameron and out the door.

Pastor? Cameron felt his eyebrows raise. That would explain why the guy didn't look like a dealer. But what was Bethany doing hanging around with a pastor? Obviously, this pastor guy didn't know much about her life.

"Hey, Ruby." Pastor Dan smiled at the girl. "I was just visiting your mom, and I promised I'd come see you next."

"You saw my mommy? Did she say she misses me?"

Dan gave Cameron a look over the top of Ruby's head. "I did see her. She's pretty sleepy, so she couldn't talk to me, but I could talk to her. And I know she'd want me to tell you she loves you very much. How are you two doing?"

"I'm bored." Ruby pouted. "Uncle Cam won't play checkers with me."

"Maybe I could play a game with you? If it's okay with your uncle." Dan gave Cameron a questioning look.

Right, like Cameron didn't see right through the pastor's plan to get into the house so he could check up on them. But if it meant a few minutes of peace for him while the pastor played with Ruby, it would be worth it.

Besides, if anyone knew who Ruby's father was, it might be the pastor. He stepped aside and gestured for Dan to come into the house.

They moved into the kitchen, where Cameron poured two cups of coffee, passing one to Dan, who'd taken a seat next to the box of paperwork. Cameron leaned against the counter next to the sink, crossing his arms in front of him as he waited for an opening to talk to the pastor around Ruby's mile-a-minute commentary.

When Ruby was finally crowned champion—thanks to a couple of "mistakes" on Dan's part—Cameron sent her to her room to get dressed, though it was already two o'clock in the afternoon. Even with his limited interaction with kids, he was pretty sure the whole who-is-Ruby's-father conversation shouldn't happen in front of the girl.

"And try to wear something that matches this time," he called behind her. Unlike the wild purple flowery pants and orange striped shirt she'd worn yesterday.

When he heard her door click shut, Cameron sought for a way to bring up his question.

"Have you taken Ruby to visit Bethany?" Dan asked before Cameron could ease into a conversation.

He shook his head, his jaw tightening. He didn't need the preacher to tell him what he should or shouldn't be doing.

"I'm not going to lie, Bethany looks pretty rough with all those tubes and monitors," Dan said. "But it might do Ruby good to see her. As long as you're with her."

Cameron grunted, his shoulders tightening. That was not in the plans.

"Look. Do you know who Ruby's father is? Because he's the one who should be taking care of her. Especially if Bethany doesn't—" He closed his eyes. Saying the words was harder than he'd anticipated. He cleared his throat. "Doesn't wake up."

Dan watched him, as if trying to decide how to respond. "I realize this must have all come as quite a shock to you."

Cameron shrugged. Shock was one word for it. Burden, inconvenience, hardship—those were others. "Yeah, well, my sister and I aren't exactly close. I didn't even know I was an uncle."

"So maybe this is your chance to get to know your niece. I've only started meeting with her and Bethany recently, but she's a pretty fun kid."

"I'm sure she is." If there was such a thing. "But I've got a job to get back to." A life. And Bethany and Ruby weren't part of it.

Ruby sprang back into the room, dressed in a rainbow-striped sundress over a pair of thick jogging pants.

Cameron rolled his eyes. Hadn't Bethany taught the kid to dress herself like a normal person?

"Nice outfit," he muttered.

"This is Mommy's favorite dress." Ruby twirled. "She says it's because I'm her rainbow after the storm."

"I can see why." Dan pulled out the chair next to him and gestured for Ruby to sit. "I was going to say a prayer for your mom. Do you want to join me?"

Ruby nodded. "Can I say one too?"

"Of course." Dan gave Cameron a questioning look. "Join us?"

Cameron shook his head. He couldn't remember the last time he'd actually prayed, but even if he were a praying man, he wouldn't waste his prayers on Bethany.

Dan waited another moment, then folded his hands and ducked his head. Ruby did the same.

Cameron remained planted at the counter, shoulders knotting as Dan began the prayer. "Dear Lord, we come before you today on behalf of your daughter Bethany."

Cameron barely resisted the urge to laugh at that. Bethany was about as much a child of God as Judas had been.

But Dan continued his prayer. "You know her hurts, Lord, and you know how to heal them. We pray that you would do so quickly, so Bethany can get back to having fun with her Doodlebug."

Ruby giggled, and Cameron worked to steel his heart against the reminder that once upon a time Bethany had been a sweet little girl too.

"Your turn," Dan said to Ruby.

"Dear Jesus—" Ruby sounded sure, confident, as if she spoke to God all the time. "Please bless Mommy and help her get better. Thank you that Uncle Cam came here to take care of me. Please bless him and help him not to be so grumpy."

A laugh burst from Dan, but he covered it with a cough.

Cameron's arms pulled tighter across his chest, but he could feel a tiny muscle at the corner of his mouth trying to lift. He forced it down.

"And please help me be a good girl and listen to him. Even when I don't want to. Amen."

"Amen." The chuckle still sat in Dan's voice, and he looked to Cameron, making no effort to disguise his amusement. "No one prays quite like a kid."

Dan turned to Ruby. "I have to go, but I'm going to keep praying for your mom. And you pray too, okay?"

Ruby nodded and reset the checkerboard, though Cameron didn't know who she thought she was going to play with.

He followed Dan to the front door, where the pastor turned to him. "I don't know how much money Bethany has saved or anything, but obviously she's not going to be working for a while. The church has some funds for emergencies like this, if she needs help covering her bills . . ."

"I can take care of it." Cameron had no desire to be beholden to anyone, even a church, on his sister's behalf.

Dan gave him a shrewd look, as if he knew exactly what Cameron was thinking, but didn't say a word. "All right. Well, let me know if you need anything at all."

Cameron stepped outside with Dan. It was worth one more shot. "You're sure you don't know anything about Ruby's father? A name, a location, anything?"

Dan sighed. "Like I said, I've only been meeting with her for a couple months. She's never said anything about Ruby's dad. And I've never seen her with a man."

Cameron spiked his fingers into his hair. So basically, he was stuck with Ruby.

"Maybe instead of seeing this as an inconvenience, it might help to see it as a blessing. A chance to get to know your niece." Dan clasped his elbow for a second.

"I don't have time for that," Cameron insisted.

"Sometimes, what we think we need time for and what we really need time for are two different things. Fortunately, God seems to have a way of showing us which is which." And with that, the pastor was gone.

And Cameron was left staring after his vehicle, trying to figure out what his words had meant.

"Uncle Cam," Ruby called from the kitchen. "Want to play checkers now?"

"No." Cam closed the front door and stalked to Bethany's room, which he'd taken for his own.

He knew where he needed to spend his time—and it wasn't in Hope Springs.

But it looked like he was stuck here. For now.

Chapter 6

"*I*'m ready."

Cameron eyed Ruby. It'd been a relief to have her at school all day the last few days, even if packing her lunch and getting her out the door in the morning had taken all his problem-solving skills, especially when she couldn't find her left shoe this morning. He'd finally given up and sent her off wearing one pink shoe and one white one, figuring it at least complemented the rest of her mismatched outfit.

"Ready for what?" He took in the tan pants and cowboy boots she'd changed into. "The rodeo?"

Ruby giggled. "You're funny sometimes, Uncle Cam."

He smirked. He hadn't been trying to be funny.

"I'm ready for my riding lesson. Remember?"

He vaguely remembered her saying something about horses at dinner last night, but he'd been in the middle of reading work updates his secretary had sent. He glanced at the document open on his computer. It still needed plenty of attention. "I don't have time to take you tonight."

He finished typing the sentence he'd been in the middle of. Because of course she couldn't have waited for him to finish his thought before she interrupted him.

"I *have* to go. The parade is in less than two weeks, and Miss Emma said we all had to practice."

He neither knew nor cared who Miss Emma was or what she'd said. But Ruby looked at him, her eyes welling with tears she wouldn't let fall.

He growled to himself. If she started crying, he would have no idea what to do. He supposed he could work in the car while she did her horse thing.

"Fine. Get your coat."

Before he knew what was happening, Ruby flew across the room and threw her little arms around his shoulders as far as they'd go. "Thank you. You're the best."

Cameron just sat there. He'd never been hugged quite like this before. He cleared his throat. "All right, come on. Let's go."

Ruby removed her arms from around him, and he shoved his chair back, something odd still buzzing in his chest over her thank you hug.

His phone rang as he was grabbing his shoes, and he pulled it out of his pocket, stifling a groan as Danielle's name appeared on his screen. Not that he didn't want to talk to her, but their calls had become painfully familiar in the few days he'd been here: she'd ask when he was coming home, he'd say he didn't know, she'd go icy silent, he'd offer reassurances that he was doing everything he could to get back to her as soon as possible, and then they'd say goodbye. She wouldn't ask how his sister was doing. Wouldn't inquire about Ruby. Wouldn't even grill him about why he'd never mentioned his family to her.

He gave an irritated head shake. It wasn't like he wanted to share all of that with her—or with anyone, for that matter. And he surely didn't need or want her sympathy.

He considered letting the call go to voice mail, but that would only open its own can of worms with Danielle.

"Uncle Cam, I'm going to be late," Ruby called.

"Just a minute." He answered the call and lifted the phone to his ear, holding it in place with his shoulder as he tugged his shoe on. "Hey, baby." He worked to make his greeting sweet. "I only have a minute. I need to get the kid to riding lessons, apparently."

"Riding lessons?" Danielle's voice was spiked with icicles. "Oh, I wouldn't want to keep you from that. Obviously, that's much more important than anything I could have to say."

Cameron rolled his eyes but concentrated on injecting extra syrup into his response. "You know that's not what I meant, baby. I just mean I may have to call you back later."

"Don't bother." Danielle's voice switched from cold to businesslike. He wasn't sure which was worse. "Just write this down. While you've been playing house, I've been doing some actual investigating into Ruby's father. Barry Anderson, 176 Howley, Sharpesville, Wisconsin."

"Really?" Cameron jumped up from his chair and snatched a pencil and a sheet of paper covered with some sort of drawing off the counter. He flipped it over and scribbled down the information. "How did you find this?" He'd searched through every piece of paper in Bethany's house and had never come across the name. He'd even finally located Ruby's birth certificate, but no father was listed.

"Simple. I managed to get a report of her credit card activity for the last several years, which led me to an apartment complex in Sharpesville."

Cameron bit his tongue against pointing out how illegal that had been.

"And from there I called the apartment manager, who remembered a Bethany Moore. Said she hung out with this Barry guy a lot. I put two and two together . . ."

"So this guy may not be—" He lowered his voice in case Ruby was listening. Though he wasn't sure why he was trying to keep it from her that he was looking for her father. She'd find out sooner or later. Sooner if this lead proved to be good. "Ruby's father?"

"That's your job to figure out, Cameron. At least it's a lead. Which is more than you've gotten. Call me when you have more information."

The phone clicked dead before he could reply.

"Uncle Cam," Ruby marched back into the room. "We have to go *right now*." She grabbed for his hand, and he shoved the piece of paper he'd written on under a stack of mail before following her to the door.

Although Ruby kept up a constant chatter on the drive to the stables, Cameron had no idea what she said. His thoughts were too busy swirling around Danielle's information. If this Barry guy really was Ruby's father, Cameron could be on his way home in days. Which he was thrilled about, of course. He pushed away the nudge of conscience that said he was flouting his responsibility. He didn't have any responsibility to Ruby or to Bethany—and certainly not more responsibility than Ruby's father.

"Uncle Cam, you passed it." Ruby's words penetrated his brain.

"What? Oh." He glanced to the left side of the road, where a homemade wooden sign reading Hope Riders arched over a long driveway. There was no way he could make the turn now.

He continued down the road, eyes straining for a good place to turn around. But the driveways were few and far between on this country road. Finally, he turned into another long driveway, this one boasting a sign for Hidden Blossom Farms. Large groves of bare trees suggested it may be an orchard of some sort, though in the dark it was impossible to tell.

When he at last pulled into the right driveway, he caught a glimpse of Ruby bouncing in her seat in the rearview mirror. "So you like riding?"

"It's the best!" Her enthusiasm reminded him again of the way she'd thrown her arms around him and called him the best, and he grinned.

Then he flattened his lips and yanked his eyes back to the big white building in front of them. He did not need to go getting attached to this little girl. After all, he'd be on a plane back to his Ruby-free life soon enough.

Chapter 7

Kayla wiped her clammy hands on her jeans and pulled in a deep breath of the animal-hay-earth-leather scent of the arena. She'd only come because Nate and Vi's friend Emma, who owned the stables, had mentioned that Ruby rode here on Wednesday nights. And after spending the past five days worrying about the little girl, Kayla had needed just a peek to make sure Ruby was all right. That her uncle was actually taking care of her.

The problem was that Nate had mentioned Kayla's fear of horses—the result of a close encounter with a kicking horse when she was a kid—and now Emma was dead-set on getting her close to one of these creatures to help her overcome her fear.

Kayla glanced toward the arena door as Emma led a giant black horse toward her. Still no sign of Ruby. Which meant that Cam had probably put his own needs before the little girl's the same way he had when he'd refused to take her to see her mom. Kayla had gone back to visit Bethany every day this week, and each time the nurse had reported that the woman's only other visitor had been Pastor Dan. Kayla didn't know why she was surprised.

She may not have known Cam long, but it had only taken that first phone call for her to know the kind of man he was—the kind who didn't worry about anyone but himself.

That's not fair, she chided herself. She tried to turn her thoughts in a more charitable direction. She supposed it would be life altering to suddenly be called to take care of your niece halfway across the country. And as much as she knew she would do it for Vi and Nate in a split second, she also prayed she'd never have to know what it was like to lose her brother or sister-in-law.

Help me have more compassion toward Cam, Lord, she prayed. Though it would be a lot easier if he did a better job with Ruby.

She rolled her eyes at herself. That wasn't exactly more charitable. She reminded herself that Cam and Ruby were really none of her business.

Except, it felt like Ruby *was* her business. Kayla had been the one to see the accident. She'd been the one to get help. She'd been the one to watch the girl until Cam could get here. And in that short time, Ruby had managed to make a home in her heart.

"This is Big Blue," Emma said, stopping a few feet in front of Kayla.

The animal was even bigger than she'd imagined, and it studied her with its enormous eyes. Kayla had to sit on her hands so she wouldn't turn her chair right back around and race out of here.

"I know he looks intimidating," Emma said, "but he's a big softie. And he's trained to respond to voice commands. So you don't need to be able to use your legs to ride him."

Ride him? Kayla gaped at Emma. She was kidding, right?

Before she could ask, the arena door opened, and Ruby came bouncing into the building. The moment she spotted Kayla, she ran into the ring, patting Big Blue on the way past like he was no more frightening than her cat.

"Kayla." Ruby's smile was wide and gap-toothed and contagious. "I didn't know you rode horses too."

"I don't."

"But she will." Emma winked at Ruby, who giggled, then turned to Kayla. "Hold out your hand and let him smell it."

When Kayla hesitated, Ruby held her own hand out for the horse. Big Blue took a breath loud enough for Kayla to hear, then nickered softly.

"See." Ruby reached for Kayla's hand. "He's nice."

Kayla followed Ruby's lead in moving her hand to the horse's velvety nose.

The animal's hot breath slid across her skin, and Kayla let a nervous giggle escape. "It tickles."

"All right, Miss Ruby," Emma said after a minute. "Why don't you go join the other dressage riders so you can go over the routine for the parade." She turned to Kayla. "Have you had enough for one night, or did you want to try to mount him?"

Kayla contemplated the animal. She hated to back down from a challenge. But maybe this was the kind of challenge that needed to be conquered in baby steps. "Next time?"

"Absolutely." Emma clicked her tongue at Big Blue, who followed her toward the other end of the arena.

"Do you want to watch me?" Ruby asked Kayla.

"Of course." Kayla scanned the handful of parents waiting on the small set of bleachers near the door. She wanted to talk to Cam anyway, encourage him again to let the poor little girl see her mom.

But she didn't spot him among the other parents.

"Where's your uncle?"

Ruby's face fell. "He's waiting in the car. He said he had to make some phone calls."

"Ah." It figured. But it didn't matter. If Cam wouldn't show his niece that she mattered, Kayla would. She popped her chair into a wheelie to cross the soft arena sand. "I'll be by the bleachers. Show me what you've got."

According to the clock, Ruby's lesson should have ended fifteen minutes ago, but still she hadn't emerged from the arena. Nor had anyone else for that matter.

With a sigh, Cameron shoved his car door open and marched toward the building. He was ready to give this Miss Emma a piece of his mind. His time was valuable, and he didn't need her wasting it by not being punctual in dismissing her classes.

But the moment he opened the door to the arena, he froze. A couple dozen parents and kids sitting on a set of bleachers swiveled his direction. A blonde woman standing in front of them turned to him and smiled. "Can I help you?"

Cameron cleared his throat. There was no reason he should feel suddenly self-conscious. It wasn't like this was the boardroom of a Fortune 500 company. It was a rinky-dink stable in a rinky-dink town. "I'm looking for Ruby Moore."

A small hand waved from the bottom row of bleachers. "Over here, Uncle Cam."

Cameron's eyes went past Ruby to the woman seated on the far side of her. What was Kayla doing here? There was no way she rode, was there, given that she used a wheelchair?

"Sorry we're running late," the blonde woman he assumed must be Miss Emma said. "We were going over the details for the parade. It's the Sunday after Thanksgiving. Lineup time is four o'clock. We'll need adults to help pass out information and candy. I hope you can be there."

Cameron opened his mouth. That sounded like absolutely the last thing on earth he would do.

But he caught Kayla's grimace. Clearly, she expected him to refuse.

"Sure," he heard himself saying. "I'll be there."

"Great." Emma spoke for a few more minutes, then dismissed the group. Instead of running to him so they could leave, Ruby sat talking to Kayla.

At this rate, Cameron was going to have the art of the annoyed sigh perfected by the time he left Hope Springs. He marched over to his niece. "Ruby, time to go."

"One minute, Uncle Cam." Ruby turned to Kayla again.

"No minutes. Now." He cut off abruptly as he realized how much like his own dad he sounded. It was a voice he hadn't heard in way too long, and it sounded odd coming from his own mouth.

"Ruby, why don't you go ask Miss Emma about your idea to braid the horses' tails for the parade. I want to talk to your uncle for a minute."

Cameron shoved his hands in his pockets. What if he didn't want to talk to *her* for a minute? Had she thought of that? But he kept his feet planted as Ruby sprinted off, though he gave Kayla a look meant to convey that he didn't have time for this.

"It's been almost a week since the poor thing has seen her mother," Kayla launched into her lecture. "Are you ever going to take her?"

He shook his head. "Not that it's any of your business, but no, I'm not."

Kayla crossed her arms, her jaw tightening. "Whatever your issue is, she's just a little girl. She needs her mom. And it might help Bethany to hear her daughter's voice. I really think you should take her."

And he really thought she should mind her own business, but he bit back the words. "Her father can take her if he wants."

"Her father?" Kayla gave him a blank stare. "She doesn't have a father."

Cameron rolled his eyes. Not this again. "Of course she does. And I think I've tracked him down."

"So you're going to just dump her off on some stranger she's never met?"

"In case you've forgotten, *I'm* some stranger she'd never met too. And this guy isn't a stranger, he's her dad."

"Well—" Kayla's eyes sparked. "Has it ever occurred to you that there may be a reason Bethany never told Ruby about her father? Like maybe he's not a great guy."

Cameron glanced away. Of course it had occurred to him. Knowing the sort of men Bethany usually dated, he was almost sure that was the case. But that wasn't his problem. His sister should have thought of that before she let this guy knock her up.

He brought his eyes back to Kayla, squaring his shoulders with resolve. "I'm sure it will be fine." He started toward the other side of the arena, where Ruby was having an animated conversation with Miss Emma.

"Cam, wait."

He didn't know why he listened, but he did, turning around in time to see Kayla tip her chair back into a wheelie and roll through the arena sand with her small front wheels in the air.

She stopped in front of him. "I wish you'd reconsider this."

"And I wish you'd butt out." The retort flew off his tongue.

Kayla's eyes widened, and he was sure she was going to yell again.

Instead, she clamped her lips tight, then spun her chair toward the door. "If that's what you want. But at some point, you might want to stop thinking about yourself and start thinking about what's best for Ruby." Her words were quiet as she rolled past him. His gaze followed her as she continued to the door, then leaned forward to pull it open and maneuvered her wheelchair through it without a backward glance at him.

Cameron collected Ruby and led her to the parking lot. Fortunately, by the time they got outside, Kayla was nowhere to be found. If he never saw that woman again, that would be fine by him.

Chapter 8

Kayla bit her lip as she contemplated the application in front of her. She'd reread every one of her answers at least three times.

"Still working on that?" Vi waddled up behind her.

Kayla sighed. "No. It's done."

"So why are you still staring at it?" Vi pulled out a chair at the kitchen table and lowered herself onto it. "Man, I will be glad when I'm carrying this little person on the outside instead of the inside."

"I don't know why." Kayla shook her head at her computer screen. "I can't make myself hit 'submit.' I keep thinking about leaving you guys just when you're bringing this amazing new life into the world. I promised I'd help out at the store, and . . ."

"We'll be fine. You know that."

Kayla nodded. She did know. "And Mom and Dad aren't getting any younger."

Vi outright laughed at her. "Kayla, your parents are currently climbing Mount St. Helens. I think they'll be okay if you leave for six months."

"What about Ruby? I mean, Cam's obviously not concerned about what's best for her. What if he does contact her father? Who's going to make sure she's all right and that—"

Vi laid her hand on top of Kayla's to silence her. "I know you care about that little girl. But Cam is technically her guardian right now.

You can't control what he does. Anyway, you don't know—he may come through after all. You have to give him a chance."

Kayla snorted. Vi only thought that because she'd never met Cam. Nor been told by him to butt out. That was gratitude for you, after all she'd tried to do to help him and Ruby.

Vi gave her a probing look. "Cam aside, you know that Ruby is in God's hands." She refused to take her gaze off Kayla, who had to look away.

"What's this really about?" Vi asked softly.

Kayla let her breath out, long and slow. "I don't know." But that wasn't quite right. "It's just, I've wanted to do a mission trip like this for so long, you know?"

Vi smiled. "I thought that was the point."

"Yeah, but what if I don't get accepted? There's a good chance they'll say the trip isn't wheelchair accessible or I'll slow them down or something."

Vi laughed as she patted Kayla's hand. "If that's the case, then they sure don't know you. Anyway, if you apply and don't get accepted this time, it doesn't mean you're not cut out for mission work. It just means this wasn't the right trip. God has a way of opening doors when and where they need to be opened, you know. But you're never going to find out if this is the door for you if you don't hit that submit button." She braced her hands on the table and groaned as she pushed to her feet. "Seriously, I don't know how women go through this whole process more than once."

As she shuffled out of the room, Kayla studied her application one more time. Her hand went to her mouse, and she hovered it over the submit button.

Then, drawing in a quick breath, she clicked.

"It's up to you, Lord," she whispered. "Is this the door for me or not?"

Chapter 9

The sick feeling that had lain heavy in his stomach since he'd driven out of Hope Springs after dropping Ruby off at school this morning intensified as Cameron stared at the apartment complex in front of him. He'd driven past it half a dozen times before he'd made himself turn into the parking lot.

This was where Ruby's alleged dad lived. All he had to do was go in there, tell the guy he was a father, ask him if he wanted to come to Hope Springs or have Ruby brought here, and then pack his bags and hop the next flight back to LA.

So what was stopping him from getting out of the car and doing just that?

Has it ever occurred to you that there may be a reason Bethany never told Ruby about her father? Like maybe he's not a great guy. Kayla's words from the other night had echoed relentlessly in his head for the past two days.

But if Bethany was friends with the pastor, then maybe that meant she had changed. And if she had changed, maybe that meant her taste in men had changed. Maybe she and her partner had split amicably—or better yet, maybe the guy was looking for an opportunity to be part of his daughter's life. Who was Cameron to deny him that?

And if things were too bad, Cameron could turn around and walk away. He hadn't committed himself to anything yet.

With a forced resolve that didn't feel like resolve at all, he pushed his car door open. At the locked entrance, he scanned the list of apartments, pressing the buzzer for the one labeled Barry Anderson. It took a moment before a guy's voice sounded over the speaker. "Yeah?"

"Is this Barry Anderson?" Cameron took a step closer to the microphone.

"Yeah. Who's this?"

"Did you know a Bethany Moore?" Cameron crossed his fingers, though he wasn't sure whether he was hoping the guy would answer in the affirmative or the negative.

"Bethany Moore? I don't think I . . . Oh wait, Bethy. Yeah. Haven't seen her in, what? Seven, eight years? Why do you ask?"

"I'm her brother. Could I come in?" He really didn't want to talk about this over the intercom. And besides, he wanted to get at least a glimpse of the guy before he told him about Ruby. He owed her at least that much as her uncle.

"Uh, yeah. I guess." The guy sounded surprised, but after a second the door buzzed open. The hallway was narrow and dark and smelled strongly of stale cigarettes and cat urine, but at least it didn't look seedy. When he reached apartment 105, Cameron gave a quick rap on the door.

Less than a second later, a guy dressed in faded jeans and a tan sweater opened the door. His hair was slightly greasy and his face weather-roughened, but Cameron let himself breathe a little easier. This guy didn't look so bad. Probably just the kind of hard-working guy who would make a good dad.

"So what's this about? Is Bethy in trouble or something, because—"

"She was in an accident." Cameron glanced past the guy into the apartment. It wasn't exactly glamorous—tired furniture, stained carpeting—but at least there weren't beer bottles laying all over the place or something. Which, given Bethany's history with men, was a pleasant surprise.

"Oh man. I'm sorry to hear that." Barry took a step back. Absently, he pushed his sleeves up. "I mean, that's terrible. Is she okay?"

But Cameron's eyes had locked on Barry's exposed forearms.

Fresh track marks.

They were unmistakable. He'd seen them enough times on Bethany to know.

Apparently catching the direction of Cameron's gaze, Barry tugged his sleeves down. "Is she okay?" he repeated.

Cameron looked him in the eye. "I'm afraid not. She died. I thought you should know." He turned and stalked down the hallway.

"Wait, man. When's the funeral?" Barry called after him. "I want to come."

But Cameron lifted a dismissive hand and picked up speed, shoving the door hard in front of him. In the parking lot, he sprinted to his car. Then he just sat there, hands gripping the steering wheel so they wouldn't shake.

He couldn't leave Ruby with a junkie. He'd give up his own future before it came to that.

As he turned the key in the ignition, an odd sense of relief washed over him. Until he realized he'd have to tell Danielle what he'd done.

Unless he didn't. He could just as easily say it had been a dead end.

Feeling unaccountably lighter than he had in days, Cameron tried to enjoy the drive back to Hope Springs. The sky was ridiculously blue today, and the few trees that still held leaves were putting on a brilliant display of color. Not to mention the lake, which he caught glimpses of every once in a while, glittering brighter than a thousand gemstones. It wasn't the Pacific, but there was something peaceful and soothing about it all the same.

Cameron relaxed into the drive, until he spotted the line of brake lights ahead of him. He slowed to a stop behind a long line of cars, grumbling to himself as he spotted the sign: "Construction ahead. Expect significant delays."

His eyes went to the clock. He'd planned his little trip so that he'd have just enough time to get to Sharpesville and back before Ruby got out of school. He'd already been cutting it close. But now there was no way he was going to make it back on time.

With a groan, he pulled his phone out of his pocket.

Too bad he only knew the number of one person in Hope Springs.

Chapter 10

*T*he nerve. One day the guy is telling her to butt out, two days later, he's calling and asking her to do him a favor and pick up Ruby from school and hang out with her. Apparently, her interference was welcome as long as it suited him.

Not that she minded spending time with Ruby. Thankfully, the little girl had known where to find the spare key under a rock in the flower bed, since Nate's band was currently practicing at his house—not exactly conducive for the homework she'd just helped the little girl with.

"What should we do next?" Ruby bounced out of her chair.

Kayla checked the time. Cam hadn't known when he'd be home, but he'd thought it would be at least an hour. Which meant they might have time for a plan that had been lurking in the back of her mind since she'd gotten Ruby from school.

"Do you want to visit your mom?"

"Really?" Ruby brightened so much that it was almost heartbreaking. How could Cam keep this little girl from her mother? "Did Uncle Cam say it was okay?"

Kayla bit her lip. "I didn't have a chance to ask him." That was true, right? "We'll be there and back before he gets home."

Ruby wrinkled her brow. "Isn't that lying?"

"Don't worry, we'll tell him when he gets back." By then, it'd be too late for him to do anything about it. And she could show him how much good it had done Ruby. Surely he'd start taking her then. "Go get your shoes. I'm going to grab my purse."

Ruby still looked uncertain, but she nodded and moved toward the closet with a little skip in her step.

"Good girl." Kayla wheeled to the kitchen counter to collect her purse. She yanked it toward her, already backing her wheelchair away—every second counted if they wanted to get out of here before Cam got home—but the purse must have snagged on the mail or something, because Kayla was suddenly surrounded by an avalanche of scattered papers.

She bent to pick them up, gathering them into a messy pile. But she paused, a lump coming to her throat as she spotted a drawing of a chair with what looked like two big wheels on the sides. In the chair sat a blob-shaped person with an overly large head and a giant smile. Too sweet.

Kayla was about to add the paper to the pile in her hand when her eyes landed on words scribbled at the bottom in messy but definitely not childish handwriting: Barry Anderson, 176 Howley, Sharpesville, Wisconsin. But it was the two words under the address that made her mouth go dry: *Ruby's dad???*

An unaccountable anger went through her. Was that where he was right now? Looking for a way to shirk his responsibility and pass Ruby off to some guy in Sharpesville. Even after Kayla had expressed her concern that it may not be in Ruby's best interest, given that Bethany had kept any and all knowledge of her father from the little girl. People didn't just do that for no reason.

So much for Vi's theory that Cam would surprise them and come through for Ruby after all.

Honestly, she didn't know why she was so angry. It wasn't like she hadn't seen this coming. Well, if Cam thought he wasn't going to hear about this when he got home . . .

It's none of your business, she reminded herself. Except, hadn't Cam made it her business when he'd decided to ask her to watch Ruby while he ran out of town chasing down someone else to take on his responsibilities?

Kayla was still clutching the paper when Ruby marched into the kitchen. "Are you coming? My shoes are on."

Kayla hastily shoved the paper to the bottom of the stack and set it on the counter. No need to upset Ruby about this. With any luck, she'd be able to convince Cam that it was wrong to take the girl to a man her mother didn't want to have her. Or better yet, the man would have turned out not to be Ruby's father.

"Yeah, kiddo. Let's go."

Kayla gave the papers one last nasty look—as if they could control what was written on them—then followed Ruby to the front door. They bundled into coats against the late fall chill, then rushed outside. But they were only halfway to her car when Cam turned into the driveway.

Ruby waved wildly to him, but Kayla groaned. There was no way they could carry out their plan now.

Cam's face was drawn as he stepped out of the car, but he gave her what she was pretty sure was meant to be a grateful smile. She returned it with a stony look. As far as she was concerned, he could keep his gratitude if he was going to involve her in his plans to send Ruby off.

"Where are you two headed?"

"We're going to see Mommy." The words rocketed out of Ruby before Kayla could open her mouth.

"Oh you are?" Cam shot Kayla a hard look, which she met head-on. She had nothing to be ashamed of.

68

"Yep. Do you want to come?" Ruby asked cheerfully.

Cam shook his head. "Go inside, Ruby. I need to talk to Kayla for a minute."

"And then can we go?" Ruby sounded so hopeful, and Kayla willed Cam to be a decent guy just this once.

"No."

"But—" Ruby's face fell, and it was all Kayla could do not to plop the little girl onto her lap and wheel right past Cam to her car and take off for the hospital.

"Inside. Now." Cam stuck his keys in Ruby's hand, then pointed at the house. Ruby nodded and dropped her head, then dragged her feet to the door.

As soon as it had banged closed, Cam rounded on Kayla. "What do you think you're doing? I simply asked you to watch her for a little bit."

"I'm doing what's best for Ruby." The words shot off Kayla's tongue. "You might consider trying it sometime."

Cam's hands fisted at his sides, but she noticed with triumph that he couldn't hold her gaze. "Believe it or not, that's what I'm doing."

Kayla shook her head. She was not going to let him get away with thinking that. "Is that why you were in Sharpesville looking for her dad today?"

Cam's head jerked toward her. "How did—"

"You left it scribbled on a piece of paper on the counter. One of Ruby's drawings, just to add insult to injury."

"Yeah, fine. Whatever. That's where I was. I told you I had a lead on him."

Kayla waited, but when Cam didn't continue, she had to ask. "Did you find him?"

Cam gave her a long look, his expression unreadable. Finally, he blew out a breath. "It was a dead end."

Relief coursed through her. "Good."

Cam shook his head. "You're unbelievable. Do you know that?" He stepped around her wheelchair and walked toward the house. "Thanks for watching Ruby."

Kayla turned her chair toward him. "You're welcome." She thought about adding another plea for him to take Ruby to see Bethany. But maybe she'd already yelled at him enough for one day. She could always butt in again another day.

Chapter 11

Cameron flopped back on the lumpy mattress that passed for Bethany's bed—his bed these days—and held his phone above him. He'd avoided calling Danielle for the past two days, but he couldn't put it off any longer, if her increasingly irate texts were any indication. He dialed her number, then pulled the phone to his ear. He was not relishing the thought of this conversation.

But Danielle sounded cheerful when she answered. "Guess what? I made us reservations at Oshiki."

Cameron pulled his phone away from his ear and stared at it. Why was she talking about their favorite sushi place?

"For Thanksgiving," she was saying when he put the phone back to his ear.

Oh right. It was Thanksgiving this week.

"Yeah, baby, listen. I don't think I'm going to make it back for Thanksgiving."

"Why not?" Her voice went hard. "When I didn't hear from you, I assumed it was because you were making arrangements with the kid's father to get her off your hands."

He sighed. "No. I'm sorry. I should have called sooner. I went to Sharpesville, to find that Barry guy."

"And?" Danielle had never been one to sit and listen to a full story. She wanted only the pertinent facts.

"I found him, but—"

"Good. Then, what, you need a few more days to get things set up? I can probably move the reservation back if I—"

"No." Cameron's fingers tightened on the phone. "I found him, but—" He hesitated. If he told her that he'd decided not to tell the guy about Ruby, she'd go through the roof. Not to mention that she might try to contact the guy herself and convince him to come take Ruby. "He wasn't Ruby's father. He'd never even heard of Bethany."

"That's— Odd." Danielle sounded like she'd gone into lawyer mode. "The guy I talked to seemed so sure. Maybe this guy is lying. We could make him take a paternity test or—"

"No, Danielle. I believe him. And you know I can always tell when people are lying. It's a dead end. I'm sorry."

Silence pulsed from the other end of the phone.

"But—" He tried for a conciliatory tone. "You could come here for Thanksgiving. Meet the kid. She's not so bad, you know. Kind of fun sometimes even." He laughed. "The other day she—"

"Cameron, I don't care *what* she did." Danielle's words were sharp. "If you want this relationship to work, I think you need to spend more of your time focusing on a way to get home. Maybe don't call me for a few days, until you make some progress."

The phone clicked dead, and Cameron dropped it and pressed his hands into his forehead. He knew she didn't mean it. He'd give her a couple of days and then call—by then she'd cool down, and maybe he'd have something to report. But as he sat up, he couldn't help but wonder: Why was he working so hard to keep Danielle happy when he'd been having doubts about their relationship even before he came here?

Because she's part of your plan for the perfect life, remember?

He pushed to his feet, tugged on his shoes, and strode for the front door, grabbing the winter jacket he'd finally broken down and purchased. Right now, he needed to do something physical.

"Where are you going?" Ruby blinked up at him from the spot where she was playing with that ridiculous cardboard dollhouse, her green plaid shirt standing out in strong contrast to her mustard-yellow pants.

"Outside."

"Can I come?"

He shrugged. "Knock yourself out."

"Really?" Her eyes widened, as if he'd given her permission to go to the Bahamas.

"Yeah. Just stay out of the way." He marched out the door and around the house, to the small shed in the backyard, where he pushed past sandbox toys and miscellaneous planters to grab a rake.

Today was as good a day as any to attack the leaves strewn across the yard. The air was sharp, but the sun was out, and the breeze was almost warm. He focused on the rhythm of the rake, letting his mind go blank. The movement felt good—and the mindlessness even better.

It took him a moment to realize he wasn't the only one working. On the other side of the yard, Ruby was struggling with a rake nearly twice her height. He watched for a moment as she managed to scatter the leaves more.

Shaking his head, he scraped a few more rakefuls onto his own pile. But his eyes went right back to Ruby, who was still wrestling diligently with her own rake.

"Try holding it like this," he called, holding his rake in front of him to show her his hand placement.

She studied him, then slid her hands into the completely wrong position. With a sigh, Cameron dropped his own rake and moved to her side.

"Like this." He pushed her right hand up and her left hand down, then moved the rake back and forth a couple times to give her a feel for the motion.

"Oh, I get it now." Ruby grinned at him, then pulled the rake across the ground herself, missing half the leaves but managing to form the start of a small pile.

"Good." He returned to his own rake.

"Uncle Cam?"

"Yeah?" He kept raking.

"Who taught you how to rake?"

"My dad, I suppose." He paused mid-stroke. "Your grandpa."

"Really?" Ruby's eyes lit up. "You knew my grandpa?"

"Of course. I'm your mom's brother. So her dad was my dad too."

"Mommy said my grandpa was funny. Was he funny, Uncle Cam?"

Cameron's heart squeezed, thinking of his dad with his corny jokes and his booming laugh. "Yeah. He was funny."

"That's good. You're funny too."

Cameron returned to raking. He'd never thought of himself as a particularly funny guy. "How am I funny?"

"You act all mean and tough. But you're really nice." Ruby giggled.

Cameron shook his head. "Keep raking."

But as he watched her wrestle with the rake, he had to admit to himself that her words had been just what he'd needed to hear. He'd made the right decision, not telling Barry about Ruby. Besides, chances were, the guy wasn't Ruby's father anyway. And even if he was . . . no, Cameron had made the right decision.

He thought of Kayla, accusing him of not caring what was best for Ruby.

The truth was, as much as he didn't want to care about anything associated with Bethany, he did.

He actually cared about this little girl quite a lot, despite his best intentions.

Then why won't you take her to see her mom? He heard Kayla, as if she were right there in front of him, piercing him with that judgmental look she was so good at.

74

He sighed, stopping to lean on his rake. "Hey, Rubes?"
She giggled. "That's a funny nickname."
"Yeah. You want to go see your mom after this?"

Chapter 12

Kayla peeked at Bethany's still form over the top of the ragged copy of *Little Women* she'd been reading out loud to the comatose woman. Bethany looked to be slightly older than Kayla, which meant she was likely Cam's big sister. Whom he didn't seem to care an iota for.

She thought with satisfaction of the expression on his face when he'd said the lead on Ruby's father had turned out to be a dead end. She probably shouldn't gloat about that, but at least it meant she could still see Ruby around sometimes. Still keep Bethany informed of how her daughter was doing. Since Cam continued to refuse to bring Ruby to visit her mother.

Kayla wasn't sure how her visits to Bethany fit into Cam's request that she butt out, but quite frankly, she didn't care. The poor woman didn't deserve to be left here alone, whatever Cam seemed to think. Besides, Ruby needed her mother back, and Kayla was convinced that the main reason she'd come out of her own coma was the love and support of all the people who'd visited her. That and all their prayers. Thankfully, she knew Bethany was covered in prayer as well. Dan had said a prayer for her in church this morning, and all of Kayla's friends had promised to continue to pray as well. *Please help her to heal, Lord*, Kayla prayed again, then dropped her eyes to the book, reading out loud.

"'I don't believe I shall ever marry. I am happy as I am, and love my liberty too well to be in a hurry to give it up for any mortal man.'"

Kayla put her finger in the book to mark her page and looked up again. "Jo sure nailed that one, didn't she?" Sometimes Kayla felt like she was the only person in the world who didn't think she needed to get married, so it was good to have this confirmation from Jo March—even if she was a fictional character.

"'I love my liberty too well,'" she repeated, opening the book again and picking up with Laurie's response: "'You think so now, but there'll come a time when you will care for somebody, and you'll love him tremendously, and live and die for him.'"

Kayla paused again. "That's not the way it is for everyone, Laurie," she murmured. Then she looked at Bethany with a laugh. "Sorry, I'll stop injecting my own commentary."

She started reading again, but after a few minutes a tap on her shoulder made her jump.

"I'm sorry." The woman talked in the low, soothing voice that was common to nurses everywhere. "Bethany has more visitors, and we don't want to tire her out with too many. Would you mind stepping out for now?"

"Of course." Kayla dog-eared the page of her book. "We'll continue tomorrow." As she followed the nurse toward the exit, she let herself hope, for only a second, that the visitors were Cam and Ruby. But as fast as the hope had entered her thoughts, it dissipated. Cam had made his feelings on that perfectly clear yet again the other night. It was probably Dan and Jade who had come.

The nurse pushed the door open, and Kayla followed her down the hallway, her wheels quiet on the smooth, shiny floor. As they rounded a corner, Kayla dodged out of the way of a bustling nurse. When she looked up, her eyes caught on two forms waiting at the end—one tall and broad, the other small and bouncy.

Her heart gave a small leap. *Thank you, Lord.*

She lifted a hand off the rims to wave to Ruby, who sent her an enthusiastic return wave. Cam looked less pleased to be here. But at least he was here, finally doing the right thing.

As she wheeled to a stop in front of them, Ruby sprang toward her wheelchair and wrapped her small arms around Kayla's shoulders. Kayla hugged her back without reserve.

"What's that?" Ruby pointed to the book in Kayla's lap.

"Oh." Kayla glanced at the book, then at Cam. Well, she had nothing to be embarrassed about. "I was just reading this book to your mom."

"Is it good?"

Kayla nodded. "One of my favorites."

"It was Bethany's favorite too." Cam's voice was low and gravelly, and he cleared his throat. "Come on, Ruby."

He started down the hallway.

"Cam." Kayla didn't mean to call after him, but there was no way to take it back.

He turned, waiting silently for her to continue.

"I'm glad you came. Do you want me to wait here, in case . . ." She eyed Ruby. Even though she was convinced that it would do the girl good to see her mom, it might be a little intense. She might not want to stay in there as long as Cam. Or she might need someone to talk to afterward.

"Yes!" Ruby immediately cheered.

Cam shook his head. "We'll be fine, thanks."

But she was pretty sure she heard the slightest tremor in his voice.

Cameron resisted the urge to look over his shoulder as he strode down the hallway toward Bethany's room, Ruby skipping at his side. He didn't need to know if Kayla was still there, still watching him with that mix of compassion and loathing.

They stopped outside the room number the nurse had given him. Cameron grabbed the door handle but found he couldn't open it. A small hand slipped into his, and Cameron looked down to find Ruby gazing up at him. His first instinct was to pull away, but the fear in her gaze stopped him.

"It's okay," he whispered, then pushed the door open.

His eyes fell on the bed. Bethany's blonde hair spilled against the white pillowcase, and a ventilator tube was taped to her mouth. An IV traveled into her arm, and other wires ran in and out of her bed, feeding into monitors that cast a slightly eerie glow on her face.

Next to him, Ruby let out a whimper that sounded like, "Mommy."

Cameron supposed he should do something to comfort the girl. But he had no idea what that would be.

A nurse bustled into the room and squatted at Ruby's side. "You can step closer. I'm sure your mom would love it if you talked to her."

Ruby nodded and let go of his hand, saying a tentative hello to her mother. The nurse gave her an encouraging smile, and Ruby started telling Bethany about school.

The nurse gestured for Cameron to come closer as well.

He looked from the nurse to Ruby to Bethany.

"Excuse me," he murmured, turning and bolting out the door. He stopped halfway down the hallway, his breaths short and quick.

She hurt you, he reminded himself. *She tore your family apart. She's the reason you don't have a mother or a father.*

But as hard as he tried to clutch his anger to him, he couldn't stop picturing Bethany's still form in the bed.

He looked at the door to her room. He shouldn't leave Ruby alone in there. But at the thought of going back in, his whole body began to tremble and his stomach heaved.

He sprinted toward the far end of the hallway, making it to the restroom just in time to lose his lunch.

79

Chapter 13

Kayla wheeled out of the visitor's lounge into the hallway, glancing at the door to the men's restroom. She didn't know why she'd stayed at the hospital after Cam had so clearly dismissed her—but she hadn't been able to shake the thought that Ruby would need her after she saw her mom. It hadn't occurred to her that maybe Cam would too.

But the way he'd run down the hallway just now, looking like he was going to be sick—maybe he needed someone too.

It was never easy to see someone you cared about lying helpless like that. And despite his earlier refusals to visit his sister, his reaction proved that he did care about her on some level. Not that Kayla expected him to admit it.

The door to the bathroom opened, and Cam emerged, looking shaky and gray. She wanted to call out to him, let him know she was here if he wanted to talk, but something stopped her. She watched as he pivoted toward the desk and said something to the nurse there. She nodded and picked up her phone. Cam stood there for a moment, then lifted his hands behind his head and made his way to the window.

Kayla peered down the hall toward Bethany's room. Ruby must still be in there. By herself.

She attempted to work up anger toward Cam at that, but she couldn't. He was obviously struggling to cope with all of this himself.

With one more glance toward him, Kayla turned down the hallway and made her way toward Bethany's room.

The nurse she'd talked to earlier was checking Bethany's monitors and smiling at a chatting Ruby. Kayla's heart squeezed at the way the girl held her mom's hand. This was obviously exactly what she'd needed.

After a moment, the nurse ducked out of the room, and Kayla pulled her wheelchair up to the end of the bed.

Ruby looked her way. "Where's Uncle Cam? He didn't say hi to Mommy."

Kayla fiddled with the blanket covering Bethany's feet. "Sometimes grownups have a hard time dealing with seeing people in the hospital. Your uncle is waiting in the lobby for you. But I'll hang out with you and your mom until it's time to go."

Ruby nodded and turned back to her mom. "When is she going to wake up? It's more fun to talk to her when she answers."

"I know." Kayla fought down the lump that tried to climb up her throat. "The doctors hope she'll wake up soon. But they just don't know." She bit her lip. Maybe that was enough for now. Anyway, it was way too early to give up hope that Bethany would wake up. "Why don't you tell your mom all about the parade next weekend?"

Ruby launched into a renewed one-way conversation with her mom until the nurse came over and said it was time to let Bethany get some rest.

Kayla could have wept when Ruby raised onto her tiptoes to kiss her mom's cheek. *Please let Bethany wake up, Lord. This little girl needs her mother.*

She followed Ruby to the lobby, where Cam was in the same spot as when she'd left him.

"Uncle Cam." Ruby broke away from her. "What are you doing?"

Cam turned, and Kayla's heart twisted the tiniest bit as she noticed his red eyes. He rubbed his nose. "I had to talk to the doctor."

"Did he say Mommy's going to be better soon?"

Cam's eyes met Kayla's and he gave a subtle head shake that made her stomach drop. "He said they're going to do everything they can to help her."

Ruby nodded as if that was all the assurance she needed. Cam looked as if he were about to say something else but then apparently thought better of it and silently led the way to the elevator. He moved to the back corner to give Kayla room to maneuver her wheelchair in the confined space.

The moment the door closed, Ruby crumpled, a big sob tearing out of her little body. "I don't want to leave Mommy."

Cam stared at her, confusion and annoyance warring on his face. "We have to."

"No," Ruby pounded her fists on the elevator door. "Let me out. I want to go back to Mommy."

"Oh, sweetie, it's okay." Kayla bent over and reached for the little girl in the cramped elevator. "You can come see her again soon. How about we go get some ice cream?"

Ruby's sobs lightened, and she turned teary eyes on Kayla. "Really?"

"Really." Kayla didn't bother to confirm with Cam. She was taking this poor little girl for ice cream whether he liked it or not.

Chapter 14

Cameron fiddled with the spoon in his empty ice cream bowl. When they'd arrived at the oddly named shop—something about a chicken—he'd insisted he wasn't hungry, but Kayla had ordered him a sundae anyway, and somehow it turned out that ice cream had been exactly what he'd needed.

Kayla had kept up a steady stream of conversation with Ruby, which had allowed Cameron's mind to wander. He only wished his thoughts didn't keep bouncing back to Bethany's helpless body lying in that hospital bed.

Seeing his sister like that had been . . . honestly, he hadn't expected to react like that. He was supposed to be angry, to never lose sight of the fact that it was all her own fault. But seeing her lying there, all he could picture was the summer days they'd spent in their tree house and the way she'd let him tag along when she went to the neighborhood pool and the way she'd taught him to sneak cookies when Mom was in the basement doing laundry.

"Told you the ice cream was good." Kayla turned to him, and he worked to pull his thoughts back to the present. Because it wasn't the past, Bethany wasn't that innocent little girl anymore, and he wasn't her adoring little brother.

"I come here every time I'm in Hope Springs," Kayla added. "Usually more than once." She ran the spoon around her own empty dish.

"You don't live here?" Cameron looked at her in surprise. He'd assumed she was a lifelong resident of this small town, but he didn't know why. Probably because she gave off that small town vibe.

What vibe, nice? his head asked.

No. Nosy, he corrected his silly thoughts.

"At the Chocolate Chicken? No."

Ruby burst into giggles at Kayla's joke, and Cameron let a reluctant smile play with his lips too. "I meant Hope Springs. But that's good to know."

Kayla nudged Ruby, then turned to Cameron. "No, I don't live in Hope Springs. I'm from Wescott, on the other side of the state, but my brother and his wife live here. I try to visit them a couple times a year."

"So you just happened to be driving by when Bethany and Ruby . . ."

Kayla shook her head. "I didn't just *happen* to be driving by. God put me in the right place at the right time."

"You believe in God?" Ruby bounced in her seat. "Me too. Pastor Dan is teaching me about him."

Kayla smiled at her, but Cameron noticed the way her eyes went to him, as if waiting for him to chime in that he believed in God too.

He kept his mouth shut. Sure, he believed in God in an existential, impersonal way. Kind of how he believed in gravity. He knew it was there and supposed it affected him, but he never gave it much thought. And he certainly didn't talk about it. Not even with Danielle.

"You're not leaving soon, are you?" Ruby licked at the ice cream dripping down the side of her cone. She had to be the slowest ice cream eater ever. "I would miss you."

Kayla grabbed a napkin and ran it over Ruby's mouth. Cameron had to admit to himself that he was impressed that she didn't flinch at the gooey mess.

"I honestly don't know how long I'm staying," Kayla said. "But for a while. At least through Christmas. My sister-in-law is expecting a baby, and I want to be here when he or she is born. I can't wait to be an aunt."

"Hey." Ruby's eyes lit up. "If you're going to be an aunt and Uncle Cam is an uncle, maybe you can be an aunt and uncle together."

Kayla's laugh rang across the restaurant as she ruffled Ruby's hair. "That's not quite how it works. But I'm happy to be a pretend aunt to you." She gave Cameron a defiant look, as if daring him to contradict her.

Whatever. She wanted to be a pretend aunt, she had his blessing. It looked like they weren't getting rid of her anytime soon anyway. For some reason, the thought didn't completely aggravate him.

"So what do you do in Wescott?" He hadn't meant to ask, but his curiosity had taken over.

Kayla looked surprised at his interest. "Actually, that's part of the reason I'm visiting for so long. The camp I worked for just closed down. I'm trying to figure out where God is going to lead me next."

"A camp? That's so cool." Ruby's face was already covered with ice cream again. "What kind of camp was it?"

"It was for kids with disabilities."

"Like you," Ruby said cheerfully, and Cameron winced, wondering if there was room for him under the table. Apparently, political correctness was another thing Bethany had failed to teach her daughter.

But Kayla smiled at the girl. "Yep. Some of the kids use wheelchairs. Some have crutches or walkers. And others look just like you. But I helped them learn how to do things independently."

"Why do you use a wheelchair?"

"*Ruby.*" Someone was seriously going to have to teach this girl some manners. "That's not—"

But Kayla cut him off. "That's a good question. I was in an accident when I was a teenager and I broke my back, so I can't walk. That's why I use a wheelchair." She said it cheerfully, as if remarking on riding a bike.

"Oh." Ruby popped the last of her cone into her mouth and spoke around it. "Do you ever wish you could still walk?"

Oh, for goodness' sake. Just when he thought her questions couldn't get more inappropriate. But he looked to Kayla. Was she going to handle this question with as much grace?

Kayla considered Ruby. "That's a pretty deep question for a seven-year-old. I guess I don't really think about it much anymore. This is just how I am now. And I like being me—"

"I like you being you too." Ruby grinned an ice cream–covered grin at her.

"That's good." Kayla returned the girl's grin. "Because I like you being you too."

All right. Before the two of them became blood sisters or something, instead of just pretend aunt and niece, it was time to get home.

He eyed Ruby. "Go wash your hands."

Kayla looked at him as if he were crazy. Well, what? He couldn't let her in the rental car like that.

"I'll go with you," Kayla said to Ruby.

Oh. He supposed sending a little kid to the bathroom alone wasn't necessarily the safest move, though in a town like Hope Springs it didn't seem like too big of a risk.

As Cameron waited for them to return, he made his way past the cozy round tables toward the shop's large window, stopping to glance at a shelf of eclectic metal sculptures—mostly of roosters, with a cow or two thrown in. He shook his head—he sure was a long way from LA.

At the window, he looked out on the street lined with specialty shops. The sidewalks were mostly empty, and he wondered how any of these small places stayed in business, though he supposed this was their off season. Even so, he'd bet most of these places were inefficient at best, bleeding money at worst. Especially if, like his parents, they let their feelings get in the way of their business sense.

"All better," Ruby announced to the entire restaurant as she made her way back to him with her now mostly clean hands held high.

He hushed her, looking around at the few other customers in the shop. But they all smiled at Ruby as if she were the most precious creature they'd ever seen.

Yeah, Hope Springs was definitely a different kind of place. One he wasn't quite sure he'd ever get used to, though he had to admit that the slower pace made a nice change from his hectic LA life.

Not a nice change, he scolded himself. *Just a change.*

And that hectic LA life was exactly what he needed to get back to.

He followed Ruby and Kayla to the exit, waiting for Kayla to move aside so he could open the door for her. When she reached for it herself and tugged it open, he stepped in front of her to grab it out of her hands.

But she didn't let go. "I've got it. I'm not helpless." Her voice was hard, and Cameron let go of the door, raising his hands.

Helpless was the last thing he thought she was. "Just trying to be polite," he muttered. He stepped through the door she still held, with Ruby behind him. Then he watched as Kayla maneuvered her wheelchair through while keeping the door open with one hand. At one point, her wheel got caught, but he resisted the urge to help, and she managed to get over the threshold. If you asked him, she could have saved herself a lot of trouble by letting him help, but whatever.

They'd parked a couple blocks down, and Ruby nattered on about wanting Kayla to ride some horse named Big Blue as they made their way to the vehicles. When they reached Cameron's car, Kayla said goodbye to both of them, then continued to her own vehicle, parked a few cars back.

Cameron pulled open Ruby's car door and waited for her to climb in, watching the long, powerful movement of Kayla's arms on her wheelchair rims.

He shook his head again at her accusation that he thought she was helpless. Honestly, she was probably the most capable woman he knew. And that was saying something, given the women he worked with. In a lot of ways, her capable looked very different from theirs. Not because she used a wheelchair but because it was tempered with a compassion he'd seen in few people. And even less in people who made it a habit to yell at him.

"Kayla." He ducked into the car to tell Ruby to stay put, then jogged to catch up with Kayla.

She gave him a curious look.

He swallowed. "I wanted to apologize for the other night. For, you know, telling you to butt out. I know you only have Ruby's best interests at heart. There are just things you—" He cut off. "Anyway, I'm sorry. You were right about taking Ruby to see Bethany. It was obviously good for her."

Kayla offered a gentle smile, though it didn't erase the surprise in her eyes. "Apology accepted."

He stuck his hands in his coat pocket. "Good." He took a step backward, then stopped. "And you were right about Ruby's dad." He kept his voice low, in case little ears had big hearing. "I found him, but there's a reason Bethany didn't want Ruby to know him. He's a junkie."

Kayla gasped. "Oh no. I'm sorry." And she truly did look sorry, though it obviously wasn't her fault. But then she frowned. "Are you sure? How do you know?"

He shook his head and laughed darkly. She was unbelievable. First she told him not to find the guy because he might not be the sort of person Bethany would want to raise her kid. Now she was questioning his judgment when he said she'd been right.

"His arms had fresh track marks." He considered telling her how he knew what fresh track marks looked like, given that his sister was a junkie too. But that wasn't really something he wanted to discuss. There was a reason he kept his family life private.

"Anyway, I just thought you should know that I won't be searching for him anymore. So you can stop yelling at me."

Kayla's laugh sparkled into the cold air, brighter than the sunshine. "I can't make any promises."

Chapter 15

She couldn't do this. Kayla looked from Big Blue to Emma to Ruby to the bleachers, where Cam sat with his phone pressed to his ear. Why in the living world were his eyes on her every time she glanced that way? Was he waiting to see her fail?

It didn't matter. There was no way she could get up on this big beast of an animal. Not even for the satisfaction of seeing Cam disappointed.

She glanced his way again. He was leaning forward now, elbows on his knees, phone still pressed to his face, forehead wrinkled as his eyes went from Big Blue to her.

Then again . . .

"Let's do this."

"Yay! I knew you could do it." Ruby did a little dance in the arena sand and Emma smiled and led Big Blue to the wheelchair-accessible mounting ramp she'd pointed out to Kayla earlier.

Kayla tipped her chair back into a wheelie, then, with one last defiant glance at Cam, who, now that she looked closer, may not have been watching her after all, powered through the sand to the ramp. A few quick pushes on the hand rims got her to the platform at the top.

Emma had positioned the horse parallel to the platform so that its side was to Kayla. She drew in a deep breath. She knew there was a lift if she wanted to use it to put her on the horse. But she'd spent the past three days practicing the transfer onto a dummy horse. This was no different. Aside from the fact that she was getting onto the back of a thousand-pound living, breathing, moving animal.

"Just a sec," Emma said as Kayla positioned her chair alongside the horse. "Where did Miss Sarah go? I need her to hold— Cam!" Emma's shout made Kayla jump, her head jerking to where Cam now stood facing the arena, his phone still pressed to his ear.

Why was Emma calling for him?

"Can you come here a second?" Emma called.

A look of impatience flashed across Cam's face, but he said something into the phone, then hung up and vaulted the low arena wall in one smooth move.

Okay, not his first time in an arena.

He strode toward them, his loafers kicking up little clouds of dirt onto his khakis.

"What is it?" He crossed his arms in front of him.

"I need you to hold the horse steady while I help Kayla mount."

Kayla was about to protest that maybe they should do it another day, when Emma could have a qualified instructor hold the horse, but Cam nodded and grabbed the horse's harness, muttering to it in a low voice as he stroked its muzzle.

That she had not seen coming, although she supposed he *had* revealed a tiny bit of his soft side the other day at the hospital and the Chocolate Chicken. She'd assumed it was a one-time thing.

"All right," Emma climbed onto the ramp and took up a position next to Kayla. "Just like we practiced."

Kayla wanted to argue, but Cam's steely eyes were on her. She wouldn't let him see her fail. And anyway, Ruby believed in her.

She glanced at the little girl, who had clambered up the ramp after her and stood watching expectantly. "You can do it, Kayla."

She could still hear Cam whispering to the horse. He looked up with an almost-smile. "I've got him."

Kayla nodded, scooted to the front of her wheelchair and pulled in three quick breaths, then exhaled and lifted her right leg with her arms, hoisting it up and over the saddle. The horse barely moved.

"Easy," Cam's low, soothing voice intoned to the animal.

Readjusting herself in her wheelchair, Kayla gripped the saddle horn with her right hand and braced her left fist against her wheelchair seat. With one quick move, she straightened her left arm, at the same time pulling on the saddle horn with all her strength.

"You did it!" Emma's cheer reached her before she even realized that it was true—she was sitting in a saddle.

"I knew you could!" Ruby was dancing at the top of the ramp.

"Good job." Cameron patted the horse's nose, leading Kayla to believe his words were more for Big Blue than for her. But that didn't matter.

She had done it. She'd conquered her fear.

Emma handed Kayla what looked like the end of a seat belt. "Clip this around your waist."

Her hand shaking just the slightest bit—though she was no longer sure if it was from fear or adrenaline—Kayla snapped the seat belt into place as Emma tucked her toes into the stirrups.

"Are you ready?" Emma asked.

Kayla didn't hesitate this time. "Yes."

"All right." Emma turned to Cam. "You can let go."

He gave the horse's nose another rub, then let go and headed back toward the bleachers.

Emma jumped down from the ramp and took hold of Big Blue's lead rope. "You know what to do," she said to Kayla.

Gripping the reins in her hands, Kayla said in as commanding a voice as she could muster, "Big Blue, walk."

Kayla gasped as the large animal moved beneath her.

And then she started laughing.

Because for the first time in fifteen years, she felt like she was walking.

Cameron had meant to do some work after holding the horse for Kayla. Mary had sent him six reminders today about a brief he needed to get filed. But his laptop remained unopened on his lap. He told himself it was because he was impressed by the large animals or by the horsemanship Ruby showed at such a young age. But that didn't explain why his eyes kept straying to Kayla.

How could they not? That look on her face—like she was in complete awe—tugged at him. He was almost envious. When was the last time he'd felt like that about anything?

He shook his head and opened his laptop. He didn't need to feel awe. He didn't need to feel anything, really. What he needed to do was get this brief done. For the next half hour, he studiously avoided looking up, though that didn't keep him from hearing Kayla's delighted laughter—until he pulled out a pair of earbuds and popped them in.

There.

Now he could focus on the documents in front of him. Black and white, logical, emotionless documents.

The work wasn't necessarily interesting—mostly tedious—but it did the job in getting his focus back where it belonged.

Until the lesson was over and both Ruby and Kayla were in front of him.

"Ruby says you haven't bought a turkey." Kayla pointed an accusatory finger at him.

"Huh?" He tried to take his attention off her pink cheeks and bright eyes long enough to figure out what she was talking about.

"For Thanksgiving." Her stern voice made an odd contrast to her cheerful glow. "What are you doing for Thanksgiving tomorrow?"

He gave her a blank stare, and the determination on her face intensified.

What was it to her what they were doing for Thanksgiving? It wasn't like Ruby was going to starve if they didn't have turkey.

"We'll probably order a pizza or something." He made sure his tone wasn't defensive. He had nothing to feel defensive about.

But Kayla's look said she disagreed. "You are *not* feeding Ruby pizza for Thanksgiving. You're coming to Thanksgiving with us."

"Us?"

"My family and friends. We're helping serve the community Thanksgiving meal right after church."

Cam eyed her. Did she think he needed handouts? "Thanks, but I don't need charity."

Kayla shook her head. "You wear thousand-dollar suits. I didn't think you needed charity. I meant you guys could come help and then join us afterward at my brother and sister-in-law's house for our own dinner."

"Oh. I don't know," Cam hedged. "We couldn't—"

"You're coming. No arguments. Thanksgiving is a day to be with family and friends, right Ruby?"

Ruby nodded, flashing Cam her best smile. "Please, Uncle Cam. Kayla said they have apple pie, and that's my favorite."

Cam opened his mouth to say no again, but Kayla caught his eyes. "Please. I'd really like you to be there."

By "you," Cam knew she meant Ruby. But for whatever reason he found himself relenting slightly. "We'll see."

Both Ruby and Kayla cheered, and Cam fought to keep his lips in a straight line. He was *not* going to be influenced by that.

"Okay, so we have church at ten, if you're interested. Then the community dinner is around noon at Hope Church. And then dinner at Nate and Vi's at six or so." She pulled out her phone, her fingers zooming across the screen. "There. I texted you their address."

"I think you need to review the definition of 'we'll see,'" he said wryly, checking his phone as it dinged with Kayla's text.

"See you tomorrow." Kayla laughed and rolled back toward the arena.

Chapter 16

" I'm interested to meet this Cam guy."

Kayla stopped arranging the vegetable tray she'd been refilling and brought her attention to her sister-in-law. She'd been ruminating on Dan's Thanksgiving sermon from this morning, about being thankful for the unknowns and uncertainties. About trusting God to work things according to his timing, rather than demanding to know everything right now. Because God unfolded everyone's life one page at a time. And though Kayla wished sometimes that her story would turn to the next page already, it had been a reminder she needed to hear. Maybe there was a reason God had kept her on this page for now.

A Ruby-shaped reason, perhaps.

"Why do you want to meet him?" Kayla was on guard. Vi tended to get these crazy ideas about Kayla and men.

"Well—" Violet didn't miss a beat in her carrot chopping rhythm. "He sounds like a study in contrasts. He acts like Ruby is an inconvenience but then takes her to her riding lessons. He doesn't care about his sister but then can't handle seeing her in the hospital. He doesn't like you but then holds a horse so you can get on it."

"He doesn't— Those were all—" Kayla spluttered. She saw exactly what Vi was trying to do.

Anyway, it wasn't like it mattered much. She'd seen the look on his face when he'd said "we'll see" to her invitation last night. He had no intention of coming to Thanksgiving with her and her friends.

And poor Ruby was going to have to eat pizza for Thanksgiving. Maybe Kayla could at least make her a plate and bring it over there later. She supposed she could consider making one for Cam too.

"He's attractive, though, right?" Vi dumped her pile of carrots onto the tray.

"What—" Kayla stared extra-hard at the veggies. "I don't know. Why do you say that?"

"Because you get two little pink spots on your cheeks every time you talk about him." Vi's voice was teasing, but there was no way Kayla was going to let her think she was even a little bit right.

"I do not." She prayed her face wouldn't heat up. But if it did, it was only because Vi's charge was so ludicrous. "I have no interest in Cam. Zero. Zilch."

"Relax." Vi laughed at her. "It's not a crime to be interested in a man."

"Well, I'm not." Anyway, she had a feeling that it might be a crime to be interested in *that* particular man.

"But seriously." Vi rubbed her rounded belly, then picked up the vegetable tray and stepped toward the other room. "I know you worry about giving up your independence. But believe me, when you meet the right man, you won't feel like you're giving anything up. More like you're gaining a part of you that you didn't know was missing."

The kitchen door swung open as Vi was about to exit, and Nate rushed in. "Need more milk." He looked from his wife to Kayla. "What'd I miss?"

"I was just telling Kayla how wonderful marriage is."

Nate smiled and bent to kiss his wife. "I'll second that."

As Vi left the room, Kayla cleaned up their mess.

"So, why were you talking about relationships?" Nate's voice came from above her.

Kayla shrugged. "Your wife has some crazy notions."

Nate laughed. "That she does." He moved to the fridge and grabbed two gallons of milk. "So this guy you invited to dinner—"

Kayla rolled her eyes. "Not you too. He's Ruby's uncle. End of story. I have zero interest in him. I just didn't want Ruby to have pizza for Thanksgiving."

"Whoa." Nate held up his hands. "I was just going to say that this is all probably a pretty big adjustment for him."

"Oh." Kayla let her shoulders relax. "Yeah, I suppose it is." Though over the last couple days, he seemed to be doing better with it than he had at first. Remarkably well, actually.

Nate stepped closer. "But now that you bring it up, *are* you interested in him?"

Kayla's fist darted to slug her brother on the arm. *That* should answer his question.

"I can't wait. I can't wait. I can't wait." Ruby danced through the church parking lot, her purple dress flapping over the nearly matching pink and white striped tights.

"Come on." Ruby sped up. "We're late."

Yeah, over an hour late—mostly because Cameron had changed his mind about whether or not to come every five minutes this morning.

And he was about to change it again. Volunteering had never been his thing. And volunteering with a bunch of strangers sounded even less appealing.

But before he could call to Ruby to come back, she opened the church doors and disappeared inside.

Cameron sighed. He honestly didn't know what had possessed him to tell Ruby to get in the car—aside from the fact that Danielle had ignored his call this morning and that Ruby had asked six billion times if they were going and that she had the next four days off of school and he had no idea what he was going to do to keep her from driving him crazy.

The moment he opened the church door, the smell hit him: turkey, stuffing, potatoes. His mouth watered even as his stomach turned.

Thanksgiving had been his favorite holiday until the year he was twelve and Bethany was seventeen. He could still remember the smell of mom's turkey, the sound of the parade on TV and Dad's jovial laugh as he wrapped his arms around Mom and danced with her right in the middle of the kitchen. They'd sent him to go let Bethany know it was time to eat.

He'd knocked once, not bothering to wait for a response before pushing the door open. But the moment he stepped through, Bethany started screaming at him. He backed out quickly, but not fast enough to avoid seeing the needle shoved in her arm. He'd stood frozen in the hallway, no idea what to do, when Dad had come up to find out what all the commotion was about. Cameron told Dad what he'd seen, Dad called for Mom, and the two of them slipped into Bethany's room, locking him out. By the time they emerged, the turkey was blackened, the potatoes stuck to the pan, the stuffing inedible.

But it hadn't mattered because Mom and Dad had left that night to take Bethany for her very first stay at a rehab center.

Cameron distinctly remembered them telling him that everything was going to be fine—that Bethany had made a mistake, but we all made mistakes. That she would go away and come home all better.

The worst part was, they had believed it. Every single time. Until it cost them everything.

"Ruby." Cameron forced his mind to his sister's daughter as she disappeared down the stairs off to the side of the lobby. He couldn't do this. Not today.

But Ruby either didn't hear him or she chose to ignore him.

99

The door opened behind Cameron, and he stepped aside to get out of the way of an older gentleman.

The man stepped through the door and looked around. "Nice place."

Cameron grunted a response. He supposed it was. Somehow, in spite of its large size, it managed to give off a warm, cozy feel, with its tall windows letting in plenty of light and the comfortable looking furniture grouped around a large fireplace on the other side of the lobby.

The man stepped to Cameron's side. "You look lost, son."

"Not lost. Just thinking."

"I s'pose this is as good a place to do that as any." The man started toward the steps. "Ya comin' or not?"

Cameron wanted to say, "or not," but he couldn't leave Ruby here by herself. He followed the older man to the stairs.

"Been a long time since I celebrated Thanksgiving," the man said as if they were old friends. "Wife died six years ago. Haven't been able to bring myself to celebrate since then. But this morning, I woke up, looked out the window, and said, 'Sam, you get your grumpy ole butt out of bed and you get some turkey. Not eatin's not gonna change anything and ya can't hide from the past forever. So here I am."

Cameron made a sound at the back of his throat, no idea how else to respond. He didn't avoid Thanksgiving because he was trying to hide from the past. It was just that it was easier not to think about it. That wasn't the same as hiding. Was it?

At the bottom of the stairs, a festive signboard pointed the way to the fellowship hall—though the sign was made unnecessary by the growing aroma of food combined with the clatter of voices and dishes.

The moment they reached the large room, the other man made a beeline for the buffet. But Cameron stopped in the doorway, scanning the dozen long banquet tables crammed into the room, each nearly full. How was he ever going to find Ruby in this crowd?

"Cam. Glad you could make it." Pastor Dan strode toward him, hand outstretched. "Kayla mentioned you might come by to help out. My sister Leah is in charge of this shindig." He pointed to a blonde woman who was scooping turkey onto an elderly woman's plate. "She can let you know what we need help with."

"Have you seen Ruby?" Cam still hadn't spotted her, and an unfamiliar uneasiness went through him. He wasn't sure he liked it.

"She's in the kitchen."

Of course. Because that would be a safe place for a seven-year-old. He started in the direction Dan was pointing.

"Don't worry. Kayla's in there with her," Dan said to his back.

Ah. Cam did an about-face and headed toward the woman Dan had pointed out as his sister. He didn't know why he was suddenly reluctant to see Kayla, but he had a feeling it had to do with the way her glowing cheeks and breathless laugh had refused to leave him alone as he'd tried to fall asleep last night. Just because things with Danielle were rocky didn't mean he wanted to be thinking about some other woman. He wasn't that kind of guy.

He was sure Ruby was fine in the kitchen. He'd stay out here and help until this thing was over. Maybe he and Ruby could grab a bite to eat here and then beg off going to Kayla's brother's house.

But he was kept so busy clearing tables and emptying garbage cans for the next few hours that he didn't get a chance to sit down, let alone eat.

Though it certainly wasn't the type of work he was accustomed to, there was something oddly satisfying about it. Every once in a while as he passed the kitchen, he caught a glimpse of Ruby talking a mile a minute to Kayla, who was always smiling.

He tried to picture Danielle in Kayla's place but came up only with the pinched look she wore whenever someone failed to get right to the point. Still, that didn't make her a bad person. Just one who wouldn't do well with Ruby's constant chatter.

"Hey." Kayla had apparently sneaked up behind him. It was the first time she'd said anything to him today, and he wondered if she'd been avoiding him as studiously as he'd been avoiding her.

He looked up from the trash bag he was tying. "Hey."

"I'm glad you came."

He shrugged. "I'm glad you kept Ruby entertained."

She laughed, bringing her eyes to his. "More like she kept me entertained."

"You have to admit she's a little exhausting."

"Who's exhausting?" Ruby skipped over to Kayla's side.

"Your uncle Cam's just a wimp." Kayla raised an eyebrow at him, but before he could respond, a whistle pierced the air.

Cameron spun to find Dan standing at the front of the room, which had emptied of everyone aside from the handful of volunteers.

"Thank you all for making this event a success. We fed over three hundred people today. And that's thanks to all of you giving so generously of your time. Now, go home and enjoy your families."

A strange surge of satisfaction went through Cameron. It was similar to the satisfaction of completing a big deal—but sweeter somehow. Even though he wasn't going to get a bonus from it—unless sore feet counted as a bonus.

Kayla turned to them. "Ready to eat?"

This was the part where he should back out, say they couldn't make it. But as he looked from Kayla's bright eyes to Ruby's bright smile, he couldn't do it. "Let's go."

Chapter 17

$\mathcal{H}$ e'd come. Kayla wasn't sure what to do with that fact.

And he'd not only come, but he'd worked hard all afternoon. She didn't think she'd seen him once without dishes or a trash bag in his hands. And he hadn't once acted like it was beneath him.

Which meant she might have to rethink some of her assumptions about him.

But she'd worry about that later. For now, there was the more pressing problem of all the delicious food being passed around the table.

Next to her, Cam filled both his own plate and Ruby's with the dishes Kayla passed his way, looking a little shell-shocked. And she didn't blame him. She'd just introduced him to nearly everyone she knew in Hope Springs.

There were Nate and Vi, of course. And then there was Vi's sister Jade, who was married to Pastor Dan, along with their daughter Hope, who was a little younger than Ruby, and their one-year-old son Matthias. Plus Dan's sister Leah, her husband Austin, and their teenage son Jackson.

And that was just family.

Most of Nate and Vi's other friends had also made it: Emma; Sophie and Spencer and their twins; Tyler and Isabel and their three kids; Ethan and Ariana and their daughter; and newlyweds Grace and Levi and Luke and May. The only ones missing were Jared and Peyton, who were currently in China to meet their adopted daughter.

"So Cam, where are you from?" Vi asked from the other side of the table.

Kayla eyed her sister-in-law, trying to decide if she was up to something, but as far as she could tell, Vi was just being polite.

"Originally, Texas. But I've lived in LA since law school."

"You're a lawyer?" Kayla didn't mean to sound surprised. Actually, it made sense, the way he was always on his phone or his computer. "What kind?"

"Corporate law. Mostly mergers and acquisitions."

"That sounds . . . interesting?" Oops. It wasn't supposed to come out as a question.

"Yeah, it's—" Cam shook his head with a slight laugh. "Really not. A few high-stress moments followed by a lot of paperwork, mostly."

"What would you rather do?" Kayla didn't mean to ask the question, but there it was.

Cam gave her a blank look, as if he didn't understand what she meant.

"You know, like what did you want to do when you were a kid?" She tried to clarify. "Like, I wanted to be Supergirl."

Cam laughed. "I never had any superhero aspirations."

But she wasn't going to let him off the hook that easily. "Okay, then. What *did* you want to do?"

Cam studied his plate so long she was sure the conversation was over, but then he met her eyes. "My dad had a landscaping company. I worked with him in the summers when I was a kid. Always loved it." He turned away abruptly and stabbed at a piece of turkey but didn't lift it to his mouth.

Kayla already knew his parents were dead, since Ruby had no grandparents, and her heart went out to him. "You should do that then. Start your own landscaping company, I mean."

Cam shook his head, looking at her like she'd lost touch with reality. "It doesn't work like that."

"Sure it does. You just have to—"

"It's not going to happen," Cam said sharply.

Kayla bit her tongue. She'd gotten carried away. It was none of her business if Cam wanted to keep doing a job he hated.

"What about you, Kayla?" Emma asked from her other side.

Kayla shot her a relieved look. Anything so she didn't have to keep talking to Cam.

"I heard the camp closed," Emma said. "Embezzlement or something?"

Cam's head lifted at that, and he gave her a hard look. Well, it wasn't like she'd been the one stealing money.

"Our director," she told Emma. "I never would have believed it if he hadn't confessed."

"I hope the organization reported it," Cam cut in, his voice blistering. "The guy deserves to be prosecuted."

Kayla shrugged. "They haven't figured out what to do yet. To be honest, I feel sorry for him. He was going through a rough divorce and gave in to temptation."

"That's no excuse." Cam's hand was clenched tight around his glass.

Why did he care so much? It wasn't like he had any involvement with the organization. Maybe because he was a lawyer?

"No, it's not," Kayla agreed. "But he has repented and asked for forgiveness."

Cam's smile looked more like a sneer. "Of course he has. That's easy enough to say. Especially when you're facing the possibility of prison."

Kayla shrugged. "It's enough for me. Personally, I hope he doesn't end up in prison, but that's up to the courts. Either way, I forgive him."

"Of course you do."

Before Kayla could decipher whether Cam's mutter was meant to be sincere or sarcastic, Emma cut in. "So what are you going to do now, Kayla? Any leads on a new job?"

"Actually, no. Or well, yes. There are a few places I've considered applying, but I don't know. I feel like God has something else for me right now. I just put in an application for a six-month mission trip to Malawi."

"That's awesome. Sounds like it's right up your alley."

Kayla dropped her gaze to her plate. "I hope the organizers see it that way. That they don't think this thing"—she tapped her wheelchair's frame—"will get in the way."

"If it hasn't stopped you from skydiving and winning marathons, I don't think it's going to stop you from this either." Jade joined the conversation.

Cam's eyes swiveled to Kayla. "Skydiving?" Was that admiration in his voice—or disapproval?

Not that it mattered.

"Twice," she said, enjoying the shock in his expression a little too much. "Anyway—" She turned back to Emma and Jade. "I'll find out if I was chosen in a few weeks. So I guess I'll figure out what's next from there."

"Doesn't it bother you not to have a plan?" Cam looked horrified at the possibility.

She shrugged. "A little bit, maybe. But I've encountered more than one unexpected event in my life." She gestured at her motionless legs. "I've found that God always has a way of working them out."

Cam opened his mouth, but Ruby beat him to speaking. "Want to play a game with me, Kayla?"

Kayla smiled past Cam. "I'd love to." Her eyes flicked to Cam. "How about it? Up for a game?"

"That's three games in a row," Cameron crowed, moving his gingerbread man onto the castle. Apparently, Candy Land was his game.

Ruby pouted at him. "Don't you know you're supposed to let the kids win sometimes?"

"What fun would that be? Then you'd feel cheated." Cameron gathered up the game cards. "I think it's time to get you home to bed."

Ruby yawned. "But I'm not sleepy."

Kayla laughed from her spot on the floor next to Ruby. When they'd first gotten out the game, the tables had still been covered with food, so Ruby had suggested they play on the floor. Cameron had been searching for a way to tactfully remind her that Kayla used a wheelchair so she couldn't just go crawling around on the floor, but Kayla had beaten him to the punch by lifting her feet to the floor, then lowering her body to the ground. Actually, she'd gotten down here more smoothly than Cameron, who couldn't remember the last time he'd sat on the floor.

As she reached for her wheelchair now, he considered offering to help. Surely he could scoop her up and set her in it in a matter of seconds.

But he'd learned his lesson when he'd tried to hold the door for her at the Chocolate Chicken.

As he watched her hoist herself back into the chair, he couldn't help but be impressed. He wasn't surprised she'd won marathons—she obviously had the arm strength for it. But skydiving?

That crossed the border into crazy-town. He was more of a two-feet-on-the-ground kind of guy.

Which was the reason he didn't go off and do something nonsensical like leave the high-paying job that afforded him the lifestyle he'd always admired to chase some dream of opening a landscaping company.

Maybe in Kayla's world not knowing what was coming was okay. But not in his. He had a plan, and he wasn't going to change it—despite this temporary hiccup in Hope Springs.

Still, he had to admit that he'd ended up enjoying the day with Kayla's family and friends.

He attended plenty of parties in LA, of course—most of them much bigger and fancier than this had been. And yet, sometimes those felt more like performances, like putting on a show so that the other guests would like you and want to do business with you. Here, everyone seemed to genuinely know and care about one another.

Why they'd extended that care to him and Ruby, he wasn't sure. But he couldn't deny that it felt nice.

Chapter 18

"So I was right." Vi passed Kayla the Santa hat she was supposed to wear to the parade.

Kayla was sure she was going to regret asking, but she couldn't help it. "About what?"

She stuck the Santa hat on her head and examined the full effect of the costume in the bedroom mirror. She still wasn't quite sure how Emma had talked her into being Mrs. Claus. All she knew was that when Emma had shown up at church this morning with the costume and a plea that the mom who was supposed to be Mrs. Claus had gotten sick, she hadn't been able to say no.

"Cam is good looking." Vi grinned at her in the mirror, and Kayla reached a hand behind her to swat at her sister-in-law, but for a pregnant lady, Vi was pretty agile.

"You're married to my brother, you know."

"And he agrees with me."

"Nate thinks Cam is attractive?"

Now it was Vi's turn to swat at her. She hit her target, knocking the hat off Kayla's head.

Vi started to squat to get it, her hand on her back, but Kayla turned her chair and reached for it.

"He agrees with me that you and Cam have good chemistry," Vi said as Kayla resettled the hat on her head.

Kayla snorted. "If by chemistry you mean we make each other want to explode, then I guess you're right."

"That's not what it looked like to the rest of us."

"The rest of–" She should have figured that Vi and her friends would jump to conclusions.

"I promise you that the only thing we have in common is Ruby."

Vi patted her shoulder. "Relationships have started on less."

Kayla shook her head. "You're impossible." She spun her chair and headed out of the room.

"I'm just saying, don't be surprised if he asks you out at some point," Vi called behind her. "And don't do what you always do."

Kayla stopped her chair and looked over her shoulder. "And what do I always do?"

"You know." Vi made a vague gesture. "Chase a guy away before he ever has a chance."

Kayla rolled her eyes. "I don't do that."

Or, well, she did, but for good reason. It was either chase them away or risk losing herself.

"I'm leaving now." She wheeled to the front door.

But Vi's words chased her all the way to the church parking lot, where they were to line up for the parade. Was her sister-in-law right? Did Cam like her? And if he did, how did she feel about it?

Not good, she decided. *Not good at all.*

Even if a little tingle went through her at the thought that he'd be here in a few minutes.

"Wear this too." Cameron passed Ruby a scarf.

She dutifully took it. "Uncle Cam, I can barely move."

"It's cold out, and I assume we're going to be out there a while." He used to walk alongside the trailer he and dad decorated with small Christmas trees every year, so he wasn't completely unfamiliar with the concept. Although that had been in Texas, where a sweatshirt had been enough to keep him warm—wouldn't Dad laugh to see him now in a winter jacket on top of a heavy flannel on top of a thermal shirt?

He shook his head as he bundled an equally well-layered Ruby out the door and into the car. He'd found himself thinking about Dad and his business a lot over the last few days. And he needed to stop—before his feelings of nostalgia convinced him Kayla had been right in suggesting that he leave law to open his own landscaping business. It wasn't logical to give up a prestigious, high-paying job in favor of the challenges and uncertainties of running a small business—no matter how much he might enjoy it.

But as he drove toward the church to line up for the parade, he found himself looking at the yards they passed with a critical eye. That one had several dead trees in need of removal. And the one over there could benefit from a new retaining wall. Not to mention that the low, squat shrubs in front of nearly every house did little to add to their curb appeal.

Cameron slowed as he pulled onto Church Street. People, horses, fire trucks, and floats lined the road, but instead of feeling crowded, it had a festive air. Cameron eased into the church lot, searching for a parking spot. His phone rang as he pulled into one, and it took him a moment of digging through his various layers before he found it tucked into the pocket of his flannel.

Danielle.

"Come on, Uncle Cam. We're going to be late."

"I know. Just a sec." His eyes fell on Emma with the horses. "Why don't you go join Miss Emma? I'll be there in a minute." As soon as Ruby had clambered out of the car, he pulled the phone to his ear, his eyes tracking his niece as she ran toward the group from the stables.

"Hey, Danielle. I'm glad you called." He didn't mention that he'd been waiting three days for her to return his last call.

"Have you made any progress?"

Cameron sighed. He knew she wanted him to come home. He wanted that too. But it might be nice if she'd ask how things were going for once. "Nothing new yet. Honestly, I'm not sure what else we can do. I think I just have to ride this out and hope that Bethany wakes up soon."

"Ride it out?" Danielle made a disbelieving click. "And what about me, Cameron? I'm supposed to sit around here waiting for you?"

Cameron rubbed at his jaw, his eyes following Ruby as she reached Miss Emma and pointed in his direction. He lifted a hand to wave, though he doubted they could see him in the dark. "You could come here. I know you have plenty of vacation time and . . ."

"Wisconsin is not my idea of a vacation, Cameron." Danielle did not sound amused.

"It's not that bad." As long as you wore layers. Cameron snickered to himself, patting at his puffy jacket. "And then you could get to know Ruby and see that kids aren't so bad. Maybe we'll even want one of our own someday."

"I hope you're not serious, Cameron." She said the words with deadly precision. "Because I've already made my feelings on that perfectly clear. As have you, I thought."

"I know." He'd been kidding—mostly. He knew Danielle would never change her mind about that. And neither would he. Right?

He spotted Ruby, now marching toward the car with a whole pack of people behind her, including Miss Emma, who appeared to be waving some kind of red fabric at him. He squinted, trying to figure out what it was.

"I'm sorry, Danielle, I have to go for now. Someone's waving a Santa suit at me."

"A what? Cameron—"

"Talk to you soon." He hung up before she could protest again.

As he opened the car door, he let out a breath. But he didn't have long to brood about the conversation as Emma, Ruby, and a group of giggling girls descended on him.

"You have to be Santa," Ruby said at the same time that Emma shoved the red suit at him.

"Please," Emma added. "You're my last hope. My Mrs. Claus canceled this morning. And now my Santa just called. Apparently there's a nasty stomach bug going around."

Cameron eyed the suit. "I don't−"

"You have to do it, Uncle Cam." Ruby and the other riders looked up at him so earnestly that he felt his resolve weakening.

"So, who's Santa?" A woman's voice called from behind him. He didn't have to turn to know it was Kayla, but he did anyway, laughing as he spotted her costume. Apparently, Emma had found her replacement Mrs. Claus.

He held up the suit. "I guess I am."

Great. Now Kayla felt self-conscious around Cam.

Thanks, Vi.

If her sister-in-law hadn't put it in her head that Cam liked her, then she could be sitting calmly next to him in this horse-drawn wagon that had been modified to look like a sleigh, waving to the crowd that had braved the frigid night. Instead of analyzing his every move and word to figure out if it held hidden signs of attraction.

The good news was that so far she'd seen nothing to indicate that Vi was right.

Even so, Kayla couldn't help weighing her own words and actions to make sure she wasn't giving him the wrong impression. The last thing she needed was for him to think she returned his feelings−if he had any in the first place. Which he didn't.

Kayla forced her thoughts off Cam and his feelings or lack thereof and scanned the group of horse riders in front of them for Ruby.

"She's a good rider." She nodded toward where Ruby was drawing her horse to a halt.

Cam directed his gaze in Ruby's direction. "I'm not surprised. We rode a lot as kids. One of my dad's biggest clients was this huge ranch."

Huh. One of the things Vi might have been right about was that Cam was a study in contrasts. He made it clear that he didn't want anything to do with his sister, and yet when he talked about his past like this, Kayla heard the nostalgia and something deeper—rawer—in his voice. She debated asking him if something had happened but decided against it. During a parade while dressed as Santa and Mrs. Claus probably wasn't the best place for a heart-to-heart.

"Are you warm enough?" Cam clapped his gloved hands together, then shifted the blanket that sat across their laps so that it covered her more.

"I'm good." She kept waving to the crowd on her side of the sleigh.

"How can you tell?" He slapped a hand to his mouth, looking mortified. "Sorry. That was a Ruby question."

"No. It's fine." She never minded answering questions about her injury—and it was always preferable to people simply staring. "I do have to be careful because I can't feel when my feet are cold. But usually as long as I don't start shivering, I know I'm okay. Plus, I'm wearing wool socks and multiple layers, and I'm pretty much as covered up as a person can be." She eyed him. "Though maybe not quite as much as you."

He laughed and pulled his gray stocking cap tighter over his ears. "Hey, give me a break. I'm still adapting to this cold climate. I don't know how you handle it. I'll be glad to get back to the California sun."

Kayla nodded, relief going through her. She was being stupid to worry that Cam liked her. He lived in California. And he'd be going back just as soon as Bethany woke up.

"Hi, Santa. Hi, Mrs. Claus."

Kayla turned her head toward the voice and found a little boy waving at them, his parents standing behind him with their arms wrapped around each other. They would have made a perfect Christmas card.

A tiny wave of sadness went through her at the knowledge that she would never sit and watch a parade with a family of her own.

But she dismissed the thought immediately. Of course she would. She'd always have Nate and Vi and her little niece or nephew.

And that was all she wanted.

She shifted away from Cam the slightest bit, mainly to remind herself that she didn't need the warmth of another person next to her.

Chapter 19

"Don't you dare." Cameron eyed the cat crouching on the floor, shaking its haunches in preparation to jump onto the bed where Cameron sat with his computer on his lap. He'd already shoved the dumb creature off him a dozen times tonight.

But with a twitch of its tail, the cat jumped, coming to a light landing next to his leg. He nudged it off the bed, then checked the clock on his computer screen. It was nearing midnight.

He should go to sleep. He'd been staring at this screen for way too long without making any progress. He had three conference calls tomorrow, and for the first time in his career, he felt unprepared.

Possibly because somehow his computer browser kept clicking over to sites about starting a landscaping company. Which was completely the opposite of where his attention needed to be.

It needed to be on his actual job. On returning to California. On Danielle, who was apparently refusing his calls again—he'd attempted to reach her four times today and gone straight to voice mail each time. He'd tried not to be relieved that she hadn't answered.

With a weary groan, he stretched, then closed his laptop. Staring at his screen more wasn't going to get him any further tonight. His eyes fell on the Bible that had sat on Bethany's nightstand since the day he'd arrived. He hadn't been able to figure out what it was doing there, since his sister had never been the Bible-reading type. He reached for it, paging through it more out of curiosity than anything else. He raised his eyebrows at the highlights and penciled notes.

A section highlighted in purple caught his attention, and in spite of himself, his eyes tracked over the words. "Do nothing out of selfish ambition or vain conceit. Rather, in humility value others above yourselves, not looking to your own interests but each of you to the interests of the others."

Cameron almost choked on his sarcastic snort. The Bethany he knew was the very definition of selfishness and vanity. She'd never put another person before herself a day in her life.

He snapped the Bible shut and shoved it into the nightstand drawer. It was time to go to bed.

He was just pulling off his shirt when he heard the door across the hallway open and little footsteps running toward the bathroom. He shook his head. It wasn't Ruby's first late-night bathroom run. He kept telling her not to drink so much water before bed.

But instead of the sound of the bathroom door closing, he heard a strange sort of coughing noise. He pulled his shirt back on.

"Ruby?" He tugged his own door open. "You— Oh." He clapped a hand over his mouth and nose as Ruby stood over the emptied contents of her stomach.

"That's— Oh—" He fought off a gag as Ruby started crying. "It's okay." Though he didn't see how. "Do you have to throw up anymore?"

She shook her head.

"All right. Go change your pajamas and get back in bed. I'll bring you some water and then . . ."

Yes, and then what?

He had no idea how to take care of a sick kid.

He pulled his phone out of his pocket on the way to the kitchen, scrolling past Danielle's name with an ironic laugh. He could only imagine what she'd say if he asked for advice on taking care of a puking kid. Instead, he tapped on Kayla's name. He had no idea if she was a night owl or not, but it was worth a shot.

You still up?

Her reply came instantly. *What's wrong?*

He shook his head. How did she know? Then again, he'd never texted her at midnight before, so it probably wasn't too much of a leap. *Ruby threw up all over the place, and I have no idea what to do.*

Does she have a fever?

Check for a fever. Yeah. That was a good idea.

He grabbed a plastic cup out of the kitchen cupboard and filled it with water. He brought it to Ruby, whose hand shook as she drank it.

A small sliver of worry slid into his gut. That wasn't normal, was it?

He hurried to the bathroom, careful to give the puddle in the hallway as wide a berth as he could without looking at it. It only took a minute of rummaging in the closet to locate a thermometer.

"Bingo." He didn't know why it should give him such a sense of achievement, but he'd take it.

He brought the device to Ruby, who moaned slightly as he tried to figure out how to operate it. Finally, he realized that it was the kind that went under the arm.

It seemed to take forever to beep, but when it did, he pulled it out. Ruby moaned again.

99.4, he texted Kayla. *She keeps moaning.*

Poor thing. It's probably the stomach bug that's going around.

That made sense. And a stomach bug was nothing to worry about, right?

Okay, thanks. I need to try to clean this up and then email my secretary to reschedule my meetings tomorrow.

He shoved his phone in his pocket and went to search out some paper towels and carpet cleaner. And hopefully a pair of gloves too.

But his phone buzzed again almost immediately. *I can come watch her for the day if you need to do your meetings.*

Cameron stared at the phone. Not for the first time, he wondered who this woman *was* that she kept helping them without asking for anything in return.

He didn't want to take advantage of her. But he really *did* need to be on those calls.

You're sure? he finally texted. *It would only be for a couple hours, and I'll technically be here the whole time.*

I'm sure, Cam. I was going to go read to Bethany, but I'm sure she'd understand if I spend the day with her daughter instead. Now get that cleaned up and go to bed.

I will. Thank you, Kayla. He hesitated, then typed out the rest of his thought. *You may really be Supergirl after all.*

She sent a smiley face emoji, and he was about to put his phone away when he got one more message. *Oh, and give Ruby a pail. Just in case.*

Cameron groaned but then grinned. Supergirl, indeed.

Chapter 20

$\mathcal{K}$ayla looked up from her book at the sound of Cam's bedroom door opening. The cat curled in her lap picked up its head momentarily, then settled back onto her legs.

"How's she doing?" he whispered, glancing toward Ruby's sleeping form on the couch.

"She seems to be doing a little better. Just fell back to sleep."

To be honest, Cam looked like he could use some sleep himself, his usually tidy hair slightly askew and faint traces of blue under his eyes.

"Did you get any sleep at all?"

He shook his head. "She puked three more times during the night, so no. I had no idea kids could be so gross."

"Or that you could worry about them so much?"

He waved off her comment, but he wasn't fooling her with that tough guy act.

"How was the call?" She'd heard the low murmur of his voice from out here, which she had to admit had made rather soothing background noise.

"Don't ask. Let's just say I'm lucky the deal didn't fall apart right then and there. Speaking of—" He pulled his phone out of his pocket and checked the screen. "I'd better get on my next call. It shouldn't be longer than an hour."

She nodded. "Take your time. I'm plenty content here." Wait. Did that make it sound like—? She quickly held up her book. "I mean, with my book."

"Thank you again for doing this, Kayla." He smiled, then disappeared into the bedroom.

Kayla settled back into her book, reading until Ruby opened her eyes half an hour later.

"How are you feeling?"

Ruby rubbed her stomach. "I'm hungry."

"I know you are, sweetie. But maybe we should wait, just to make sure you aren't going to get sick anymore." Poor Cam had already cleaned up after her so many times. And Kayla was quite sure that was outside his usual wheelhouse, though she was proud of him for stepping up.

"I'm bored." Ruby sat up partway, and Kayla wheeled closer to the couch so she could adjust the pillows behind the girl.

"We can fix that. I can read you a book or we can watch a movie or play a board game."

"Can we play Barbies?"

"Sure. How about we play right here, though, so you can rest. I'll bring them over." She crossed the room and grabbed the box that held Ruby's Barbie collection. She wheeled back to Ruby, positioning herself so that she faced the girl. "You have a lot of these. Who do you want to be?"

"I'm Barbie." Ruby dug in the bin. "And you can be Ken." She passed Kayla a Ken doll.

"All right. What should Ken and Barbie do?"

Ruby gave her a goofy smile. "Go on a date."

A laugh burst from Kayla. They were starting young these days. "A date, huh?"

Ruby nodded but giggled. "They're boyfriend and girlfriend."

"Ah, I see." Kayla pretended to walk Ken across the couch, then made her voice deep. "Hello, Barbie. Would you like to go on a date with me?"

"Yes, Ken." Ruby made her voice even higher pitched, then dissolved into giggles.

But after a moment, she stopped and laid back on the pillows. "My tummy hurts again."

Kayla brushed the hair off her forehead. "Maybe no Barbies for now. How about I read to you instead?"

Ruby nodded, and Kayla moved to the small bookshelf in the corner to choose a book.

"Do you have a boyfriend?" Ruby's question came out of nowhere, and Kayla turned to peer at the girl over her shoulder.

"Nope."

"Do you want a boyfriend?"

Kayla turned back to the bookshelf. "Nope."

"Why not?"

Kayla paused, her finger on the spine of a book. "I'm too independent, I think."

"What does independent mean?"

Kayla pulled a book off the shelf and flipped through it. "It means I like to do things for myself. Make my own decisions."

"And you can't do that when you have a boyfriend?"

Kayla put the book back, pulling another off the shelf. "I suppose you can, but—" How in the living world was she supposed to explain this to a seven-year-old? "It's just different."

"Well, I still want a boyfriend." Ruby sounded so earnest that Kayla had to laugh.

"No boyfriends for at least another twenty years." Cam's voice from the other side of the living room made Kayla jump.

Heat rushed to her cheeks. How long had he been standing there? And how much of their conversation had he heard?

Not that it mattered. Anyone who knew her knew she wasn't interested in a relationship. It was no secret.

She set the book on her lap and turned her chair to face him. "We were just about to read."

He nodded, but the way he was looking at her was odd. He shook his head as if clearing away a thought. "Actually, my last call got canceled, so if you want to go, I've got it from here."

"Oh." How did she say she'd like to stay without it coming across the wrong way?

She didn't, that was how. "Okay." She set the book on the arm of the couch. "Feel better, Ruby."

"I will. Thank you for taking care of me."

"Anytime." She brushed the girl's hair off her forehead, then collected her bag and wheeled to the front door, Cam following behind her.

"Wait!" Ruby's call was urgent, and both she and Cam spun toward her.

"What's wrong? Do you have to throw up again?" Cam made a face but stepped toward Ruby.

But she shook her head. "I have a great idea."

Cam stared at her. "All that commotion was for an idea?"

"Yep." Ruby was unapologetic. "It's a really good idea. Kayla should come to the zoo with us on Saturday."

"Oh. Uh—" Cam glanced over his shoulder at Kayla for a millisecond before turning away. "I thought you wanted to bring a friend."

"Kayla is my friend," Ruby insisted, and Kayla's heart went all syrupy.

"I'm sure Kayla has other—" Cam looked over his shoulder again, his expression a clear plea to help him out.

But there was no way Kayla could say no to such a sweet invitation. "I'd love to come if you don't mind."

Cam studied her for a long moment. Then he shrugged. "We'll pick you up at nine."

Chapter 21

" It's zoo day! It's zoo day!" Ruby danced around the kitchen. She'd made a remarkable recovery after Tuesday's illness, and she was definitely back to her old, noisy self. Cameron was surprised at the intensity of his relief about that. It was odd to him how unsettling it had been to see her sick.

He gave her a mock frown and pointed to her soggy bowl of cereal. "Eat. Or we're not going anywhere."

Which, honestly, might be the best course of action. What had he been thinking, letting Ruby invite Kayla along?

But he supposed he did owe her, after the way she'd come to his rescue watching Ruby so he could make his conference calls.

And he'd overheard her telling Ruby that she wasn't interested in dating, so he didn't have to worry that she'd get the wrong impression about their relationship. Not that it even was a relationship—more like an acquaintanceship.

"When can we see Mommy again?" Ruby followed her question with a big slurp of the milk left in her cereal bowl.

"We just went yesterday." This time, Cameron hadn't run out of the room, though he'd remained planted in a corner while Ruby talked up a storm to her mother.

"I know, but the doctors said it's good for her to hear my voice. It will help her wake up."

Cameron held in a sigh. The doctors also said that if Bethany was in the coma much longer, her chances of coming out of it fell dramatically. Though that part he hadn't shared with Ruby.

What if Bethany didn't wake up? The thought had been circling his head all night.

What would happen to Ruby? Since he was Bethany's only living relative, did that mean the state would automatically give Ruby to him? And did he want her?

The truth was, he didn't know. He never would have guessed it three weeks ago when he arrived, but there were parts of taking care of her that weren't all bad. Kind of enjoyable, even. Like the way she gave that goofy gap-toothed grin or made a surprisingly witty comment that forced a chuckle out of him. Or wrapped her little arms around him in an unexpectedly powerful hug.

But did he want to give up his whole life, everything he knew—including, quite possibly, his girlfriend—to become a father to her? That was a big step. One he wasn't sure he was prepared—or qualified—for.

"I'm ready." Ruby wiped the back of her hand over her milk mustache.

He sighed. Figuring out the future could wait.

For now, they had a trip to the zoo to get on with.

Cam seemed different today, but Kayla couldn't quite put her finger on what it was. She'd noticed it almost the moment he'd picked her up this morning, and it had lasted through the hour-long car ride and the past two hours at the zoo.

Maybe it was the fact that he was wearing jeans instead of his usual dress clothes. Or that he didn't have his phone attached to his ear. Or that he actually smiled every once in a while.

Whatever it was, it gave him a relaxed, less aloof air. And for some reason, that was making her uncomfortable, though she was more than happy to see Ruby enjoying herself.

"Can we get some popcorn? And then go see the giraffes? They're my favoritest favorites." Ruby skipped between them, and Kayla caught the look of envy a woman walking past with two screaming toddlers shot them.

Kayla was tempted to call out to the woman that they weren't the happy family they must look like. Even if it almost felt like they were.

That was it. That was what was making her so uncomfortable. The fact that they looked like all the other families here—and that she couldn't convince herself that she didn't like it.

"That popcorn does smell good." Cam veered toward the popcorn stand off to the side of the path. "Three bags."

"Make that two," Kayla cut in. "I'll get my own."

Cam gave her an odd look. "I've got it." He turned back to the teenager working the cart. "Make it three."

"Cam, I said I'll get it myself." She didn't know why it was such a big deal to her, but it was.

"Kayla, it's fifty cents. I think I can spring for it. I owe you for watching Ruby the other day."

The teenager looked uncertainly between Cam and Kayla. "So a dollar fifty, then?" He passed three bags of popcorn through the window.

Cam paid, then passed a bag to Ruby before grabbing up the other two and carrying them toward a table on a stone terrace that overlooked a small pond.

Kayla let out a huff as she followed. She was being stupid, but for some reason it really bothered her that Cam had bought the popcorns. She knew he was right that she'd more than paid him back by watching Ruby. But that was something a friend or even a babysitter did. Buying popcorn was something a date did. And this was *not* a date.

And she didn't want it to be one.

At the table, Cam passed her a bag of popcorn, but she set it down.

"I'm going to run to the restroom while we're stopped." She needed a minute to herself. Besides which, since she couldn't feel her bladder, she'd had to train her body to follow a schedule, and it was almost time.

"Do you need to go, Ruby?"

The little girl shook her head. "I went before we left home. Uncle Cam forgot to tell me, but Mommy always does, so I knew."

Kayla smiled at the girl, then wheeled away, feeling Cam's eyes on the back of her head. She didn't look over her shoulder.

Thankfully, by the time she'd finished in the restroom, she had managed to talk some sense into herself. She could even laugh at herself for getting so freaked out at the thought of family and dating. Neither Cam nor Ruby were thinking like that. She'd just let her imagination get away with her—or, more like Vi's imagination.

She'd go back out there and they'd continue on with their trip to the zoo—just an uncle and his niece and their friend.

She maneuvered out of the bathroom and toward the terrace where she'd left them.

Cam sat at the table, his phone pressed to his ear, and Kayla rolled her eyes at herself. All those worries about why Cam was acting so differently today—and here he was on his phone again.

She scanned the terrace for Ruby but didn't spot her among the few other families gathered there. She craned her head over her shoulder in both directions but didn't see her there either.

She sped toward Cam's table.

"Cam!" Her voice was sharp, but he didn't stop talking or even look up.

She shoved her chair closer and yanked the phone out of his hand.

That got his attention. "What are you—" He cut off as his eyes fell on her. "What's wrong?"

"Where's Ruby?" She barely managed to keep the panic out of her voice.

"She went to throw her popcorn bag away." His eyes darted across the terrace. "She was just here . . ."

His eyes met hers, horror-struck. "Where'd she go?"

"It's okay." Kayla needed him to stay calm, which meant she needed to stay calm herself. "We'll find her."

Cam sprang up from the table so quickly that Kayla had to roll her wheelchair backwards so he wouldn't plow into her.

He grabbed his phone from her and lifted it to his ear. "I'm going to have to call you back."

Without waiting for a response, he hung up, then spun in a slow circle, his eyes tracking across the landscape.

The moment he turned toward the pond, he froze, then sprinted toward it.

Kayla's heart leapt to her throat.

A thin sheen of ice skimmed the surface, not thick enough to hold a mouse, let alone a child.

Ruby wouldn't have . . .

Would she?

Kayla took off after Cam, who had scrambled down the side of the embankment that rimmed the shore.

He looked up, relief mingled with fear in his expression. "She didn't come down here." He rushed back up the bank.

"She couldn't have gone far. It's only been a few minutes." She focused on keeping her voice calm to steady both of them. "You go that way—" She pointed over her shoulder. "I'll go this way. Make sure you ask anyone you see. Find someone from the zoo if you can, and have them let the rest of the zoo's employees know."

He gave a terse nod, already striding away.

"Cam!" she called to his back.

He turned but didn't stop walking.

"We'll find her. Call me the second you have anything."

Chapter 22

Cameron raised his voice, fighting to call his niece's name over the pulse thumping hard and fast in his throat. His sister, the perennial screw-up, had managed to keep Ruby alive and intact for seven years. And now he'd been with the kid for less than a month and he'd already lost her.

"Ruby!" The name came out as a sharp gasp, and a woman holding a little girl's hand gave him a strange look. He jogged over to her, half expecting her to run away at his likely crazed expression.

But she stood her ground, tugging the girl closer to her.

"Sorry, ma'am. But have you seen a little girl walking around? She's wearing a—" What had she been wearing? Her coat, right? He saw it hanging on the hook by the door every day, watched her put it on before school. It was . . . "A blue coat. With snowflakes on it."

The woman shook her head. "Sorry. I haven't."

"Okay. Um." Why couldn't he think straight? He dealt with crises at work on a daily basis. And they'd never clouded his head like this. He took a breath. He had to take the emotion out of the situation. What he needed was some logic. Except, somehow that was a lot harder to pull up when it came to his missing niece than a stranger in a boardroom.

"Why don't you give me your number, and if I see her, I'll call you." The woman's voice was kind as she passed him her phone.

"Yeah. Okay. Yeah, that's a good idea." It took Cameron three tries to type his number in with his shaking hands, but he finally passed the phone back to the woman.

"What's your daughter's name?" the woman asked.

"Oh. She's not my— It's Ruby. Her name is Ruby."

"That's a pretty name." The little girl who had remained quiet throughout his exchange with her mother smiled shyly at him. "I'll say a prayer that you find her."

"Uh—" Cameron scratched at his cheek, backing away. He shouldn't be wasting time chatting. He needed to keep looking for Ruby. "Thanks."

He turned and set off at a jog again. "Ruby!"

A bear in the enclosure next to him lifted its head.

But there was no sign anywhere of his little niece.

Please, God. Let us find her. He didn't know where the prayer had come from, didn't remember the last time he'd prayed, but it was the only thing he could think to do.

Ten minutes later, Cameron's feet dragged to a stop. Prayer or not, they were never going to find her.

What if someone had kidnapped her or—

No. He couldn't let his thoughts go there.

He'd alerted zoo security, and they were checking every visitor who left the zoo.

His phone rang, and he snatched it out of his pocket, exhaling hard as he read Kayla's name on the screen.

"Please tell me you found her."

"By the giraffes." Her laugh was shaky and weak. "We should have known."

"I'll be right there."

The moment he hung up, his feet kicked into a sprint, and he followed the signs that pointed the way to the giraffe enclosure.

When he finally spotted Ruby and Kayla watching a giraffe amble past, relief and anger collided in his chest. How could the little girl put him through something like that?

He slowed to a walk, though his heart continued to pump like mad.

"Hi, Uncle Cam." Ruby's oblivious greeting sent him over the edge.

He opened his mouth to yell at her. But her eyes, a perfect reflection of his own, welled with tears, and next thing he knew, he was crouching and pulling her to him in a hug. "Are you okay?"

Ruby nodded against his jacket, her little arms squeezing his neck. "I'm sorry. Do you forgive me?"

Cameron hesitated, then nodded. "Don't ever do that again, okay?"

As Ruby nodded again, then skipped back to the giraffes, Cameron could only look at Kayla and shake his head. He wondered if she was thinking the same thing he was: parenting sure was heart-wrenching work.

It was one more reminder of why he didn't want to do it permanently. He'd never be able to handle all the messes. All the cleaning up. All the sleepless nights.

All the smiles. All the hugs. All the giggles.

He shook off the thought. Sure, that stuff was nice. But it didn't make up for the hassle of having your days completely consumed by caring for another human being.

Did it?

Chapter 23

Cameron strained for a glimpse of Ruby among the children flooding out of the school Monday afternoon. Ever since almost losing her at the zoo the other day, he'd found himself fighting off a sense of unease whenever he didn't know right where she was. He knew it was silly—she was obviously among these talking and giggling kids. But that close call had left him more than a little shaken.

If he'd lost her, he didn't know . . .

Cameron shook his head. He *hadn't* lost her, thanks to Kayla.

Finally, he spotted Ruby trailing behind the other kids, head down and feet dragging. Cameron frowned. That wasn't the Ruby he knew at all—the one who was always at the center of the group, laughing and talking away. He hoped she wasn't sick again.

He waved as she got closer to the car, but she didn't look up.

Now what did he do?

He'd gotten used to dealing with happy, bubbly Ruby—even when he got annoyed sometimes at *how* cheerful she could be. But he had no idea how to deal with sullen, sulky Ruby.

She kept her sullen expression as she slid into the back seat.

"Hey, Rubes." He injected an extra note of cheer into his greeting. "Feeling okay?"

"Yes." Her voice was flat.

"Oh." If that wasn't the problem, then what? "How was your day?"

"Terrible." Ruby clicked on her seat belt, then crossed her arms in front of her.

"I'm sure it couldn't have been that bad." He pulled out of the parking spot. "What was so terrible about it?"

"I'm a sheep."

Cameron angled his head so he could see her in the rearview mirror. "You look like a girl to me."

"Very funny." She didn't bother to stick her tongue out at him, instead sinking deeper into her seat. "In the play. I wanted to be the star. But Cassidy got it. Like always. I'm just a dumb old sheep."

"Oh." Cameron was at a loss. He didn't have the vaguest idea how to deal with a problem like this. "I'm sure the sheep is important too."

Ruby made an impatient noise. "I hardly even say anything. I crawl onstage, baa, and then crawl back off. It's the lamest part ever."

Cameron nodded. It did sound a little bit lame, but even he was smart enough to know he shouldn't say that. What would Kayla say if she were here? Something that would cheer Ruby up for sure.

But whatever it was, he couldn't come up with it.

They drove the rest of the way home in silence.

"Do you want a snack before homework?" They'd settled into an afternoon routine that was as normal to him now as reading the daily briefs had been only a few weeks ago.

"No." Ruby was still sulking as she unzipped her backpack. "Here. I forgot to give you this the other day."

Cameron took the note, frowning. A note from the teacher? Maybe there was more going on here than a bad part in a play.

"Our school bake sale is Tuesday, December 4," he read aloud. "You are signed up to bring—" His mouth opened, and he jerked his head up to Ruby. She looked at him blankly, and he lifted the paper again. "Six dozen cutout cookies."

She nodded.

"Ruby, December 4 is—" He pulled out his phone to confirm. "Tomorrow."

She nodded again.

"How long have you known about this?"

She shrugged. "I lost the paper in my desk."

"Where are we going to get six dozen cookies on short notice?" He pulled out his phone. "What's the name of the bakery?"

"We have to make them." Ruby gave him a look like that should have been obvious.

He shook his head, tapping the word "bakery" into the search bar. "I don't know how to make"—he glanced at the paper again—"cutout cookies." Actually, he didn't even know what cutout cookies were.

"I know how. Mommy makes them with me every year."

Cameron looked up from his phone. Bethany made cookies? He had such a hard time, sometimes, trying to reconcile the Bethany he knew with the one Ruby seemed to know.

He glanced back down at the phone, clicking on the website for the bakery. *Please let it still be open.*

He frowned at the listing. It had closed twenty minutes ago. "The grocery store probably has some. Maybe not six dozen, but . . ."

"I told you, Uncle Cam. We have to *make* them. Everyone else does. I can't be the only kid who walks in with grocery store cookies."

"I'm sure you won't be the only one—"

But she stopped him with her look. The one that said he was disappointing her again.

He sighed. "Fine. We'll figure it out. But if they end up tasting like feet, don't blame me."

She giggled, then clapped a hand over her mouth and refastened the frown on her face. But he let a grin lift his lips at the temporary reappearance of the Ruby he knew and loved.

Wait.

Loved?

He let the shock of the word go through him.

Yeah, he loved his niece. The wonder of the revelation nearly stole his voice.

But he pulled out his phone and managed to say, "I think we're going to need some backup."

Chapter 24

Kayla's arms quaked with fatigue, but she didn't ease up, instead pushing harder to spin the wheels of her racing wheelchair on the rollers that acted like a treadmill for the chair.

But as hard as she tried to focus on nothing but the rhythm of her gloved hands against the rims, her thoughts kept getting caught in a loop. A loop that involved Ruby, Bethany, and way too much Cam. Cam steadying her horse. Cam asking if she was warm enough at the parade. And most of all, Cam hugging Ruby to him at the zoo the other day. She was willing to bet that even he hadn't realized how much he cared about the little girl until that moment.

She had to admit that if ever her heart had been in danger of falling for Cam, it had been then. Fortunately, she'd withstood the test.

"Training again?" Vi waddled into the room.

Kayla didn't answer, knowing full well that her sister-in-law hadn't come in here to discuss her training regimen.

"You know it won't help, right?"

Giving up, Kayla straightened, letting the wheels spin on their own. Her lungs pumped with hot breaths, and she ran her forearm over her hairline. "What won't help?"

"Running away."

Kayla gestured at her wheels, which were still spinning, slowing as the friction of the rollers worked against their momentum. "Hard to run away when the wheels aren't going anywhere."

"You know that's not what I meant."

"I have no idea what you meant," Kayla said honestly.

Violet laughed. "All right. I'll spell it out for you. You like Cam and you're freaked out and you're trying to ignore it, but it's driving you crazy so you're throwing yourself into your training to try to convince yourself you're happy alone."

"I *am* happy alone."

Vi studied her. "Maybe. But there's a part of you that wonders if you could be even happier with him."

Kayla made a noise that was supposed to indicate just how far off Vi's theory was. She was just the right amount of happy the way she was.

"Why not see where it goes at least?" Vi asked. "Give him a chance."

Kayla rolled her eyes. "For one, he hasn't asked for a chance." Was that what was bothering her? Kayla pushed the thought away. That was preposterous.

"And for another, he lives in LA."

"I think Hope Springs is growing on him. Or you could always move. I hear it's sunny in California."

Kayla shook her head. "Honestly, Vi, I don't even know what I want with *my* life right now. Let alone getting involved with someone else's." That was the biggest issue. Until she figured out what she was going to do next, she didn't feel equipped to figure out who she wanted to do it with—if anyone.

"That's fair enough." Vi lowered herself slowly onto Kayla's bed, her belly bulging in front of her. Apparently their conversation wasn't over. "Just remember that there are very few things you can't do with another person at your side. In fact, most things are easier that way.

'Two are better than one, because they have a good return for their labor: If either of them falls down, one can help the other up.'"

Kayla knew it didn't pay to argue with Vi when she used Scripture—especially the verse from her wedding. Instead, she gestured to Vi's belly. "How's our little one today?"

The distraction worked. Vi rubbed a hand over her belly, with a rueful laugh. "I think he might be a musician like his daddy. He's decided my ribs are a xylophone."

Kayla laughed with her. "You think it's a boy then."

Vi bit her lip but nodded. "Yeah. I don't know why, but I just get a feeling."

"Well, I still think it's a girl."

The opening notes of Nate's song "He Holds Me" rang out from Kayla's phone, which was on the bed where she'd left it before she'd folded herself into her racing chair.

Vi reached for it, then looked at her with an impish grin. "It's Cam."

"Yeah, right."

"No, really." Vi held up the phone so Kayla could see the screen. "Told you he was interested."

"And I told you *I* wasn't interested. Let it go to voice mail."

"You're answering this." Vi held the phone out to her, but Kayla shook her head. "Or I am."

Kayla studied her sister-in-law. But she knew Vi didn't bluff.

"Fine. One second." She used her teeth to grab the Velcro that held her thumb against her glove, then tucked her hand under the opposite armpit to pull the glove off.

"It's going to go to voice mail," Vi warned.

Kayla shrugged but quickly unwrapped her other gloved hand and held it out.

Vi hit answer before dropping the phone into Kayla's hand, then waved and waddle-flounced out of the room.

Kayla stuck her tongue out at her sister-in-law's back before lifting the phone to her ear.

"Are you there?" Cam was asking.

She tried not to let the sound of his voice play with her heart. And failed.

"Yeah. I'm here."

"Good." Relief seeped from Cam's voice, and she was instantly on alert.

"Why? What's wrong?"

"I have to make six dozen cutout cookies by tomorrow." Panic laced his words. "Those are the ones in different shapes, right? Oh, and Ruby didn't get the part she wanted in the play, and I didn't know what to say to her."

A relieved laugh escaped Kayla's mouth, both because nothing was wrong with Ruby and because Vi had been wrong. Again.

Cam wasn't calling because he liked her. He was calling because he needed her baking skills. Or what there was of them.

"Do you need some help over there?"

"Yes, please." His voice was warm, and it wrapped around her like a hug.

She shook off the feeling—she didn't need a hug—and focused on the task at hand. Six dozen cookies and cheering up a disappointed little girl.

"Do you have everything you need?"

"I have no idea. What do I need?" His cluelessness was slightly exasperating—and slightly endearing.

"Just a second." She set the phone down so she could extricate herself from her racing chair and transfer to her regular wheelchair, then grabbed the phone again and brought it to the kitchen.

"Do you have a good cutout cookie recipe?" she asked Vi.

Her sister-in-law gave her a knowing look that Kayla pointedly ignored, then pulled out a recipe book that had to be about a hundred years old. She flipped to a page near the back. "This was my grandma's recipe."

Kayla thanked her, then read off the ingredient list to Cam. She could hear him searching Bethany's cupboards in the background.

"I have everything except powdered sugar."

Kayla pulled the phone away from her ear and turned to Vi. "Do you have powdered sugar?"

Vi gave her that same knowing look and nodded.

"All right. I can be there in twenty minutes," she said into the phone.

"Thank you, Kayla. You're my hero. I think we might have to promote you from Supergirl to Superwoman."

She snorted and hung up. She could barely look at Vi, who had not wiped that knowing expression off her face.

"Don't look at me like that. I'm helping out for Ruby's sake."

"I know." Vi winked and Kayla couldn't help but laugh, even as she snatched a towel and tossed it at her sister-in-law.

Chapter 25

"Kayla's here!" Cameron called from the spot he'd taken up at the window when every attempt to get Ruby to smile again had failed.

Ruby simply nodded from the spot where she'd plopped on the couch. Cameron had half a mind to march down to that school and give whoever had decided his niece wasn't good enough to play anything but a sheep a piece of his mind. But he had a feeling that wouldn't help. He could only hope Kayla would know what to do.

He watched as she reached across to the passenger seat and grabbed her wheelchair, attached the wheels and cushion, and transferred into it.

It wasn't the first time admiration for her—for the way she dealt with her disability, the way she never complained, the sheer strength she showed every day—had struck him.

She opened the back door of the car and reached inside, pulling out a plastic bag, which she set on her lap before wheeling toward the house.

Her eyes landed on him, standing in the picture window, and she waved.

He supposed he should be embarrassed that she'd caught him watching her. But he waved back, then moved to open the front door.

"I hear we have some cookies to bake." Kayla popped the front wheels of her chair over the doorframe, carrying the scent of the cold, but also something sweet and coconutty. He moved to close the door, but she had stopped dead right inside it.

"What do you have against Christmas?"

He blinked at her—why would she think he had anything against Christmas? "Nothing. Why?"

She waved a hand wildly to encompass the whole room. "Where are your Christmas decorations?"

He pulled out his phone and checked the date. "It's only December 3." Honestly, decorations hadn't even occurred to him.

"Exactly. Christmas is only three weeks away. What do you say, Ruby? Should we decorate after we make the cookies?"

Ruby gave a listless shrug, and Cameron gave Kayla a helpless look. There was no getting through to Ruby tonight.

But with a determined set of her mouth, Kayla opened the bag on her lap and rummaged in it. She pulled out a bag of powdered sugar and passed it to Cameron, then wheeled over to Ruby and reached back into the bag. This time she came out with a white headband with woolly ears attached. She held it out to Ruby, who shook her head and crossed her arms.

"I heard you get to be a sheep in the play," Kayla said brightly, "so I thought this might help you get into character."

"I don't want to be a sheep."

Kayla shrugged and stuck the headband on her own head. It should have looked ridiculous, but she actually looked kind of cute like that.

"Did I ever tell you about the time I auditioned for the role of Dorothy in The Wizard of Oz?" Kayla steered her wheelchair into the kitchen, and Ruby followed. Cameron brought up the rear.

"Look how organized this is." Kayla shot Cameron an approving smile. "There might be hope for you yet."

Yeah. He'd gotten ingredients out of the cupboards. He was practically a master chef. Still, he had to appreciate her attempt to be nice. Sure beat all the times she had yelled at him in the past few weeks.

"Anyway—" She turned back to Ruby, the sheep ears bobbing. "I wanted the role of Dorothy so badly. I practiced every day. My mom even got me a pair of red sparkly shoes that I wore everywhere. I thought I did a good job at my audition, so I was sure the part would be mine. I wore my red shoes to school the day they announced who got what parts. And when they called my name, I stood up, all ready to take the stage as Dorothy. Except I didn't get the part of Dorothy."

She paused dramatically, and Cameron had to hand it to her. She had certainly drawn Ruby into her story. Him too, if he was being honest.

"What part did you get?" Ruby whispered.

"A tree," Kayla said, keeping a straight face. "Not one of the cool talking trees. One of the trees that stood in the background and didn't do anything."

"That's lame. Almost as lame as a sheep." Ruby collapsed into a chair.

"Lamer," Kayla said. "But you know what I did?"

"Quit?"

"No." Kayla tapped Ruby's nose. "I decided that if I was going to be a tree, I would be the best tree there ever was. I would eat, sleep, and breathe being a tree. I only wore brown and green. And I made people call me 'Tree' instead of Kayla."

Ruby giggled, but Kayla kept a serious face. "And you know what? It worked. I was the best tree anyone had ever seen. And the very next year, I got to be the big bad wolf when we did a play of the three little pigs."

Cameron couldn't help bursting into laughter. Kayla was tough and feisty, sure, but the big bad wolf?

She gave him a look of mock hurt. "I'll have you know that people are still talking about my performance as the wolf."

Cameron raised an eyebrow. "What people?"

She shrugged. "My parents, mostly."

He laughed harder, and Kayla grinned as she tapped the headband on top of her head. "That's why I thought you might like this. To practice being the best sheep this town has ever seen. What do you say?"

Ruby eyed the headband, then nodded. Kayla pulled it off her head and slipped it onto Ruby's.

"Baa," Ruby said immediately.

Cameron and Kayla laughed together, and Cameron's heart lightened. That was one crisis averted.

Now for the next. "Should we make these cookies?" He moved to Kayla's side at the table. "Tell me what to do."

She pulled a ratty old book out of her bag. "I brought Vi's recipe. She said it's been in her family for like a hundred years. Why don't you mix the dry ingredients? Ruby and I will get the wet ingredients going. Then we'll put it all together."

Ruby baaed at her.

"Oh, sorry. Sheep and I will get the wet ingredients started."

Ruby gave a satisfied nod and let out another baa. Cameron suppressed a groan. That was going to get old fast.

But as he glanced at Ruby and Kayla with their heads bent close together, he had to admit, it was a small price to pay.

The oven timer dinged, and Kayla looked up from the artificial branch she'd been trying to wrangle into some semblance of an actual tree.

"I'll take care of the cookies. You two keep figuring this thing out." She backed her chair carefully through the scattered piles of artificial pine branches.

"I can get them." Cam started to get up from the floor.

"Absolutely not." Kayla gestured to the mess surrounding them. They were having a doozy of a time trying to figure out how this tree went together. "This is your job."

And anyway, she needed a second to remind herself that none of this was real. Because with the sugary sweet scent of baking cookies filling the house, soft Christmas music playing in the background, and the Christmas decorations scattered around them, it'd almost started to feel like she, Ruby, and Cam were a cozy little family.

"I'm not sure when you became boss," Cam muttered.

"Right about the time you called in a panic and said you needed help with the cookies."

"Touché." Cam shrugged, then attempted to fit his branch into the tree's thin trunk. It snapped into place with a satisfying click.

They all looked at each other in surprise, then let out a cheer.

"Smooth sailing from here," Cam said. "Could you pass me another one of the long ones, Rub—sheep?"

Ruby baaed, then passed one to him. Cam threw Kayla an exasperated look. "Thanks for that."

But she could tell that he was grateful to see Ruby back to her cheerful self.

In the kitchen, Kayla pulled the golden cookies from the oven. She took her time scooping the cookies onto the cooling rack and loading the pan with another batch of reindeer and candy canes and angels, working to talk some sense into herself as she did. This was all an illusion. Yes, she was friends with Ruby. And maybe with Cam. But there was nothing beyond that. And there never would be. But every time she almost had herself convinced, a Ruby giggle or a Cam rumble tickled her ears, and she had to start all over again.

When she finally returned to the living room, any sense she'd managed to talk into herself disappeared in the face of Cam's and Ruby's wide grins. They stood in front of the tree, holding their arms out toward it as if they were models showcasing a masterpiece rather than a scraggly, precariously leaning Christmas tree.

Kayla clapped her hands. "It's beautiful."

Cam looked nearly as pleased as Ruby.

Kayla reached into a box of decorations. They needed to focus on getting this done so she could go home and stop letting herself get carried away by this little fantasy family.

She pulled out a clump of tangled lights and passed it to Cam. "Here's your next job."

He groaned. "You really do like being the boss, don't you?"

Kayla nodded without looking at him. If he meant, did she like being independent and not losing herself to any man, then yes, yes she did.

She and Ruby wrapped the tree in garland, then sorted through the ornaments. There weren't a lot, and they were largely homemade, but Kayla could tell that each one meant something to Bethany. But every time she asked Ruby about one, the little girl just baaed at her.

"Serves you right." Cam laughed when she sighed after the fifth time it happened.

Kayla shot him a fake glare, then turned to Ruby. "What if you were a talking sheep, so you could use words *and* baas?"

Ruby tilted her head, then said. "Baa. I'm hungry, baa."

"Well, that's a slight improvement," Cam muttered, pulling out his phone. "No wonder. It's 7:00. How about a pizza?" He gave Kayla a defensive look. "We don't have it every night."

She gave him a gentle smile. "I didn't think you did."

"Baa. Sometimes we have cereal. Baa," Ruby said cheerfully.

Kayla laughed as Cam ducked his head. "Yeah, that's true."

"Cereal for supper sounds tasty." She wanted to tell Cam that he had nothing to be ashamed of. He was taking care of Ruby, making sure all her needs were met—but more than that, he was providing her with a happy home even in the worst circumstances any kid could be asked to go through. That was worth a lot.

They continued decorating as they waited for the pizza, then cleared a space at the kitchen table to eat.

"Baa. Can I pray? Baa?"

Cam looked to Kayla with a question in his eyes.

"I would love that." Kayla folded her hands, noting that though Cam didn't fold his, he did give his attention to Ruby.

"Dear Jesus. Baa," Ruby began. "Thank you for our supper. Baa. And thank you for Mommy. She's the best mommy in the world, and I really want her to be better for Christmas. Baa. Oh, and thank you that Uncle Cam was smart enough to call Kayla for help with the cookies. Amen. Baa."

Kayla's laugh joined Cam's as she looked up, accidentally meeting his eyes. He held her gaze for a moment, but fortunately Ruby knocked her milk over, giving Kayla an excuse to look away.

Dinner was easy and fun, the conversation flowing mostly from Ruby, with Cam and Kayla piping in here and there. They were just putting away the leftovers when there was a loud crash from the living room.

"What in the living world?"

All three of them froze for a second, then flew toward the living room.

"Mrs. Whiskers," Ruby cried. "Baa."

"Oh no." Kayla pressed a hand to her mouth to hold back the giggle. It wasn't funny. Only, it kind of was.

The cat had obviously attempted to climb the tree and gotten herself tangled in the garland, which was still draped around her. Her tail was puffed out to twice its normal size, and her ears lay flat against her head. The tree was toppled against the far wall.

Cam let out the first laugh, and Kayla couldn't hold it in any longer. In a moment, Ruby's infectious little girl laugh joined theirs.

The cat looked at them all as if they were crazy, then stalked off, the garland trailing behind her—which only made them all laugh harder.

It took a full five minutes to get their giggle fit under control, but at last Cam stood the tree back up. A few ornaments had fallen off—fortunately, none were breakable—and the tree leaned even farther now, but other than that, it was none the worse for the wear.

When they'd finished fixing the tree, Cam announced that it was time for Ruby to get ready for bed.

"Baa," the little girl pouted around a yawn. "What about frosting the cookies?"

"I'll stay and help Cam frost them." The words blurted from Kayla's mouth. She should really take them back. More alone time with Cam was *not* what she needed.

But between Cam's grateful look and Ruby's content yawn, she couldn't bring herself to change her mind.

"Baa. Baa. That means, will you tuck me in?" Ruby set her sleepy eyes on Kayla with a sweet smile.

Warmth filled Kayla's chest at the question, but she looked to Cam to see how he felt about it.

He nodded with a smile almost as sweet as Ruby's. "That's a great idea. I'll go get things ready to frost the cookies."

"But I want you to tuck me in too, baa. I want you and Kayla to do it together."

Kayla let herself peek at Cam out of the corner of her eye. She half hoped he'd say no.

"Yeah. Okay." Cam started toward Ruby's room, and Kayla fought to remind herself yet again that though Cam and Ruby were family, she was not. She was just a friend lending a hand.

But as they read Ruby a story together and listened to her say her prayers and turned on her night light, that family feeling only grew stronger. And when Ruby hugged first Cam and then her, Kayla was pretty sure she'd lost the fight right then and there.

Chapter 26

Keep your eyes on your cookie.

But even that didn't erase the thought Cameron had been fighting off all night: *This was what family felt like.* He remembered the feeling from his childhood—from before Bethany ruined everything—and it brought a sharp but almost pleasant ache to his chest to feel it again now.

Except they weren't a family. Sure, Ruby was his niece. But he was only taking care of her temporarily. And Kayla was . . . a friend, he realized with surprise. He certainly hadn't come to Hope Springs seeking to make friends. But Kayla had been a force to reckon with as she muscled her way into their lives. And right now, he was glad she had.

Because otherwise all the cookies would look like the one in front of him, with frosting blobs oozing over the sides and obscuring the cookie's shape so that it looked more like a frog than an angel.

He examined the spread of perfectly frosted cookies in front of her. "How do you do that?"

She looked up from the snowman she'd been giving a red scarf and smiled. "Natural talent, I guess."

"Yeah. I guess I got skipped in that department."

Kayla studied his cookies. "I mean, they have . . . They're really . . ." She bit her lip, as if searching for something nice to say.

He loaded his spoon with a big glob of blue frosting. "Think faster." He angled it toward her and used a finger of his other hand to pull it down, like a loaded catapult.

"You wouldn't." But Kayla dropped her own spoon and held up a hand to shield herself. "Your cookies are really interesting."

"Interesting?" Cameron pulled the spoon back farther. "That's a nice way of saying you can't think of anything nice to say."

Kayla's laugh bounced off the walls, and she clapped a hand over her mouth, glancing toward the hallway. But it'd been at least an hour since the last time Ruby had gotten out of bed to say she needed to go to the bathroom or get a drink or check her backpack, so he was optimistic she was finally asleep.

He couldn't resist. He let the spoon fling forward, sending the frosting straight for Kayla's face.

She shrieked and covered her head, catching most of the frosting on the back of her hand, although a small splatter landed on her cheek.

"You did not just do that." But she was laughing even as she licked the frosting off her knuckles.

"I think I did." He smirked at her, wondering what had come over him. This was so totally not like him. It was way too spontaneous and loose and . . . fun.

Huh.

When had he stopped being fun?

He loaded up another spoonful. If he was going to have fun again, he might as well go all in.

"Cam," Kayla shrieked. "We have so many cookies to do yet." But she grabbed her own spoon and loaded it full of red frosting.

Cameron glanced down at his blue t-shirt. "Wait. This is my favorite shirt."

Kayla blinked at him. "It's just a plain shirt. There's nothing on it."

"But it's comfortable."

She shook her head. "Should have thought of that before you started this."

Frosting flew through the air toward him, and he lifted an arm to block it while also flinging his spoonful at her. Apparently, this time he caught her by surprise because the frosting splattered right on her cheek. He ended up with an armful of frosting, but none hit his shirt.

"Missed me." He grinned and reached for another cookie to frost.

But he was just loading his spoon with frosting—for the cookie, not a weapon—when a wet blob plopped onto his forehead.

He looked up slowly, already feeling the frosting sliding toward his eyes. A blob dropped onto his shirt.

"Really?" But he couldn't help the giant laugh that burst out of him when he saw the expression on Kayla's face. Triumph mixed with amusement mixed with . . . he didn't know exactly what that was, but it made her look almost sparkling. Or maybe that was the tears falling on her cheeks as she laughed so hard.

She held up a hand as he reloaded his spoon. "Truce?" she gasped.

He studied her. She was wiping at her eyes and not paying attention to him at all, which meant he could easily get another shot in. But maybe there was such a thing as *too* much fun. Especially when they were supposed to be getting these cookies done. "All right. Truce."

They fell silent as they returned to frosting the cookies, but every once in a while, one or the other would let out a low chuckle.

"Can I ask you something?" Kayla's question came out of the blue, and he looked up at her as she set aside the angel she'd expertly decorated and started on a snowman.

He dropped a glob of frosting on his own reindeer. "Shoot."

"What happened between you and Bethany?"

Oh.

That question he wasn't prepared for. He'd managed to avoid talking about his sister with anyone in nearly twenty years. But the way Kayla was looking at him with those big, warm eyes full of compassion made the words tumble out against his will. "It started when she broke her arm in volleyball and had to have surgery. I guess that would have been her junior year of high school because I was twelve at the time. They gave her pain meds after the surgery, and I guess she liked how they made her feel." He swallowed.

Kayla's hands stilled on the cookie she was decorating.

He made himself go on. "A few months later, I caught her shooting up. Heroin. My parents were devastated. They checked her into rehab, even though they couldn't afford it."

He snatched for a cookie and started decorating it to give his hands something to do.

"It became a cycle. They'd check her in, she'd check out. They'd welcome her home, tell her everything was forgiven." He shook his head. "The last time, they gave her a job at Dad's landscaping company. She was out of rehab for so long that time that even I started to believe she was better." Bitterness coated his tongue. How could he have been so foolish? He'd *known*, in his head, that she couldn't have changed. But he'd *wanted* so badly, in his heart, to believe that she was still the big sister he'd adored. "They'd put her in charge of accounting because she'd always been good with numbers, and they thought it would give her confidence if they showed how much they trusted her." He set his mutilated cookie aside. "Turns out she was playing them. They had no idea that she knew how to forge my dad's signature. She'd write out checks to bogus accounts, her dealers, herself. . . . She was smart enough to cover it all up. By the time they realized, it was too late. Things had already been tight, but this was the last straw. They lost the company. And—" This was the worst part. "They let her get away with it. They didn't want to press charges. Said they just wanted her to get the help she needed."

He lifted his eyes to find Kayla watching him.

"It looks like she did." She gestured around the small kitchen.

But Cameron shook his head and dropped a fist onto the table. "No. She didn't. She ran away to who knows where. Left us with her mess." He stretched his neck, staring at the ceiling. "Dad had a heart attack the month after he filed for bankruptcy." Cameron didn't dare to look away from the ceiling. "Mom lost everything. I tried to help her out, but I was putting myself through college by then, and . . . Anyway, she had a stroke a couple years later." He blew out a hard breath. This part killed him every time he thought of it. "She was alone. A repairman found her body a few days later."

"Oh, Cam." Kayla's hand landed on his, sending warmth up his arm. "I'm so sorry."

"Yeah." He cleared his throat. "Sorry. I shouldn't have— I've never—"

"I'm glad you told me." Her hand left his.

"So that's the story of me and Bethany." He tried to make his voice light. "More than you bargained for when you asked, I'm sure."

Kayla backed her wheelchair away from the table. "Maybe, but all families have their share of problems."

Somehow, he doubted that hers did. She was voluntarily staying with her brother right now, wasn't she?

She grabbed a plastic food storage container off the counter and passed it to him. "I guess that explains why you weren't so keen on coming when I first called you to tell you about Bethany."

He laughed softly. "Yeah. Not so keen at all. But I'm glad you bullied me into it. It's been good to get to know Ruby."

"Hey." She pointed at him. "I didn't *bully* you. I just told you what you needed to hear."

"If that's what you need to tell yourself."

Her expression softened. "You know you're doing a good job with her, right?"

He shrugged. "Honestly, I'm just trying not to screw her life up too badly."

Kayla bit her lip.

"What? You think I'm screwing it up?"

She shook her head with a gentle laugh. "No. I'm just wondering if you've thought about what you're going to do if Bethany doesn't wake up."

He sighed roughly. "I've thought about it. But I honestly don't know. Finding Ruby's father was supposed to be the answer, but obviously that didn't pan out. I just don't know if I'm the best one to raise her permanently, you know? I'm still hoping Bethany will wake up and I can . . ."

"Get back to your life in California," she filled in.

He shrugged. He supposed so. That was where his life was, wasn't it? Even if Hope Springs was starting to feel more like home every day.

Kayla wheeled slowly toward the front door. She didn't know why she was so reluctant to leave.

But for some reason, that conversation with Cam had been so real and so raw and so . . . she didn't know what, but it made her want to keep talking to him. To learn more about how he ticked and why he was the way he was. To encourage him to see that even in all those terrible things his family had gone through—was still going through—God had a plan.

"You know—" She spun around so suddenly that she nearly ran Cam over. He took a step back, giving her a mildly curious but not annoyed look. "God has a plan even in this."

Cam looked skeptical. "How can you know that?"

"Because he promises that in his Word. And also because I've seen him working out his plan in my own life."

"By sticking you in that thing?" Cam gestured roughly at her wheelchair, horror overtaking his face a second later. "I'm sorry, Kayla. I don't know why I—"

"It's okay, really." She patted her seat cushion. "And actually, yes, by sticking me in this thing."

He studied her, disbelief written in his eyes. He leaned against the wall, arms crossed in front of him. "How so?"

"My parents brought me up in the church, taught me to be a good girl, all that. But I always felt like I had such big expectations to live up to. Nate was like this, I don't know, uber-Christian, always at youth group, in a Christian band, living for Jesus, you know? So I decided since I couldn't live up to all that, I'd be the exact opposite. I started going to parties, drinking . . ." She closed her eyes, remembering how close her path had cut to the one Bethany ended up on.

When she opened them, she found Cam's wide eyes on her. She didn't want to ruin his opinion of her, but she needed him to realize how God could work even their failures to his glory. "When I woke up after the accident, I was mad. Mad at God, mad at Nate, mad at my parents. Mad at the doctors and nurses, even. But now I can see how God used all of this to woo me back to him. To show me that he is the source of all good things in my life. Plus, because of my accident, I ended up at a job I really loved."

"Which you no longer have because of someone else's greed," Cam pointed out.

Kayla shrugged. "I admit I haven't figured out how God is using that yet. But I trust that he is. Anyway, it gave me a chance to meet you and Ruby—" She cut off and looked away, heat rushing to her face. She hadn't meant that how it sounded. "I mean— You know, so I could rescue you when you need to make cookies and such."

Worst save ever.

But she had a feeling that trying to fix it more would only make the situation worse, so she spun her chair back toward the door. At least she could still make a graceful exit.

Except she turned too sharply and knocked into the small table that held a vase with artificial flowers and a small lamp. Flinging her upper body forward, she was able to catch the lamp, but the sound of shattering glass told her the vase's fate.

She closed her eyes. So much for that graceful exit.

"Do you happen to have a broom?" She didn't dare turn around to look at Cam as she asked.

"Don't worry about it." His voice was kind. Overly kind? The kind of kind that meant he knew how flustered she was? "I'll get it."

But she shook her head. "I'm not helpless, Cam. I can clean up my own mess."

"Suit yourself."

As his footsteps retreated, Kayla forced herself to sit up straight and push her shoulders back. She had nothing to be embarrassed about. Accidents happened.

Especially when you have a crush on someone.

A crush? No way. Her feelings for Cam were more like—

Nothing. Her feelings were more like nothing because she had no feelings for Cam.

"Here you are."

A broom appeared at her side, and she grabbed it out of the air without looking at the person who held it there. It was a lot easier to convince herself she didn't have feelings for him when she didn't look at him.

She swept the glass fragments as quickly as she could, maneuvering her chair to make sure she got all of them. She kept her eyes on the job, though she was pretty sure she could feel Cam watching her.

Her suspicion was confirmed when he stepped in front of the pile she'd swept together the moment she brushed the last pieces onto it.

She held out a hand for the dust pan, but he squatted in front of her, holding it angled behind the pile of glass.

"I can get it, you know." She didn't mean to sound so testy. But really, she just needed to finish this up and go home and bury herself under the covers. And not come out again until she got her stupid heart to stop thinking it wanted something she knew for a fact it did not want.

"I know you can. And I know you're Superwoman. But that doesn't mean you have to do everything yourself. Sometimes other people want to be useful too, you know."

"Have it your way." But as she swept the glass onto the dust pan, she had to admit that it was much easier this way. The verse from Ecclesiastes that Vi had quoted earlier popped into her head. "Two are better than one, because they have a good return for their labor." She pushed it right back out.

"I think we got it all." Cam straightened. "And it didn't kill you to let me help." His smile landed on her, and the verse popped right back in.

She handed Cam the broom, then skirted around him to the front door. She had to get out of here before she started believing that maybe that verse applied to her after all.

Chapter 27

"Wow, Ruby, these look great." The white-haired teacher who had introduced herself as Mrs. Klein shuffled the containers Cameron had handed her, subtly shifting the one with the cookies he had decorated to the bottom of the pile. She turned to him. "So it's twenty-five cents a cookie."

"Oh, uh— Okay. I guess I'll take four then." He pulled out his wallet. It seemed a little odd that she'd expect him to buy the cookies he'd spent all night making, but whatever. He could spare a buck.

Mrs. Klein took his money and stuck it in a small metal box. "So this is the money box. It should have enough change."

He nodded again. This woman really was an over-sharer. He'd just made the cookies. He didn't need all the details of how they'd be sold.

"If you can, try to go for the upsell. I mean, don't be pushy about it, but you know, encourage them to buy a plate of brownies too or something."

"I can—" Wait. What? "You want me to sell the cookies?"

Mrs. Klein blinked at him. "You're signed up to do it this morning."

"I am?" He glanced at Ruby, who was grinning up at him. "I think someone may have forgotten to mention that."

"Oh dear." Mrs. Klein consulted a clipboard on the table. "I don't have anyone else coming in until lunchtime. Oh dear . . ." Her white eyebrows knit together. "I don't know. I guess we could . . ."

"I can do it." Well, now, what was he doing? He had at least three cases that needed his attention today. But the woman seemed so distressed, and it wasn't like it would be that hard to stand here and peddle cookies to kids. He could probably even manage to make some calls at the same time.

"Oh, can you really? That would be wonderful. Absolutely wonderful." The older woman patted his arm. "We'll be right in that classroom if you need anything."

"I'm sure I'll be fine."

Ruby skipped over to give him a hug, and he took the opportunity to whisper in her ear, "A little heads-up next time, please."

She giggled. "You're funny, Uncle Cam." And then she was skipping off to class behind Mrs. Klein. But she turned around after a few steps to add, "Baa."

Cameron gave her a thumbs-up. Thank goodness Kayla had known how to bring Ruby out of her funk yesterday. And how to make cookies. And how to listen to him talk about Bethany.

He didn't know what had possessed him to tell her so much. He'd always considered his past—and especially his sister—his biggest secret. And yet, it hadn't felt odd telling her. It had been a relief, actually. He'd woken up feeling lighter this morning than he had since he'd gotten here. Longer than that—since Dad had died, maybe.

He contemplated telling Danielle too.

But he quickly dismissed the idea. Danielle detested listening to other people's sob stories. And besides, maybe the reason it had been so easy to tell Kayla was that he knew he was leaving eventually and wouldn't see her anymore.

The thought drew him up short.

He'd grown so accustomed to seeing Kayla while he'd been here that he hadn't even considered what it would be like when he went back to California and she went wherever she ended up going. It made him a little sad to think about.

But he shook off the feeling. He had his life, and she had hers. They'd just happened to intersect at this small point in time.

He pulled out his phone to return a call from a CFO who was a real pain, but before he could dial, he had a line of students at the table.

"Whoa." He whistled to himself, fighting off the urge to run, until he remembered that they were just customers who wanted a product he was selling. Somehow, through all the jostling, shouting, and general chaos, he managed to get everyone what they wanted. When the bell rang for students to be in class, he let out a sigh of relief. The rest of the morning was much slower, and Cameron managed to make all the calls he needed to. When he'd finished, he found himself again perusing articles about starting a landscaping business. It looked like it would take a significant outlay of cash, which wouldn't necessarily be a problem since he'd always been a saver. The bigger issue was the risk. And the fact that Danielle would laugh him right out of the room if he suggested he'd like to make a career change.

At lunchtime, Cameron handed the cookie selling job off to a woman who introduced herself as the mother of one of Ruby's friends.

"You must be Ruby's uncle," she said. "I've heard so much about you."

She had?

"Good luck," he told her as kids swarmed the table. "These kids are little fiends when it comes to sugar." They'd already sold out of the cookies Kayla had decorated—and some desperate kids had even bought one or two of his monstrosities.

The woman laughed and touched his arm.

"Uncle Cam!"

He turned at the sound of Ruby's voice, using the opportunity to free his arm from the woman's hand.

"Hey there, little sheep."

The woman gave him an odd look, but he ignored her and squatted to be at eye level with his niece. "How was your morning?"

"Good. Want to come to lunch with me?"

Cameron debated. He still had those documents waiting on his computer. And yet . . . he was much more in the mood for lunch with his niece than for dealing with paperwork.

"That depends." He grinned at her. "What's for lunch?"

As he walked with her to the lunch room, Ruby grilled him. "Why were you talking to Mrs. McGregor? That's Cassidy's mom."

"The one who got the lead in the play?"

Ruby nodded.

"Well, it's not her fault her daughter got the part. And anyway, you can't be mad at Cassidy forever."

Ruby put a hand on her hip. "Yes, I can."

He started to argue, but then they were in the cafeteria, and she was leading him through the line. Turned out, it was spaghetti day.

When their trays were filled, he followed her to a table already holding six girls and one boy.

"You can sit there." Ruby sat in the chair next to the boy, pointing to the chair across from her.

Cameron squeezed past the close seats and took the spot she'd indicated, eyeing the boy. He didn't trust any boy who chose to sit at an all-girls table. He was definitely a ladies man.

"This is Jenna, Bree, Sierra, Maria, Libby, and Haley." Ruby pointed around the table at the girls. "And this is Braxton. My boyfriend."

Cameron choked on the drink he was taking from the tiny milk carton. "Your what?"

The girls at the table all giggled, but Braxton gave Cameron an impish smile. Cameron debated how much trouble he would get in for laying out a second-grader.

He kept an eye on Braxton for the rest of the meal, but fortunately the kid didn't attempt to make a move on Ruby. In fact, he seemed pretty oblivious to the fact that she was there at all. Mostly, he spent the meal staring longingly at a table full of boys who were having a contest to see who could down their milk the fastest.

By the end of the meal, Cameron nearly felt sorry for the kid. Ruby had clearly strong-armed him into this relationship.

"All right, Rub— Sheep. I have to get going." He slid his tiny chair away from the table and stood, grateful for the chance to stretch his cramped back. "Thanks for lunch."

"You're welcome." Ruby skipped next to him as they went to clear their trays. As he was setting his down, his phone buzzed in his pocket.

He pulled it out, giving the screen a quick look. A groan slipped unintentionally from his lips. He scolded himself silently. That should not be his reaction to a call from the woman he was supposed to marry. It was just that most of her calls these days involved either yelling or icy silence.

"Who is it?" Ruby asked.

"Huh?" He glanced at her. "Oh. My girlfriend."

Ruby stopped dead in the middle of the hallway. "You can't have a girlfriend."

He slowed to a stop as well. "Why not? You have a boyfriend."

She rolled her eyes. "That's different."

Yeah, because *he* was an adult. She was a second-grader.

"Okay, look, I have to take this. I'll see you after school." He reached to give her a quick hug, but she wriggled out of his arms.

"But you can't have a girlfriend because you have Kayla."

"I have . . ." He scrubbed his hands over his face. Oh boy. "Ruby, you know Kayla and I are just friends, right? Actually, mostly she's your friend. I just happen to be there too."

Ruby gave him a penetrating look. Fine, he and Kayla had become friends too. Pretty good friends if the way he had spilled his guts to her last night was any indication.

But that didn't change the fact that he had a girlfriend. An almost-fiancée.

He waved goodbye to Ruby, swallowed hard, and answered the call as he burst out the school doors into the gray day, determined to have a nice conversation with Danielle.

"I thought you were going to ignore me again," Danielle said by way of greeting.

"Sorry about that." He worked to sound placating. "You would not believe the morning I had. We were up all night frosting cookies, and then I get her to school this morning and find out that I'm supposed to be the one selling them." He laughed. All in all, it hadn't been such a bad day. And he felt a little more connected to Ruby now that he had spent some time in the place she hung out every day.

"I think I've been more than patient, Cameron." Danielle's words crashed like bricks through the phone.

So much for a nice conversation.

"I know. You've been the best." Well, maybe not the best. But she was doing the best she could.

"It's been a month. When are you going to be home?"

He rubbed his temple. "Danielle, you know I just can't answer that. I would if I could, but my sister's condition hasn't shown any improvement, and the doctor's don't know if . . ."

He trailed off as he reached his car and leaned against it instead of getting in. Just once, he wished she'd ask how he was doing. Ask if he needed anything. At least offer a semi-sympathetic comment about what he was dealing with. Listen to him like . . . like Kayla had last night.

He shook off the thought. Danielle wasn't that kind of person, and he knew that.

"Can you at least tell me if you'll be home by Christmas? I want to plan our engagement party, but I don't want to be humiliated a second time."

Cameron sighed. "I mean, if there's a miracle, maybe. But otherwise, I don't see how."

"I see." Danielle clipped the words. "I'm not sure how much longer I can do this, Cameron."

Do what? he wanted to ask. He was the one who was here, taking care of a little girl every day while managing his work schedule and her riding lessons and even cleaning up vomit.

And suddenly, he realized—he didn't know how much longer he could do it either. Not taking care of Ruby—he'd realized last night that he'd do that as long as needed.

"Then maybe we shouldn't do this anymore." The words popped out without warning, but once he'd said them, he knew they were exactly what needed to be said.

"So you'll come home?" Danielle's voice wore the triumph of scoring a major deal.

But Cameron shook his head, scrubbing a hand down his face. "No. I mean, maybe we shouldn't do *us* anymore." He bit his lip. He didn't want to hurt her.

"What?" Danielle sounded more dismissive than upset. "Cameron, don't be stupid. Just come home, and everything will be fine."

He watched the gray clouds above him. "No, Danielle, it won't. I saw it before, but I didn't want to admit it to myself." Absence hadn't made his heart grow fonder. It'd only made him more certain of what he'd already known that day Kayla's call had rescued him from going through with the proposal. "We're just not right for each other."

"Is this about the ring?" Danielle made the clicking sound she always made when she was annoyed. "Because I told you, I never met your mom. And anyway, there's an expectation that someone in our position would have a certain quality of—"

"It's not about the ring, Danielle." He drew himself up short. "Well, actually, it is. About what the ring means. About the fact that I've never told you about my family because I was afraid of what you'd think. About the fact that I've never even told you my dreams."

"Your dreams?" Danielle's tone was cavalier. "We have the same dream. Success. Money. Prestige. And in case you haven't noticed, we're well on our way."

Cameron shook his head. "I think I want more than that." Though he honestly didn't know what that would be. Only that somehow Hope Springs was offering him a taste of it. "I'm sorry." And he really was. "I never wanted to hurt you."

"You're not hurting me." Ice tipped Danielle's words. "Call me when you come to your senses."

After the line went dead, Cameron stood staring at the school building for a long time. Had he really just given up the life he'd had all laid out? His plan for a perfect job, perfect promotion, perfect wife? After this, there was a decent chance George would fire him.

He sighed as he climbed into his car. What was it Kayla had said when he'd asked if it bothered her not to have a plan? Something about God always having a way of working the unexpected out?

Well, good luck to you, God, he thought as he pulled out of the parking lot.

Chapter 28

Kayla chewed her lip, eyeing the phone in her hand as she sat up in bed Sunday morning. Ruby had mentioned wanting to go to church more than once. It would make total sense for Kayla to text Cam and invite them. So why was she having such a hard time making her fingers tap on his name?

It wasn't because she was afraid he'd reject her invitation. That was up to him, and he hadn't seemed too resistant when she was talking about God the other night.

It was more that she was afraid he'd get the wrong impression and think she was looking for an excuse to see him.

"Stop being so stupid," she muttered to herself. "Are you really going to let that keep you from inviting him and Ruby to hear the Gospel?"

She tapped out the invitation, then hit send before she could change her mind.

Rather than staring at the screen to wait for a reply, she clicked over to her email. She gave a cursory scroll through the various marketing messages before she noticed a message from the organization running the mission trip she'd applied for. Her mouth went dry as she tapped to open it.

The moment it appeared on the screen, her eyes darted over the words. Then she sat staring at her phone, dumbfounded.

She'd been accepted.

"Thank you for answering my prayers, Lord," she whispered. "Now I know what you want me to do next."

It was a relief, but also—

Something felt off. The excitement that should be sending her into a happy dance was tempered by the fact that she would have to leave Hope Springs behind—right when Nate and Vi had their baby, right when she was getting to know everyone here so much better, right when Ruby needed her.

She shook off the feeling. Her visit to Hope Springs had never been intended to be permanent. If she didn't go on the trip, she'd have to find a job somewhere. And that likely wouldn't be Hope Springs.

Well, she didn't have to make a decision right now. She had a few weeks before she needed to let them know.

Using her arms to scoot to the edge of the bed, she transferred to her wheelchair to get ready for church.

The decision still weighed on her as she wheeled into the kitchen, where Nate greeted her with a cup of coffee.

"Thanks." It was just what she needed. "Where's Vi?"

"Still getting ready. Moving a little slow this morning."

"You try hauling a watermelon in your belly." Kayla shot to her sister-in-law's defense. "You'd be moving slowly too."

Nate held up his hands. "Trust me, I know. I don't know how she does it. She's pretty amazing."

"*Very* amazing," Kayla corrected, though she knew her brother was head over heels for his wife. "Only a few weeks yet. Are you getting excited?"

Nate's eyes lit up at the same time that he shook his head. "Nervous."

"You'll be a great dad, you know that."

"I do?"

"Yes, you do." Kayla set her coffee on the table and rolled closer to him. "Or if you don't, I do."

Nate blew out a breath. "I hope you're right."

"I know I am. After all, you're a great brother."

He gave her a thoughtful look, and she knew he was thinking about the accident. Even though he'd finally forgiven himself for it, she knew he still struggled to let go sometimes.

But after a moment his eyes cleared. "I am, aren't I?"

She swatted at him but then grew serious. "Speaking of which, can I ask you for some advice?"

Nate regarded her. "Of course you can. About Cam?"

"What? No." Kayla smacked his arm again. "About the mission trip. I was accepted."

"What? Kayla, that's great." He set down his own coffee to hug her. "I know how much you wanted—" He hesitated as he pulled back and his eyes fell on her face. "What is it?"

She shook her head at her own maddening confusion. "I *do* want it, but— I don't know. I also want to stay here."

"Here?" Nate raised an eyebrow. "As in, in Hope Springs?"

"No. Yes." She sighed and laughed at herself. "I don't know. But I mean, if I got accepted for the trip, I should do it, right? It's pretty clear that's what God wants me to do."

Nate picked up his coffee and took a slow swig, watching her over the rim. Kayla knew he was using the time to process her question and formulate an answer, but she wanted to tell him to just say something already.

Finally, he set the mug down. "I guess I would say don't confuse God giving you an opportunity with God telling you what to do. He's given you a free will and a brain and a heart for a reason. Whether or not you go on the mission trip won't change anything."

Right. Except possibly her whole life.

"Pray about it," Nate advised.

"What are we praying about?" Vi shuffled into the room, a hand pressed to her back. The poor woman looked so uncomfortable that Kayla hoped for her sake the baby would come sooner rather than later.

"Kayla got accepted for the mission trip." The pride in Nate's voice filled Kayla's heart. "Now she has to decide whether or not to go."

"I knew you'd be accepted." Vi patted her arm. "I'll pray for you. Are we ready for church?"

Kayla nodded, pulling out her phone on the off chance that Cam had responded to her invitation.

She told herself she was glad there were no new messages.

She was confused enough the way it was.

Chapter 29

"They smell funny. Baa." Ruby wrinkled her nose at the waffle Cameron dropped onto her plate.

He didn't know what had possessed him to try making them this morning. He'd barely conquered the fine art of peanut butter and jelly for Ruby's school lunches, yet for some reason, he'd thought it'd be a good idea to graduate right to breakfast pastries.

Maybe it was the nervous energy that had gripped him ever since he'd broken up with Danielle the other day. It wasn't that he thought he'd done the wrong thing. But blowing up his carefully laid plans—leaving himself with no clue of what was going to come next—had him a little shaken. He'd spent most of Wednesday debating whether he should call and beg Danielle to take him back. But that wouldn't have been right—not when he knew they weren't right for each other. Fortunately, by Thursday, he'd poured his energy into a new project: decorating the yard. But he'd finished that on Friday and spent yesterday restlessly pacing the house. Which had brought him to baking this morning, apparently.

"Yeah." He scooped the waffle back off Ruby's plate. "You don't have to eat that." He crossed the room and dumped the three waffles on his plate into the trash, then dolloped the remaining batter in there too. "The usual?"

"Yes, please."

He grabbed two bowls and the cereal box. Ruby closed her eyes and whispered to herself. Praying. He'd gotten used to it and, out of politeness more than anything else, waited to dig into his own cereal until she'd finished.

He saw her nod, the signal for when she had finished, but this time she didn't open her eyes.

"Ruby?"

She held up a finger to signal for him to wait a minute. He rolled his eyes but sat silently.

When she finally looked up, she grinned at him. "Sorry, I was saying an extra prayer."

"Ah." He scooped a generous bite onto his spoon. "What for?"

"That you would say yes to what I want to ask you. Baa."

Cameron shook his head. This girl was something else. "And what is that?"

"Can we go to church? Baa?" Ruby's eyes were full of pleading, and Cameron laughed in relief. That was an easy question. And an easy answer.

"Yes."

"Really?" Ruby's eyes widened.

Wait. He had meant to say no—in spite of Ruby's pleading eyes and Kayla's friendly text this morning. But he couldn't deny that Kayla's conversation the other night—about how God had used her injury for her good—had him intrigued. How long had he wondered what good could possibly come out of what had happened to his family?

He sighed. "Really. But you have to hurry up and change. Church starts in—" He picked up his phone and checked Kayla's text. "Twenty minutes."

Ruby shoved another bite of cereal into her mouth. "I'm already changed," she said, mouth full of food.

"Chew." Cameron eyed her flowery pants and taco print shirt, then let it go.

Twenty minutes later, as he pulled into the church parking lot, he had a brief flash of panic. Though his family had gone to church until Dad died, he hadn't been to one in years.

Maybe it had been a mistake to come.

"How about if I drop you off and come pick you up when it's done?"

Ruby made a face at him. "You have to come in with me. I'm seven."

All right. She had a point there.

He parked the car and let her lead him toward the church doors.

"There's Kayla." Ruby waved wildly toward the sidewalk, where Kayla was approaching the church with Nate and Violet, but the three appeared to be caught up in conversation and didn't look their direction.

Good. Though Cameron didn't know why he felt that way. He actually quite enjoyed spending time with Kayla.

Which may have been the problem.

"Can we sit with her, baa?" Ruby grabbed his hand and tried to tug him forward, but he maintained a steady speed.

"No. And I don't think sheep are allowed at church." He could use a break from all the bleating.

"Pastor Dan said I'm Jesus' little lamb." Ruby gave him a mischievous look. "Baa."

He couldn't help the laugh that burst out at that.

Apparently, the sound caught Kayla's attention because she suddenly turned her head in their direction, then sent them a wide smile. She said something to Nate and Violet, who waved to Cameron and Ruby, then continued toward the doors.

But Kayla started toward them, which made Cameron's stomach do a weird sort of dip he couldn't explain.

"Good morning." Her greeting was as bright and cheerful as always, and Cameron relaxed. Just because he'd confessed his deepest, darkest secrets to her the other night didn't mean anything had to be different between them.

"Can we sit with you, baa?" Ruby bounced up and down as Kayla reached them, then spun her chair to wheel next to them toward the building.

"Of course. I'd be honored." Kayla glanced at Cameron. "If it's okay with you."

He nodded reluctantly. It wasn't like he had any good reason to say no.

When they reached the door, Cameron hesitated. After the argument over the broom the other night, he wasn't sure Kayla wouldn't bite his head off for opening it for her. But he glanced around at the other worshipers filing into the building. He didn't need everyone here to think he was the kind of guy who wouldn't open a door for a little girl and a woman who used a wheelchair.

He pulled it open. Instead of reaming him out, Kayla offered a quiet "thank you" as she slid through the door. Cameron nodded silently, almost wishing she'd yelled instead. At least that he knew how to deal with.

He followed Kayla and Ruby through the lobby and into the sanctuary, surprised by the number of people who stopped to greet them—both people he'd met at Thanksgiving and others he'd never seen before. He didn't remember his childhood church being this friendly.

"I want to sit next to Kayla," Ruby said as they reached a row filled with several of the people who had been at Nate and Violet's house for Thanksgiving.

That was fine by Cameron. He slid into the row, taking a seat next to Violet as Ruby pounced onto the seat on his other side. Kayla remained seated in her wheelchair at the end of the row.

"Glad you could make it," Vi whispered, before folding her hands and resting them on her belly.

While she prayed, Cameron took the opportunity to examine the space. A large cross hung on the front wall, and windows that reached nearly to the vaulted ceiling lined the wall that looked out over Lake Michigan. Cameron's eyes rested on the rolling waves, and a sort of peace he wasn't accustomed to washed over him.

The haunting melody of a piano solo drew Cameron's attention to the front of the church.

After a moment, the piano was joined by a guitar and a bass, then drums.

"Today he calls you." The lone male voice was strong and somehow familiar.

Cameron peered more closely, then leaned toward Violet. "Is that your husband?"

She nodded, clearly enthralled with his singing, and Cameron sat back, letting the music wash over him. The style wasn't his usual music preference, but he found he enjoyed it.

When the song was done, Pastor Dan welcomed the congregation, then began the day's readings.

Cameron tried to pay attention, though it wasn't easy with Ruby wiggling next to him and his gaze constantly attempting to stray to Kayla. Though a slight smile lifted her lips, he couldn't help thinking that she appeared to be deep in thought about something. And for some reason, he wanted more than anything to ask her what it was.

As the congregation finished singing another hymn—which Cameron had only listened to, though Ruby had joined in on the refrain in her surprisingly powerful seven-year-old singing voice—the little girl leaned over and whispered, "Thank you."

Cameron looked down at her in surprise. "For what?" he whispered.

"For bringing me here." She leaned her head on his arm.

Cameron froze for a second. "You're welcome." He resisted the urge to pull his arm away, instead letting the warm, steady weight of Ruby's head anchor him in this moment.

At the front of the church, Dan approached the podium. But instead of standing behind it, the pastor slid it to the side and stepped in front of it, moving closer to the first row of seats.

"Fool me once, shame on you. Fool me twice, shame on me," Dan began. "Ever heard that saying?"

Heard it? Cameron shook his head. He'd lived it. As had his parents. Thanks to Bethany.

"Here's the thing," Dan continued. "That saying may be clever, with its play on words, but it's not what Jesus calls us to. He says, "Fool me once, I forgive you. Fool me twice—" The pastor paused, glancing around the church. "I forgive you. Fool me three times, I forgive you again. In fact, in our reading for today from Matthew 18, Peter asked Jesus if he should forgive someone who had sinned against him even *seven* times."

Dan pulled a Bible off the podium, flipping it open. "I mean, that sounds pretty generous to me. Someone hurts you seven times, and you forgive them every time? You deserve a medal. But as Jesus answers Peter, you can almost see him shaking his head. Because Jesus has a slightly bigger number in mind. He says, 'I tell you, not seven times, but seventy-seven times.'" Dan closed the Bible and looked up at them. "Can't you just see Peter's eyes going big? Seventy-seven times? That's a lot."

Cameron glanced at Ruby, whose eyes were on the pastor, her mouth open the tiniest bit, the same way Bethany's always had been when she was concentrating.

Seventy-seven times, huh?

Cameron had easily forgiven his sister that many times. Not that he wanted to pat himself on the back or anything. But if Jesus was counting . . .

"Seventy-seven is a lot," Dan continued. "But actually, the phrase used here can also be translated another way. It could be translated as seventy *times* seven. In other words, four hundred and ninety times. Is there anyone you'd be willing to forgive *four hundred and ninety times*?"

Honestly, Cameron had probably come close to forgiving Bethany that many times—before she'd crossed the line and cost his family everything. At some point, enough was enough. Why should he keep forgiving someone who obviously didn't have any intention of changing, who would only hurt him again and again and again?

Dan peered around the congregation, as if he couldn't believe what he'd just said. "Surely Jesus was exaggerating here. He doesn't really want us to forgive people who have hurt us almost five hundred times, does he? That would be ridiculous, foolish, unrealistic, unreasonable, right? Right." Dan nodded. "Jesus *doesn't* want you to forgive anyone almost five hundred times."

Cameron shifted in his seat. He'd known Jesus couldn't possibly expect that.

"Actually," Dan continued, "he wants you to forgive them *endlessly*. His use of the number seventy-seven or seventy times seven wasn't meant to give you a benchmark. He was basically saying, 'However many times they sin against you, forgive them that many times.'"

Cameron let out a quiet, disbelieving breath. This preacher was obviously crazy—or Jesus was. No one could forgive someone who kept hurting them over and over. And no one deserved to be forgiven for that.

"If you're like me, that probably rubs you the wrong way." Dan paced to the far side of the sanctuary. "After all, aren't there some people who should never be forgiven? People who have hurt you so much, who have hurt you so many times. . . . People you'd be fine with never seeing again. . . . People you've forgiven before but who have basically spit in your face and gone on to do the very same thing to you again and again and again. . . . People you'd be better off if you'd never known."

Dan moved toward their side of the church, looking right at Cameron. He shifted in his seat, unable to shake the eerie sensation that the pastor knew he was thinking of Bethany.

He tried to tune out the sermon. He didn't need any more exhortations to forgive someone who didn't deserve to be forgiven, whatever the pastor said. But Dan's next words hit him right in the gut. "The hardest part is when that person is someone who is supposed to love you. A friend. A parent. A sister or brother."

Ruby wiggled against his arm, and Cameron glanced down. She grinned up at him, her smile so much like Bethany's that he had to look away, clenching his jaw tight. Bethany may have managed to produce a pretty good kid. But that didn't change the fact that she'd destroyed his life, destroyed the lives of their parents, with her selfishness. The same selfishness she'd said she was sorry for again and again and again. Yeah, fool him once . . . But after a while if you let someone keep fooling you, that just made you a fool.

"'Love your enemies,' Jesus says." Dan was still going. "It sounds like a paradox, right? But sometimes loving our enemies is easier than loving those who are supposed to love us but have hurt us. I mean, how often do you see your enemies? But your friends and family—the people who sometimes hurt you the most—they're right there all the time. And they have more opportunities to hurt you every day."

Cameron swallowed. Not anymore. Bethany would never hurt him again. He wouldn't give her a chance. A tiny pang went through his middle as Ruby shifted her head on his arm. He'd tried so hard not to let his sister's daughter work her way into his heart. But somehow she had, and he was going to miss her when he eventually went back to California. But that didn't change the fact that he wanted nothing to do with his sister once all of this was over.

"Think of Joseph," Dan said. "His brothers threw him into a cistern, sold him into slavery, and told their dad he was dead. But he forgave them. Or the prodigal son's father. His son took his inheritance while his father was still alive, then told his dad he didn't want anything more to do with him—until the money ran out. And his dad forgave him. Welcomed him home with open arms."

Not the brightest dad ever. Cameron couldn't help picturing his own father welcoming Bethany home.

"Or Jesus himself. His own family said he was crazy and tried to get him to stop preaching. Or even better—or worse, I suppose—he was betrayed by one of his closest friends. And what did Jesus do?" Dan looked around the sanctuary. "He forgave them. Even though they didn't deserve it. None of these people deserved it."

Dan paused so long that Cameron wondered if the sermon was over. But then he said quietly, "The next time you're struggling to forgive someone, whatever they've done to you—something big or something small—I want you to remember that there is someone else who doesn't deserve forgiveness. You. Me." Dan picked up his Bible, flipping it open near the end. "It's easy enough to think that we're a good person, that we aren't anywhere near as bad as those who hurt us. But James 2:10 tells us, 'For whoever keeps the whole law and yet stumbles at just one point is guilty of breaking all of it.'" Dan looked up. "I don't know about you, but I have stumbled at far more than one point. And because of my sin, I deserve death. Romans 6:23 says, 'For the wages of sin is death.'"

His pause was only the length of a heartbeat. "Fortunately, that verse doesn't end there. It goes on, 'but the gift of God is eternal life in Christ Jesus our Lord.'" Dan's smile beamed around the church. "You don't deserve forgiveness. I don't deserve forgiveness. The person who hurt you doesn't deserve forgiveness. But God gives it anyway. Because his Son came into this world to keep the law perfectly—without stumbling at a single point—and then to die a sinless death in our place. He did that so we could have the forgiveness that none of us deserve." Dan shook his head slowly. "And if God, who has never done even one thing wrong, can forgive me for my many wrongs—so many more than seventy-seven or even seventy times seven—even though I don't deserve that forgiveness, surely I can forgive those who sin against me even though they don't deserve it. God calls us to that forgiveness when he says, 'Forgive as the Lord forgave you.' Amen."

Cameron lifted his head as the people around him began to stand. He pushed slowly to his feet too.

The sermon had been good. He could admit that. But that didn't mean he thought Pastor Dan was right.

Sure, maybe Jesus could forgive people even when they didn't deserve it. It was probably easy for him. But Cameron was only human. It wasn't reasonable to ask him to simply forget what Bethany had done to their family.

Not now.

Not ever.

As they settled back into their seats for the final hymn, Cameron slid farther away from Ruby. He knew Bethany's sins weren't her daughter's fault. But right now he needed a little distance from any reminders of his sister.

The moment the service ended, Ruby broke into conversation with Kayla, who looked past the little girl and caught Cameron's eyes with a smile. It was only for a moment, but it was enough to make his heart do a strange sort of leap. Cameron ignored it.

He nudged Ruby out of the row, and they followed Kayla toward the back of the church. But instead of exiting into the lobby, she stopped at the back row, where a couple was busy wrapping a baby in blankets.

Kayla squealed and returned the hugs the couple offered. "Let me see your little bundle."

"This is Ella Lynn." The man held up a squirming baby, probably not quite a year old, though Cameron knew better than to trust his own judgment when it came to children's ages.

Kayla rubbed a finger over the baby's tiny hand, and something about the movement was so tender that it tugged at Cameron.

"How old is she?" Ruby asked.

"She's nine months."

Well, who knew? He must be getting better at determining ages than he thought.

"Come on Ruby. We should get going." He tried to step around Kayla's wheelchair, but she glanced up, as if she'd forgotten he was there.

"Oh. Sorry. Jared, this is Ruby's uncle, Cam. Cam, this is Jared and Peyton and their brand-new daughter Ella Lynn. Jared is one of the paramedics who responded to Bethany's accident."

"Oh." Cameron wasn't quite sure how to react to that. He held out a hand. "Thank you."

Jared shook his hand. "How's your sister doing?"

Cameron's eyes flitted to Ruby. "She's doing . . . okay. Still about the same, but . . ."

Jared nodded solemnly. "We'll keep praying for her."

"Yeah." Cameron shifted awkwardly. "It was nice meeting you. Congrats on your little one."

He took a step toward the lobby, grabbing Ruby's hand to tug her with him.

"Wait. You're coming to lunch at the Hidden Cafe, right?" Kayla's eyes landed on his.

"Oh. Uh. Thanks, but—"

"Please, Uncle Cam," Ruby half-whined. He gave her a look, and she changed tactics. "I'm hungry. Your waffles were bad and I didn't have time to eat much cereal."

Kayla lifted an eyebrow. "You made waffles? I'm impressed."

"Don't be. They looked like shoe leather."

"And smelled like feet," Ruby added with a giggle.

Cameron couldn't hide his own laugh. "They kind of did."

"That settles it." Kayla clapped twice. "You two are coming to lunch with us."

Cameron considered arguing more. But the truth was, he was hungry. And enjoying his time with these people.

And, between Kayla and Ruby, he had a feeling he would have lost any argument anyway.

Chapter 30

"Oh, for crying out loud." Kayla gave an exasperated laugh at herself. That was the fourth time she'd dropped her napkin during this one meal. She started to roll her wheelchair back from the end of their long table at the Hidden Cafe, but Cam beat her to it.

"I've got it." He leaned over, giving her a full breath of his fresh, slightly spicy smell.

As he sat up, she tried not to notice how good he looked in his dark suit and the sapphire tie that brought out the flecks of warmth in his eyes. Or the way his suit hugged his shoulders, emphasizing their width. Or the way a lock of his hair fell onto his forehead, giving him a more playful appearance than usual.

A strange tingle went straight up the back of her neck—the same tingle that had been plaguing her every time he looked at her since they'd gotten here.

It had been a long time since she'd allowed herself to acknowledge attraction to any man, but Cam sure was making it rather difficult not to today.

Which was a problem.

Because she had no intention of giving up her independence for any man. Not even one as charming and attractive and funny and . . .

She stopped herself. Listing his good qualities was not going to help here.

"So, Kayla," Emma said from her other side.

Kayla turned to her friend with such a profound feeling of relief that she was afraid Emma would read it on her face.

But Emma seemed oblivious as she gave Kayla a huge smile. "I have a proposition for you."

"Yeah? What's that?"

Emma's grin grew. "I've been looking into starting a social interactions program at Hope Riders. But I don't have time to oversee it myself, and I was thinking . . ." She waggled her eyebrows at Kayla.

"Me?" Kayla stared at the other woman. Was Emma offering her a job?

"Of course, you."

"You'd be perfect for that." Cam cut in, and Kayla swiveled her head toward him in surprise. "I would?"

"Of course she would," Emma said to Cam, who gave a satisfied nod.

"And then you could stay in Hope Springs forever," Ruby added.

Kayla smiled at her but then turned back to Emma. "Is this something you want to start right away?"

"The sooner the better. Our grant funding just came through, so I need to get it going pretty quickly."

Kayla bit her lip. "I really appreciate the offer, and I'm definitely interested, but can I think about it a bit? I just found out this morning that I was accepted for the mission trip, so . . ."

"You were?" Emma popped up to hug her. "Oh, Kayla, that's wonderful. And no pressure at all. Whatever you decide, I know God is going to bless."

"Looks like you're in high demand." Cam gave her a warm look—or maybe it wasn't his look that was warm so much as her cheeks.

She ducked her head.

She had more important things to think about right now than her ridiculous feelings. Like how in the living world she was going to make this decision.

She spent the rest of the meal trying to weigh the pros and cons of each opportunity—but only ended up with a swirling head.

"All right, Ruby, time to go."

Kayla looked up in surprise at the sound of Cam's voice. She hadn't even registered that most of the others had left already.

"Bye, Kayla." Ruby jumped up from her seat and threw her arms around Kayla's neck.

"Bye, sweetie." Kayla was seized by the ridiculous urge to tell the two of them not to go. After spending so much time with them over the past couple of weeks, it felt odd not to be certain when she'd see them again. But it would be odd to invite them to the movie she'd been planning to see with Nate and Vi, so she simply lifted a hand and waved as they started for the door.

"You're just going to let them walk out?" Vi hissed from next to her.

"Yes, I am." She turned to her sister-in-law, whose hand was pressed to her belly. "And so are you."

Vi snorted. "You don't know me very well, do you?" She lifted her head to look past Kayla, raising her voice to call, "Cam! Ruby!"

The two of them stopped, their matching eyes falling on Vi.

"We're going to the movies. If you want to join us." Vi's voice seemed overly loud in the small restaurant.

Kayla dropped her eyes to her lap, then to the floor, then to the table—anywhere that wasn't Cam.

But after a moment, she couldn't bear not knowing his answer, so she looked up.

Ruby was already on her way back toward the table. Cam stood frozen to the spot, though his hand was extended toward Ruby, as if he'd tried to stop her.

His eyes met Kayla's, and she held her breath, one hundred percent unsure what he would do. One hundred percent unsure what she wanted him to do.

After a moment, he shrugged, dropped his arm, and followed Ruby.

"If you need to work, we can take Ruby without you." Kayla didn't know why she blurted the words. But at least this way Cam couldn't think the invitation had been directed at him.

"Nah, that's okay. I'll come."

The way Ruby's eyes lit up went straight through Kayla. And the fact that Cam looked nearly as pleased only made the feeling grow stronger. Somehow, over the last few weeks, Ruby's uncle had gone from complete indifference toward his niece to adoring her—even if he maybe wasn't quite ready to admit it to himself.

As they slipped out of the restaurant into the gray December afternoon, Vi gave Kayla a sly look. "Why don't you ride with Cam, Kayla?" Her sister-in-law's voice was all innocence. "Nate and I need to stop at the antique shop on the way to pick up a table I want for the house."

Kayla shot her sister-in-law a look that should have burned the sweet smile right off her face. But Vi seemed completely unperturbed. Right, as if Kayla hadn't heard the stories about how Vi had contrived to get her best friend Sophie alone with Spencer so the two could realize they were still in love.

Well, if that was Vi's plan here, she was going to be sorely disappointed.

"Sure." Kayla made her voice breezy and calm. No need to let Vi think it ruffled her in the least to spend more time with Cam and Ruby. Because it didn't. She turned to Cam. "If you two don't mind."

Ruby jumped up and down. "Come with us! Come with us!"

Cam's smile was sincere. "That's fine with me."

"All right then, that's settled." Vi took her husband's arm and waddled toward their car. "We'll see you there in a little bit."

Kayla followed Cam and Ruby to Cam's vehicle. When they got to it, Cam stepped in front of her to open the passenger door.

She gave him a look and prepared to tell him that she was perfectly capable of opening a car door on her own, thank you very much, but then he moved to open Ruby's door as well, poking her lightly in the side as she climbed past him, eliciting a giggle from her and a hearty chuckle from him.

Kayla laughed too—she couldn't help it. She moved into position to transfer into the car, trying not to feel self-conscious as Cam stood by, watching her first lift her legs into the vehicle, then boost her torso inside.

But he smiled as he reached for her wheelchair. She'd shown him how to take it apart when they went to the zoo last weekend, so they could stow it in the trunk.

As Cam got into the car, he gave Kayla another smile—he really needed to stop doing that—then looked over his shoulder at Ruby. "All buckled?"

"Baa. Let's go."

Kayla smirked at Cam when he huffed out a breath. Apparently Ruby was taking her acting advice seriously.

They had just pulled into the theater's parking lot when Kayla's phone dinged with a text from Vi.

Not feeling so great. I think we're going to head home. Have fun though!

Kayla rolled her eyes. She should have seen this coming. It was straight out of Vi's playbook.

But there was nothing she could do about it now.

Her fingers tapped out a quick reply. *I know what you're up to. And it's not going to work.*

Though as she glanced at Cam's smiling lips, she realized—she was going to have to take care to make sure that was true.

Cameron hadn't felt this relaxed in a long time.

Maybe it was the dark of the movie theater or the fact that he'd turned his phone off completely so that even its buzzing vibration couldn't interrupt his afternoon. Or maybe it was the sound of Ruby and Kayla giggling together all through the movie.

He'd tried to be annoyed—their laughter had made him miss more than one line of the movie. But instead he found himself smiling every time he heard them.

Ruby's full-bellied laugh was almost contagious—and Kayla's lighter, more lilting one wasn't far behind.

As the credits rolled and the lights came up, Ruby leaned over. "Uncle Cameron." Her whisper was urgent.

"Yeah?"

"I have to go to the bathroom." She squinted her eyes, as if she were in agony.

"Oh. Uh. Can you wait until we get home?"

She shook her head.

"I'll take her," Kayla offered.

"Thank you." Cameron honestly had no idea how a person was supposed to parent a child alone. He could definitely see that parenting was easier as a tag-team sport. Not that he and Kayla were parents. Or even a team.

As he cleaned up their garbage, his thoughts drifted back to Kayla's friends at lunch. So many families—all happy and whole and content.

But not all families were that way. And there was no guarantee that those that were would stay that way. He knew that better than anyone.

He threw away the trash, then waited in the hallway for Ruby and Kayla. Three other guys stood there too, apparently doing the same thing.

A young woman came out of the restroom, a toddler in her arms, and walked up to one of the men, smiling. He pushed off the wall and fell in step with her, wrapping an arm around her back and leaning over to tickle the toddler.

Something clenched in Cam's gut—a brief flicker of doubt. Was it possible that he did want that?

"Can we go look at the lake?" Ruby bounced toward him and slipped her little hand into his. Hers was still wet from washing it, but he didn't pull away.

Cam shrugged. He had plenty of work to catch up on, but honestly, he was in no rush to get to it. "It's up to Kayla."

"That sounds fun. I haven't been down to the marina since I got here."

They emerged from the theater to find that the cloudy afternoon was already dimming. As they made the short trek to the top of the hill that led down to the marina, Cam hesitated, glancing at Kayla in her wheelchair. That was a steep hill.

"You can manage this?" He didn't want to insult her, but he also didn't want to watch her lose control of her wheelchair and go plummeting into Lake Michigan.

"Yep." She popped her front wheels up, balancing on the large back wheels, then started down the hill at a controlled pace.

Cam shook his head as he followed her. He shouldn't have doubted her. The woman seemed to have no concept of just how extraordinary the things she did were.

At the bottom of the hill, they made their way onto the wide breakwater that extended into the lake, creating a safe harbor. A sharp wind blew off the water, and Cam reached over to pull Ruby's hood up.

By the time they'd made their way to the end of the breakwater and back, he could barely feel his fingers. He glanced at Kayla, who was now going to have to wheel all the way back up the hill.

But this time he knew better than to ask if she could do it. Instead, he walked alongside her as she attacked the hill as if it were nothing more than a speed bump.

"I can see how you've won marathons." He paused at the top of the hill to let Ruby, who had fallen behind after stopping to examine every crack in the sidewalk, catch up.

Kayla smiled, her breathing only a hint labored. "Honestly, I'm pretty out of shape right now. I've been starting to train again, although if I go to Malawi, I guess I won't be doing any races."

For some reason, the thought of her going that far away drew Cam up short. It made no sense—he'd be going back to California sooner or later, so what did it matter to him where she wound up?

"Does the Chocolate Chicken have hot cocoa?" He looked from Kayla to Ruby. "Or am I the only one who needs to warm up?" And who was having too much fun to go home quite yet.

Kayla grinned at Ruby. "I believe it does."

Chapter 31

$\mathcal{D}$arkness was already falling as they exited the Chocolate Chicken, and though the evening was chilly, Kayla had to admit that she couldn't remember ever feeling so warm and cozy and . . . content. And the Christmas lights twinkling from all the storefronts only added to the peaceful atmosphere.

The sound of bells jingling carried in the clear air, and Ruby pointed down the street. "That's the carriage that went past our house three times last night."

Kayla read the chalkboard sign on the sidewalk. "Carriage tours nightly until Christmas Eve. Tour the best of Hope Springs' Christmas lights." She turned to Cam. "Why does it go past your house?"

Cam gave her a mysterious smirk. "Wouldn't you like to know."

"That's why I asked. Ruby?" She'd certainly have better luck with the little girl. "Did your neighbors decorate their houses?" When Kayla had left their house the other night, she hadn't noticed any decorations—or at least not any that would qualify as "the best of Hope Springs."

Ruby giggled and shook her head but didn't say anything.

"Seriously, what's the big secret?"

Both Cam and Ruby burst into laughter.

"I guess we'll just have to show you." Cam gestured to the carriage as it pulled to a stop in front of the Chocolate Chicken, the horses' breath steaming the air in front of them.

Yeah, she could probably be persuaded to extend this day a little longer. But after this, she *had* to go home, before Vi's plan really did work.

They waited for the current passengers—a young couple with pink cheeks and arms wrapped adorably around each other—to disembark. Then Cam boosted Ruby into the carriage. Once she was settled, he moved out of the way to let Kayla get into it. She eyed the narrow foot rest. There was no way she'd be able to get her feet stable on there and pull herself up. Maybe if she skipped it and hoisted herself directly onto the floor of the carriage? But it was high, and the opening was narrow. She doubted she could get the leverage she needed.

But she'd never been one to give up without a fight. She maneuvered her wheelchair into the best position she could manage, then reached for the side of the carriage and put her considerable arm muscle into pulling herself up. But the angle was off, and after a moment, she let herself drop back into her chair. She readjusted and tried again, but after another half-dozen attempts, she rolled her chair back from the carriage.

Given enough time, she knew she'd get in there eventually—she hadn't yet met the vehicle she couldn't transfer into. But it was cold, and she wasn't going to make Cam and Ruby wait here all night.

"You two go." She kept her eyes directed toward her lap. She knew she shouldn't be embarrassed, but she was. After Cam had been so impressed with the way she'd powered up the hill. Well, now he knew she wasn't Superwoman, after all. "I'll drive down your street later and see what's so mysterious that you can't tell me."

"Don't be stupid." The roughness of Cam's voice caught her by surprise, and she looked up to find him glowering down at her. "If I didn't know how stubborn you were, I would have offered to help long before now."

She gave a shaky laugh. "I'm not stubborn. I'm independent."

He shook his head. "Part of being independent is knowing that there's no shame in asking for help. You're stubborn."

"Please come, Kayla." Ruby's plea was much kinder than Cam's.

Kayla lifted her eyes to his. "All right, fine. Would you mind helping me?"

His glower transformed into a grin. "Thought you'd never ask. Just tell me what to do."

She let out a long breath. She didn't like the feeling of being carried—the lack of control—but it was the only option. "I can't get the right angle to transfer myself. I think you're going to have to lift me."

Cam nodded as if she'd asked him to do something totally normal, then stepped forward and slid one arm under her legs and the other behind her back. She inhaled sharply as he lifted, having no choice but to wrap her arm around his shoulder, telling herself that she didn't feel a tiny tingle all the way through her skin and down to her fingertips. That she didn't notice the ripple of muscle as he pivoted toward the carriage.

"I'm really sorry about this." She turned her head away from him so she wouldn't be staring at his firm jawline, wouldn't be awash in his spicy scent.

"Don't be silly." At least he hadn't called her stupid this time.

With a slight grunt, he angled her through the opening and raised her onto the carriage seat, setting her down as gently as if she were made of porcelain.

Then he stepped back and pushed her wheelchair underneath the awning of the Chocolate Chicken. "I assume that will be fine there for a little bit?"

Kayla nodded. "Yeah." She tried to get herself to think straight, but Cam's eyes were on her, and she wanted suddenly to know what he was thinking. Had he felt the same electricity she did when she was in his arms?

But then he looked away and climbed into the carriage, settling next to Ruby.

Kayla let out a sigh—of relief, of course.

Cameron fisted his hands in his coat pocket, working hard to look anywhere but at Kayla. Holding her in his arms for those few moments had been disconcerting. The way her warm, coconutty scent had cloaked him, the way her hand had rested lightly against his neck, the way her hair had brushed his cheek—it had all thrown his senses, not to mention his feelings, into confusion.

Be logical, he reminded himself.

Logic said that what a woman smelled like—or looked like sitting in the moonlight or sounded like laughing with Ruby or felt like in his arms—had nothing to do with anything. Feelings might get caught up in those things. But logic didn't. Logic said this was just a carriage ride. Logic said they were both doing this for Ruby. Logic said Kayla didn't have feelings for him any more than he did for her.

Logic said the only reason he was thinking like this at all was because of Ruby's ridiculous suggestion the other day that he couldn't have a girlfriend because he had Kayla.

You don't have a girlfriend anymore.

That was true . . . but it also didn't mean he was looking for one.

The driver made a clicking noise to his horses, and the carriage started forward with a slight jerk, leading Ruby to squeal and Kayla to lurch forward. Instantly, his hand was out of his pocket and on her arm, steadying her.

Only for a second, but it was long enough for him to feel the jolt.

"Thanks," she murmured.

"It's fine." He cleared his throat and pulled his hand back, even as his heart took up the rhythm of the horses' clattering feet.

As the carriage turned away from downtown toward the residential streets, he forced himself to focus on the decorations glinting from the houses. But the closer they got to the house, the more he felt the anticipation building. He didn't know why he was so excited for Kayla to see what he'd been working on, but he couldn't keep his grin from growing as the carriage approached their street.

Ruby apparently felt the same way, as she started bouncing on the seat next to him. "Close your eyes," she said to Kayla.

"Seriously?" Kayla's eyes flicked from Cameron to Ruby, and now he felt his smile reach for his ears.

"Really." He reached across the space between their seats and pulled her hat over her eyes.

"Hey." But she laughed and held her hands over her eyes as well. "This had better be good."

When the carriage finally arrived at the house, Cameron asked the driver to stop for a minute.

"All right, open your eyes," Ruby said.

"Are you sure?" Kayla kept her hands over her face.

"Yes!" Ruby stood and pulled Kayla's hands down, then shoved her hat onto her forehead.

Cam watched as Kayla's expression went from confused to surprised to delighted. "Wow! You did this?" She turned to him, and he couldn't deny the warmth that went through him at the admiration in her gaze.

He shrugged. "You're not the only one who knows how to put up Christmas decorations."

"Clearly not. Wow, Cam. This is amazing."

"Thanks." Cam let his eyes go to the yard, where he'd wrapped the trunks of every tree in blue lights, then draped white lights from the branches. He'd also created his own trees by stabbing shepherd's hooks into the ground, wrapping them in lights and then extending more lights from them in a pyramid shape. But his favorite part was the tunnel of lights he'd created along the walkway to the front door. Icicle lights on the eaves completed the effect.

It wasn't too bad, if he did say so himself.

"I take it you entered the decorating contest. Seriously, you might give Leah and Austin a run for their money this year. I have to get a picture of this." Kayla readjusted in her seat to dig into her coat pocket.

"There's a decorating contest?"

Kayla stopped rummaging for a second and stared at him. "You didn't know about the contest? You just did this for fun?"

He shrugged. Was it that hard for her to imagine him doing such a thing? "I always loved decorating the yard with my dad. This brought back good memories. And Ruby insisted on the icicles. We had to go back to the store to get them."

"Got it!" Kayla held up her phone triumphantly. She pulled off her glove and tapped the screen, then frowned. "Oh. I turned it off during the movie. One second. You guys move over so I can get you in it with the house in the background."

Cam and Ruby shifted. "Is this good?"

"You need to get closer. Maybe Ruby should sit on your lap."

All right. He'd never held a kid on his lap in his life, but sure, why not? Ruby got up, and he shifted to the far edge of the seat, then boosted her onto his lap and wrapped an arm around her so she wouldn't fall off. To his surprise, it didn't feel odd at all to be holding a kid. "How about this?"

But Kayla was staring at her phone, one hand pressed to her mouth, shaking her head.

"What's wrong?" He leaned forward, nearly dumping Ruby off his lap, but cinched his arm tighter so she wouldn't fall and gently took the phone from Kayla's hand.

He flipped it around to read the text that was open.

Took Vi to hospital. The doctors said placental abruption. They want her to deliver right away. Pls pray.

"That was from an hour ago. Why didn't he call me?" Kayla's voice was teary as she grabbed the phone back out of Cameron's hand and examined the screen. "Oh. He did. Six times." She glanced at Cam, fear pooling in her eyes.

A sick feeling settled in his stomach as Kayla tapped her screen, then pressed the phone to her ear. There had to be something he could do to help.

He set Ruby back on the seat next to him, then turned and tapped the carriage driver's shoulder. "We need to get back to where you picked us up."

"We haven't gone down Church Street yet." The driver spoke in a low-key monotone.

"Skip it. Take us back to the Chocolate Chicken."

The driver nodded and clicked to the horses.

Cam settled back into the seat, then leaned forward and took Kayla's free hand in his. "It's going to be okay." He had no idea what possessed him to whisper the words. He had no way of knowing that.

She gave him a weak smile as she left a message.

When she'd hung up, she turned to him. "Do you think you could drop me off at the hospital?"

He shook his head. He was absolutely *not* going to drop her off at the hospital.

"We're coming with you."

Chapter 32

Kayla numbly took the coffee cup Cam held out to her.

Shell-shocked. That was the only way to describe how she felt.

Like she had just watched everything in her world blow up in her face.

The doctors were still working on Vi, but they were pretty sure she'd make it.

The baby, though.

Tears came to Kayla's eyes again, and she swallowed them down with a scalding drink of coffee and a swipe at her cheeks.

The poor baby.

And poor Vi and Nate.

Grief for the hole that Vi would feel when she learned what had happened to her baby—it had been a boy, they'd learned—tore at Kayla's ribs.

"Do you want to stay or go home?" Cam's voice was low and soothing, and Kayla wondered yet again if this was the same man who had come barreling into this same hospital only a month ago, no interest in seeing his own sister, clearly impatient at the idea of caring for his niece. Now he leaned over and tucked Ruby's jacket under her head, which was pressed against the arm of a chair. The little girl had brightened them all for a while, until she'd grown too sleepy and curled up in the chair.

"I'm going to stay. But I can get a ride with Nate or someone else." The small waiting room was so crowded with friends that a nurse had come in a while ago and asked if some of them might like to come back another time—but not a one had budged. "You go. Get Ruby home to bed."

Cam's eyes held hers. "Ruby wouldn't want to leave you."

She swallowed. What about him? Did he want to stay too?

"Really, Cam. I'll be fine. Thank you for bringing me."

He nodded, then stood and slid his arms under Ruby's sleeping form. Kayla tried not to remember what it'd felt like to have those arms around her, lifting her into the carriage.

She should have been humiliated, disgusted at herself that she'd needed to ask for help. Instead, all she'd felt was warm—safe.

It was a feeling she couldn't let herself get used to.

She was plenty warm and safe all by herself. She didn't need a man to make her feel that way.

"Call me tomorrow," Cam said. "Let me know how they're doing."

On his way out of the room, he rested a hand briefly on Nate's shoulder, and Kayla's heart squeezed so tight she didn't know how it didn't pop.

Then Cam and Ruby were gone, and Kayla was left feeling . . . alone. Which made absolutely no sense, seeing that she was surrounded by friends.

She wheeled her chair in front of Nate's seat. Her brother looked up, his eyes bleary. "What am I going to do, Kay?"

She took his hand. The truth was, she didn't know. "We're all here for you, Nate. And for Vi."

The waiting room door opened, and a tired-looking doctor entered the room. "Mr. Benson?"

Nate gave Kayla a panicked look, and she squeezed his hand, closing her eyes and trying to issue a desperate prayer as Nate stood. But her soul drew a blank.

"Is she all right? Can I see her?"

The doctor ran a hand down his face, and Kayla's heart went cold. But the doctor nodded. "She's stable. You can see her now."

Nate let out a whoosh of air, as if he'd been punched, and fell back into his seat. "Thank you, Lord." But then he lifted his eyes, meeting Kayla's in horror. "How am I going to tell her?"

Kayla opened her mouth, grasping for the words of comfort she knew he needed to hear. But she was empty. Her quick prayer for something helpful to say went unanswered, and an unsettled feeling stirred inside her.

How could God have allowed this to happen to the people she loved most in the world? To people he'd already asked so much of? Who served him faithfully day after day?

None of it made any sense.

As she looked at Nate, she could only shake her head and swipe at her own eyes. "I'm so sorry."

She'd let her brother down.

And God had let them all down.

Chapter 33

Cameron growled at the document open on his laptop. For the life of him, he couldn't remember why he was supposed to care about it.

All he could picture right now was Kayla. Kayla smiling. Kayla laughing. Kayla crying over the loss of her little nephew.

That last one was the one he kept getting caught up on. The way she'd wiped the tears off her cheeks as fast as they fell. The way she'd tried to hide her face from him. The way every fiber of his being had ached to pull her into his arms and hold her tight and tell her it was okay to let them see her hurt.

She'd texted early Monday morning to say Vi had pulled through, and he'd been amazed by the power of the relief that had gone through him. How was it that these people he'd only known for a month had come to mean so much to him?

It wasn't logical.

But then, it seemed that nothing here was logical. It wasn't logical that his thirty-six-year-old sister had had a brain aneurysm, wasn't logical that Vi and Nate had lost their baby, wasn't logical that though it had only been five days since he'd seen Kayla, he missed her with a fierceness he'd never experienced before.

He closed his laptop. The house was too quiet, and Ruby wouldn't be home from school for two hours yet. His eyes fell on the picture

Ruby had been drawing this morning—of her mother playing with her in the snow.

All week, Cameron's conscience had asserted itself louder and louder, Dan's sermon knocking around his thoughts like Ruby's super ball. Was the pastor right? Was it time he forgave Bethany? Time he was there for her the way Kayla and her friends had been there for Nate and Vi?

With a sudden decisiveness, he shoved the dining room chair back and jumped to his feet, sending the cat that had been curled up on his lap flying with a scolding yowl.

He grabbed his jacket and keys and twenty minutes later was standing in Bethany's hospital room, hands jammed in his pockets. Now what? He glanced around the room, then grabbed a chair from the far corner and pulled it up to the bed.

He stared at his sister for a long while, too many memories swimming through his thoughts. Memories of playing hide and seek with the whole family. Memories of movie nights gathered around the small TV in the family room. Memories of telling her everything would be okay when her first boyfriend broke up with her.

Memories of the first time she'd returned from rehab, promising she was all better. And of the second time. And the third. Of Mom and Dad welcoming her back every time.

Memories of the day he came home from school to find Dad in tears—his strong dad in actual tears—because Bethany had betrayed them.

Abruptly, Cameron shoved to his feet, sending his chair skidding across the floor behind him. "I'm sorry. I just can't." He spoke the words out loud, right over the top of his sister. "I can't forgive you for what you did. Mom and Dad gave you everything. They forgave you and welcomed you back and picked you up every time you fell. And because of you, they weren't there—" He tipped his head back to stare at the ceiling, his vision blurring. "They weren't there to do any of that for me. I had to figure it all out myself." His voice cracked, but he wasn't done. "You took them from me, Bethany, and nothing can change that."

He watched her still form for another minute, warring against the part of himself that felt sad and scared for her. She didn't deserve that.

"You managed to raise a pretty amazing little girl, I'll give you that." He pinched the bridge of his nose. "And I'll keep taking care of her as long as I need to. But it's not for you—" He shook his head, wiping away a single tear that had managed to creep onto his cheek. "It's for her. And for Mom and Dad."

Chapter 34

S he shouldn't have let Nate and Vi talk her into coming to dinner at Dan and Jade's house tonight. They'd said being around friends would help, and though she doubted it, she'd come along, because if Nate and Vi could see everyone and talk and handle their grief, then what right did she have to stay home and be sad? But the cloud that had hung lower and lower over her all week felt like it was pressing on her now, stifling her, pushing her into the ground.

She forced a smile onto her face as she picked up Vi's empty plate to bring to the kitchen. She had to be strong for her sister-in-law.

"I can get that." Vi reached for it, but Kayla shook her head. It was the least she could do.

"You sit. I've got this."

Vi gave her a grateful pat and returned to her conversation with Sophie.

Kayla kept the smile plastered in place as she maneuvered past the others to the kitchen, not looking toward where Cam was handing Ruby a piece of cake. Tonight was the first she'd seen of him since he'd left the hospital last Sunday, and she didn't know why she felt like she had to avoid him now.

She suspected it was because as hard as she'd tried not to let him, he'd seen her cry. Seen her weak. Seen her in need.

Something she worked hard not to let anyone see—ever. She was supposed to be the strong one. Didn't people always tell her that—how much they admired her strength?

Straightening in her chair, she made her way to the kitchen, where Jade was loading the dishwasher. Jade directed a discerning look her way as she added the dishes to the machine. "How are you doing?"

"Me?" Kayla put on her toughest strong-girl smile. "I'm doing fine. Just trying to keep Vi off her feet."

"Good luck with that." Jade squeezed Kayla's shoulder. "They're going to be okay, you know that, right?"

Kayla swallowed painfully. "Of course. I'll go grab some more dishes."

But as she reached the living room, her eyes caught on Vi, absently rubbing a hand over her stomach, the same way she'd done when she was pregnant. With a silent shudder, Kayla left the room and wheeled down the hallway to Dan's office. She knew he wouldn't mind—she just needed a few seconds to pull herself together.

The moment she'd closed the door, she dropped her head to her hands and loosed the dam of tears she hadn't allowed herself to cry at the funeral they'd held for her little nephew—Isaac Matthew—three days ago. The same question that had plagued her since then swirled through her head: Why?

She could see the good that had come out of her accident, but how could babies dying possibly be for anyone's good, let alone Nate and Vi's? Why would God let something like that happen?

The part that hurt the most was that she had no answer. Just a profound sense of sadness that something had been taken from her that she was afraid she might never get back.

It made no sense. She kept trying to talk herself out of the feeling. She'd already gone through her crisis of faith once, a long time ago. She couldn't have a second one. Now she was supposed to be the one who was there for others through their own crises.

The creak of the door behind her made her wipe her eyes quickly. "I'll be out in one second." She worked to make her voice bright, but even she could hear the tears in it.

She heard the door click shut and offered a silent thank you. At least whoever it was had realized she wanted to be alone.

But footsteps crossing the wooden floor abolished that hope. She wiped her eyes harder. Dan must need something from his office. "Sorry, I didn't mean to—"

"Are you okay?" It wasn't Dan's voice. It was Cam's.

Kayla kept her head down, unwilling to let him see that she'd been crying. Again. "Of course. I just needed to . . ."

A wooden desk chair rolled up in front of her wheelchair, and through her eyelashes, she watched Cam sit in it, then slide it closer to her.

His hands moved toward her, and she couldn't find the wherewithal to move out of the way. She let out a long breath as his hands wrapped around hers.

"You're not okay. And that's okay." His voice was gentle. "Someone told me that after my dad died—I don't remember who. And I remember thinking at the time what a load of hogwash that was. But after a while, I realized it's kind of true. It's okay not to be okay. And it's okay to let others know you're not okay."

Kayla let herself look up at him. He was watching her with those clear blue eyes, warmer than she'd ever seen them but also filled with compassion.

"I feel silly," she admitted. "Nate and Vi are handling this better than I am. I should be the one supporting them, you know? The strong one."

Cam's thumb caressed the top of her hand. "You don't always have to be the strong one."

"Yes, I do. That's who I am. People tell me all the time—you're so strong, Kayla. I never could have gone through what you did, Kayla. You're an inspiration, Kayla."

Cam studied her. "Even inspirations are allowed to be sad sometimes, I think. Especially when something bad happens to someone they love. Right?"

Kayla's eyesight went bleary again, but she managed a small smile. "Maybe." She pulled her hands out of his to wipe her cheeks, then immediately wished she hadn't. The feel of his hands on hers had given her a warmth and hope she'd been needing all week. "I just— I gave you that whole speech about how God has a plan in everything. And I'm really struggling to believe that right now. Honestly, it feels like everything I believe has been turned upside down, and I don't know how to right it again."

She clapped a hand over her mouth. It was one thing to let him see her weak but another to let him know she was questioning her faith, especially when his own seemed so tender. The last thing she wanted to do was lead him away from the Lord. "I'm sorry, I didn't mean that. I just mean—" She closed her eyes. "I don't know what I mean." Defeat pulled on her shoulders.

"Maybe that's okay too," Cam said softly. His hands went around hers again, and she shivered a little. "Actually, it's a relief to see you struggling."

Kayla lifted her head to him. "That's . . . mean?"

He laughed. "Sorry. No, I mean, I'm not glad you're struggling. But I'm glad you told me. It makes me feel better to know I'm not the only one who ever has doubts. Because the other day at church . . . man, I was sure I was the only one. But it's nice to know you're human too."

Kayla gave him a slow, sad nod. "The humanest, unfortunately."

Cam leaned forward, lifting a hand to wipe a tear off her cheek. "I don't think that's such a bad thing." His voice was low, barely above a whisper, and as Kayla's eyes came to his, she found herself leaning forward. His hand was still on her cheek, and she closed her eyes.

What is happening here? What are you doing?

But she was tired of questions. She let her lips part.

Cam's hand slipped from her cheek and the sound of chair wheels on the wooden floor accompanied his throat clearing.

Kayla's eyes sprang open as her face spontaneously combusted.

What had she been thinking?

He hadn't wanted to kiss her. He'd only been trying to offer some simple comfort, and she'd read way more into it than she should have.

"Kayla, I'm—" He scooted his chair closer again, but she shook her head and held up a hand.

"We should get back out there. I have to check if Vi needs anything."

She spun her wheelchair toward the door without waiting for a response. She was in the hallway before she heard him push the desk chair into place.

But she didn't look back.

You are quite possibly the world's biggest idiot.

Why hadn't he kissed her?

His heart was hammering angrily at him, but his head told it to chill out. He hadn't kissed her because, for one, he'd just gotten out of a relationship and wasn't looking for another. And for two, he hadn't been at all sure that she really wanted to kiss him. She'd never given any indication of having feelings for him before. Likely, she had only leaned in because he'd offered her some measure of comfort in her grief. And he didn't want to take advantage of that.

Idiot. Apparently his heart didn't agree with his reasoning. *It* had definitely wanted to kiss her, even if his head said no.

Next time, he bargained. If she ever gave him a next time.

He followed her to the living room, trying to ignore the curious—maybe somewhat distrustful—look her brother sent his way. Cam tried to offer him an innocent looking smile as he took a seat next to Ruby at the table where she was coloring with the other kids.

He picked up a crayon and started coloring a picture of some princess or another. Though Ruby watched those movies all the time, he couldn't keep them straight.

But his eyes kept going to Kayla, who was either studiously ignoring him or completely unaffected by what had just happened. He found himself hoping it was the first.

"So Ruby—" Emma turned to his niece. "Did you write a letter to Santa?"

Cameron's head jerked up. Christmas. Santa. He hadn't even thought about that. Unless Bethany had some hidden store of gifts he hadn't run across, he needed to get Christmas presents for Ruby.

"Baa." Ruby grinned. "That means, 'nope.' Mommy always says Santa knows, so I don't need to ask for anything. And he always does. Last year, he got me the bike I wanted."

"If you did write a letter, what would you ask for?" Cam kept his question casual.

Ruby shrugged. "I don't know. Whatever Santa wants to bring me. Baa."

He groaned silently, thanking Bethany in his head for teaching her kid not to be greedy.

Surreptitiously, he pulled out his phone and tapped Kayla's name. *Help! I didn't think about Christmas presents. What do I do?* He added lots of panic face emojis, then sent the message.

He watched as Kayla pulled her phone out, read it, laughed to herself, then lifted her eyes to his, looking slightly bemused but not at all awkward. Thank goodness. They could move on and pretend his idiotic move of dodging her kiss hadn't happened.

Go shopping, I guess?

He rolled his eyes at her response. Thanks, Einstein. *Where do I shop? What do I get? You have to help me. Please!!!*

As he waited for her to read it, he fired off another message. *I don't want to ruin her Christmas.* There. Let her try to resist that.

He could tell the moment she got the second message, because she stopped tapping and looked up at him, biting her lip.

Then she dropped her head and tapped again.

Please, he urged silently.

All right. I'm free Tuesday. When her text came through, he let out a quiet exclamation of triumph, and Ruby gave him an odd look.

"What, Uncle Cam?"

"Oh. Nothing. Something for work." He ducked his head and picked up another crayon.

But when Ruby went back to coloring her own picture, he let himself glance toward Kayla. She looked a little brighter as she talked with Vi and Jade, and he let himself wonder: Would he get a chance to kiss her on Tuesday?

Chapter 35

*K*ayla was going to chew a hole through her lip. She'd been staring at the email from the mission organization for the past half hour, trying to convince herself to respond.

She knew what she had to do.

She couldn't go on the trip.

Because as much as she'd always wanted to do this, now wasn't the right time—not when she was questioning everything, wrestling with her own doubts. How was she supposed to spread the Gospel when she felt like her own faith was so fragile that all it would take was a feather to knock it down? When she couldn't even put two sentences together to pray right now? When the whole time she'd sat at church on Sunday, she'd been wondering if God really did care?

The doorbell rang, and Kayla set her laptop aside gratefully.

Until she realized that meant she had to see Cam. But he'd been at church on Sunday too, and things hadn't gotten awkward. Sure, that was mainly because they hadn't said a word to each other. But what was she going to say: *Sorry I almost kissed you the other night?*

It was better if they both acted as if it had never happened.

Kayla took a breath and pulled the door open. Today was going to be a totally ordinary day. Just two friends shopping together to make sure that a little girl had a good Christmas.

Ordinary, aside from the flippy thing her stomach did the moment she spotted him standing there in his jeans and sweater. She forced herself to ignore it.

"Good morning." Cam pulled a coffee cup from behind his back. "This is a bribe."

Kayla's fingers accidentally brushed his as she took the cup from him, and she pulled her hand back quickly, telling herself the warmth was from the coffee, not his touch. "I'm not sure you understand how a bribe works. You're supposed to give it to convince the other person to say yes. Not *after* they've already agreed to help."

"Ah, well. Then consider it a thank you." Cam's eye twitched, and she almost could have sworn it was a wink—but that was crazy.

She reached for her jacket and slipped her arms into it. Cam watched, waiting patiently, but didn't step in to help, she noted with satisfaction.

"So, where to?" he asked as she joined him outside.

Kayla bit her lip. She'd been debating that very question. Hope Springs had a plethora of shops—but they were mainly specialty places like Vi's antique store and Ariana's fudge shop and home decor places. If they wanted toys, they were going to have to go to the mall—which was over an hour away.

She wasn't sure she could handle being alone in the car with him for that long.

But then she thought of the look on Ruby's face Christmas morning. She supposed she could put up with a little awkwardness for Ruby's sake.

"Let's go to the mall." She followed him to the car and transferred into the passenger seat, then leaned down to take apart her wheelchair at the same time as he did. She caught his spicy scent as their heads almost collided, and she sat up quickly.

"Sorry," Cam mumbled. "You get it."

"That's okay. You know what to do." She picked up her purse and pretended to dig for something until he grabbed the wheelchair and brought it to the trunk.

This was not off to a non-awkward start.

And it didn't get any better when Cam got into the car and pulled out of the driveway. An odd, sort of electric, silence hung between them as Cam followed her directions out of town.

Kayla tried to focus on the scenery. But the silence only grew more charged.

They could not go through the whole day like this.

Which meant they were going to have to talk about it. It might make things more awkward for a minute or two—but then they could get back to normal.

She drew in a breath for courage, but before she could say anything, Cam turned to her. "What did you think of Dan's sermon on Sunday?"

Kayla's mouth snapped shut. Okay, they could talk about that instead.

"It was good." That was a safe answer—Dan's sermons were always good—though she honestly wasn't sure how much of it she'd caught. As hard as she'd tried to focus on what he was saying, the weight of her doubts had drowned out everything else, even the refreshment of the Word she knew she so desperately needed to hear. "What did you think of it?"

"He sure does harp on forgiveness a lot, doesn't he?"

Kayla laughed. Now she remembered—the sermon had been based on the parable of the unforgiving servant, who was forgiven his large debt but then refused to forgive the man who owed him a smaller debt. "Yeah, I suppose so. But that's because forgiveness is kind of the whole point. Without God's forgiveness, won for us by Jesus, we'd all be condemned to hell."

Wow, where had that come from? Kayla had been so sure that her doubts would keep her from sharing God's Word. But to her relief, she realized that whatever else she was wrestling with, she still believed this.

Cam nodded, but his face creased into a frown as he turned onto the road she pointed to. "I went to visit Bethany the other day. Without Ruby."

Kayla tried to keep up with the thread of the conversation. Was he done talking about forgiveness? She felt like there was so much more she should have said. But maybe what he needed right now was someone to listen. "How was it?"

He gave a dry laugh. "Pretty awful."

Her heart went straight to him. Despite his issues with Bethany, she knew he cared about his sister. "I'm sorry. I know it has to be difficult to see her like that." As much as it hurt that her brother and sister-in-law had lost their baby, at least she still had *them*. Cam didn't know if his sister was ever going to wake up—and what kind of state she'd be in if she did.

But Cam shook his head. "I yelled at her." His eyes flicked to Kayla, then back to the road, as if he wasn't sure he wanted to see her reaction. "I meant to go there to forgive her. But then there were all these memories. They weren't all bad, but somehow that made it worse, you know? I just don't see how—" He broke off, reaching to turn the heat down a notch. "I try to tell myself that she's different now. She's going to church and as far as I can tell from her house and the way she's raised Ruby, she's probably changed. But that's not the Bethany I know. The Bethany I know tore my family apart. Am I really supposed to forgive her for that?"

Kayla considered his question. It would be easy to offer a simple, "Yes, of course." But she knew better than anyone that it wasn't as easy as that. "If you mean, do I think it's what we're called to do as Christians, then yes, I do," she said finally. "But if you mean, do I think it's always possible—that takes a greater strength than we have. We can only do that through Christ in us."

"Well, then, I'm not sure I have enough Christ in me." Cam sounded impetuous, and Kayla let out a soft laugh.

"It's not about how much Christ you have in you, Cam. It's about letting him work in your heart. And it takes time."

For goodness' sake, she might as well be talking to herself. Wasn't that what she needed to do with her doubts? Let Christ work in her heart?

Cam nodded, and they fell into silence again. But this time it wasn't that electric, charged, awkward silence. It was the silence of two people contemplating hard truths.

"How about this?" Kayla held up a unicorn necklace, grateful that navigating the stores had dispelled any lingering awkwardness between them, putting them squarely back in the friendship zone.

Which was right where they belonged.

Cam glanced up, his arms loaded with the bags of gifts they'd already purchased. His smile may have made her insides do a little flippy thing again, but she was getting better at ignoring that. Soon enough, it would go away entirely.

And she wasn't even *thinking* about almost kissing him anymore.

"It's perfect." Cam grinned wide enough that she had to look away.

"What do you think? Are we set?" she asked after they paid, counting off in her head. They'd found books, a doll stroller, a plush pony, and now the necklace.

"There's one more thing I thought of. But I don't know. I mean, I think she would like it, but . . ."

"Maybe if you actually tell me what it is, I can help."

"I'll show you." Cam started down the crowded corridor of the mall, and Kayla fell in next to him with her wheelchair, trying not to notice how mindful he was to lead them on the path with the fewest obstacles.

"What is it with you and all the mystery? Why can't you just tell me?"

"I like surprises." His eyes sparkled as he turned into a large department store. "And so do you."

"You don't know that." But she couldn't deny that he was right, and in spite of herself a little flutter of pleasure went down her neck at the fact that he knew that about her without being told.

"I saw this online, and it made me think of Ruby and that box she has." He followed the signs to the toy department, glancing down each aisle until he'd apparently found what he was looking for.

"What do you think?" He held out his arms the same way he and Ruby had when they'd shown off the scraggly tree they'd put together. But this was no scraggly tree. It was a three story dollhouse, nearly as tall as he was.

"Wow, that's . . ."

"Don't you dare say interesting," Cam warned.

Kayla laughed. "No. I was going to say big."

He turned to look at it, frowning. "Is that a bad thing?"

"Not necessarily. But where would she put it? I'm not sure it would fit in her room. Or the living room."

Cam's shoulders fell. "You're right."

He looked so sweet, pouting about not being able to get his niece the gift he'd chosen, that Kayla wheeled closer. "It was a really nice thought, though. What about a smaller dollhouse?" She scanned the shelves and pointed to one that was more reasonably sized but still cute. "Like that one."

"That one's puny."

"Well, Ruby's pretty small herself. Unless you were planning to play with it?"

He hit her with a surprised laugh. "What do you think I do all day?" But he examined the smaller dollhouse more closely. "I guess this one is nice too." He picked up the box and started back down the aisle. "Come on. We have one more stop."

"Another?" Kayla never would have guessed Cam could outshop her—not that she was going to give him the satisfaction of telling him that. "Now where?"

"You'll see." He grinned at her.

She treated him to a dramatic eye roll but couldn't deny that her curiosity was growing as she followed him back through the mall. They'd already hit every store that could possibly have anything for Ruby.

Without warning, Cam slowed to a stop. "Hold on a second." He took a step backwards and peered in the window of a jewelry store. Kayla backed up her wheelchair to see what had captured his interest. It was a display of Christmas gifts for men—mostly watches, but also some rings and cuff links.

"My dad used to have a compass like that," Cam said quietly, pointing to a silver circle etched with the cardinal directions. "My mom gave it to him when they first started dating. It was engraved with his favorite verse: 'Be strong and courageous.' I always wondered what had happened to it. I didn't find it when we cleaned out the house after mom died. Bethany probably . . ." He shook his head, giving her a rueful glance. "Sorry. Let's keep going."

"Do you want to go in and look at it?"

Cam gave it one more look, then shook his head again. "No. Come on, let's keep going."

"And where are we going again?"

He laughed. "Nice try."

She frowned as he turned right. According to the sign, all that was in this direction was the food court. "I don't think there are any stores down this way."

"I know." Cam's grin grew. "But there's lunch. My treat."

Nope. No way. She'd never agreed to lunch. That was too much like a date. "We don't have to get lunch. I'm not hungry . . ." Okay, that was a total lie. She'd worked up quite the appetite with all their shopping.

Cam waved off her argument. "Well, I'm starving. And I don't want to eat alone. So what'll it be? Personally, I'm leaning toward one of those gigantic cinnamon rolls."

"For lunch?"

"Yep. Come on, you know you want one."

Kayla shook her head, but her mouth watered. Fine, he was right about this too.

Ten minutes later, as the fluffy dough, aromatic cinnamon, and sweet frosting melted on her tongue, she couldn't remember for the life of her what her objection to eating with him had been.

Until she caught a glimpse of him watching her with a warm smile.

She cleared her throat to keep that earlier awkwardness from creeping over her again. "I assume you know how to wrap the presents?"

Cam laughed. "A bold assumption. But, yes, I think I can handle the wrapping. I'm not completely helpless. Unless you want to−" He broke off as his phone cut through the noise of the food court.

"Sorry." He pulled it out of his pocket. "I would have turned it off, but I wanted Ruby's school to be able to reach me, just in case . . ."

Kayla waved off the apology. "That was a good idea." Man, when had this guy become such a good parent? And why did it make her heart do all those extra cartwheels just when she'd gotten it under control?

But Cam's smile faded as he looked at the screen. "It's not the school. It's the hospital." He lifted his head, his eyes meeting hers, panic lasering out of them.

"It will be okay," Kayla said out of habit, even though she was less certain of that than she'd ever been. Her heart thundered for poor Ruby. For Cam. For Bethany.

Please, Lord. It was only two words, but it was two words more than she'd managed to pray in over a week.

Cam lifted the phone to his ear, his other hand falling onto the table, and instinct drove Kayla to grab it before she realized what a bad idea that was. But Cam was her friend, and she needed to be here for him—and right now, taking his hand was the best way she knew to do that.

She watched his face as he listened. His forehead creased, but he nodded. "Okay," he finally said. "What does that mean?"

He listened some more, his fingers clutching at hers. Kayla swallowed, silently wishing for him to hurry up and finish the call so she'd know what was going on too.

"Thank you. We'll be there as soon as we can." As he lowered the phone from his ear, he slid his other hand out of Kayla's to hang up the call.

She let him sit staring at the phone for a full three seconds before she couldn't stand it any longer. "What is it?"

He looked up at her with an odd expression. "Bethany opened her eyes."

"Oh my goodness. Cam!" Before she could consider her reaction, Kayla was wheeling around the table and throwing her arms around his neck.

She heard him swallow as he leaned closer and squeezed her to himself. "They said it doesn't necessarily mean she's waking up. But they're hopeful."

Kayla nodded against his shoulder, trying to blink away the ridiculous tears that insisted on puddling in her eyes.

This was exactly the kind of news she'd needed today. It didn't make everything better, didn't erase all of her doubts—but it did ease the ache in her heart.

"Come on." She didn't even try to hide the tears as she pulled back. "Let's go get Ruby and take her to see her mom."

Chapter 36

The elevator dinged at Bethany's floor, and Ruby dove out of it, followed by Kayla. But Cameron was paralyzed. As much as he'd been waiting for this moment, he wasn't sure he was ready for it. Wasn't sure he was ready to face his sister awake. Wasn't sure he was ready to give up Ruby. Wasn't sure, even, that he was ready to return to his real life.

Kayla spun her wheelchair, apparently realizing he wasn't with them. "You coming?"

"Yeah." He forced his feet to step off the elevator, barely making it through as the doors closed.

"Ruby, hold up," Kayla called, and Ruby skipped back to them.

"Hurry up, Uncle Cam," the girl commanded. Apparently the excitement of getting pulled out of school to see her mom had made her forget that she usually communicated in baas these days.

"I will. Come here a second, though." He'd been trying to figure out all the way here how to explain to his niece what the nurse had told him on the phone.

He crouched down to be at eye level with her. "I don't want you to be upset if your mom doesn't open her eyes right now. The nurse said she's still really sleepy. And even if she does open them, she might not be able to do anything else, like smile or talk. She might be confused and not know who we are. Do you understand?"

Ruby nodded solemnly. "It's fine if she doesn't know who I am because I know who she is."

Cameron hesitated. Maybe this wasn't a good idea, after all. What if it traumatized Ruby to see her mom like this? But it might traumatize her more if he made her go home now. It wasn't the first time he'd wished for some sort of manual to tell him what to do.

"Okay," he finally said. "Let's go see her." He straightened slowly and let Ruby take his hand. They started down the hallway but after a second, he realized that Kayla wasn't with them.

He turned around to find her with her hands on the rims of her wheels—but she wasn't pushing them. "Aren't you coming?" He could understand if she didn't want to, especially given the memories it must bring back of her own accident. But he could really use her in there.

"Only if you want me to." She tucked her hair behind her ear, looking unusually vulnerable as she waited for his answer.

"Yeah." He gestured for her to catch up with them. "I really do."

Her smile was bright and gentle and supportive all at the same time, and together, the three of them made their way down the hall, Cam's heart picking up speed the closer they got to Bethany's room. Ruby might be able to handle this, but could he?

His gaze went straight to Bethany as they entered the room. But her eyes were closed, her form as still as always.

Well, the nurse had warned him that was likely.

Still, his heart broke a little for Ruby, who had made her way to the bed and picked up Bethany's hand. "Mommy?"

Bethany's eyes remained closed.

"I'm sorry, Ruby. They said—"

His words got caught in his throat as Bethany's eyes fluttered open.

"Mommy!" Ruby jumped up and down.

But Bethany's eyes skimmed right past her, past all of them, as if they were nothing more substantial than air.

"Mommy?" Ruby's voice shook. "It's me, Ruby."

But Bethany's eyes didn't go to her daughter, instead staring blankly at the far wall.

"Ruby—" Cameron took a step forward as Ruby turned away from the bed. He crouched just in time to catch her in his arms as she broke into tears. He ran a hand up and down her back, his tight throat barely managing to squeeze out the words, "It will be okay."

The much louder voice in his head was shouting that it would *not* be okay. In some ways, it had been easier to see Bethany when her eyes were always closed. At least that way, they could pretend she was only sleeping. But seeing her like this—eyes open but completely unaware—was surreal. Or maybe too real. It was like the time he'd walked in on her and her boyfriend in their parents' basement, both so strung out on who knew what that neither of them realized he was talking to them when he was standing right in front of them, yelling for them to turn down the music, which had been blasting at levels that should have burst their eardrums. Finally, he'd turned the music off himself and stalked away—and still neither had acknowledged his presence. It was like they were somewhere else entirely, completely oblivious to the real world around them.

A sudden, fresh surge of anger went through Cameron. It was one thing for Bethany to put him through that. But how could she put her little girl through it too?

He pushed abruptly to his feet, grabbing Ruby's hand. "I think we should go."

"But Uncle Cam, I don't want—"

"We're going." He pulled her toward the door.

Kayla backed her wheelchair out of the way. "Cam, don't you think—"

"No." He stepped into the hallway. "No, I don't think we should stay. It's obviously upsetting Ruby. And there's nothing we can do right now. We need to go home so Ruby can do her homework and we can have dinner and she needs to shower yet and brush her teeth and—" He couldn't stop talking. If he just kept this list going, then they could get back to all the things that had become a normal part of his day.

"Cam—" Kayla's fingers brushed his hand. "It's okay. You're right." She turned to Ruby. "Your mom would want you to get your homework done and be all rested for school tomorrow."

He nodded, hoping Kayla could read the gratitude in his eyes. "Yep. Come on, little sheep. You've got a date with some addition problems."

He waited for the giggle Ruby usually gave when he talked about her having a date with homework, but she stared at the floor silently. He cursed himself for bringing her in to see Bethany. He should have known it would be too much.

"I don't want to be a sheep anymore." Ruby scuffed the toe of her tennis shoe against the tile floor.

"Of course you do. The play is in three days. You need to be in character." He could hardly believe he was saying it, after all the times it had driven him crazy that she wouldn't break character to so much as eat breakfast.

"I don't want to be in the play," she said, putting out a lip.

"Why not?" Kayla wheeled closer to the girl, giving Cam a questioning look.

He raised a shoulder. Sometimes he forgot how in over his head he was here—and then something like this came along to remind him.

"Because Mommy's not going to be there." Her eyes filled, and Kayla reached out a hand to take one of Ruby's. Cam squatted on the little girl's other side.

"I know, sweetheart, and I am so sorry that she can't be. But your uncle Cam is going to be there. And I'm going to be there." Kayla's eyes went to his, and he wanted to tell her suddenly how much it meant to him that she was always there for them. But she kept talking. "And I told Vi and Nate about it, and they can't wait to see you. And I think Jade and Dan are bringing Hope and Matthias. And you know Jonah and Jeremiah and Gabby are in the play, so Isabel and Tyler will be there too. And you know what?"

Ruby lifted her eyes to Kayla, who grinned at her.

"You are going to get the loudest cheer any sheep has ever gotten." Kayla winked at her. "It'll be so loud that everybody will think you're a movie star."

Ruby's giggle was tiny, but it brought Cameron such relief that he could have gathered them both up in a hug.

Instead, he gave Kayla's arm the briefest squeeze, then stood and took Ruby's hand. "Now, about that date with your homework."

This time Ruby's giggle was stronger. "You can't have a date with homework, Uncle Cam."

He feigned shock. "Why not?"

"Because dates are for people."

He glanced at Kayla as they made their way toward the elevator.

Yes, dates were for people.

Chapter 37

*K*ayla tucked the pearl barrette into her hair, giving a satisfied smile at the effect of the white gems against her dark locks.

"Don't you look nice."

Kayla jumped at the sound of Vi's voice behind her. "I will never know how you get around so silently."

Vi gave a gentle laugh. "I see you went all out tonight." She gestured to Kayla's hair, the makeup she rarely bothered with, the black leggings and soft blue sweater she'd chosen after spending way too much time in front of the closet, the black boots that took a wrestling match to pull onto her feet.

Kayla shrugged. "It's a special night. I want Ruby to feel like it's a big deal."

"Mmm." Vi nodded, but Kayla could read the amusement in her eyes. "It's for Ruby. Not her uncle."

"What?" Drat. That sounded too rehearsed. She tried again. "Of course it's not for Cam."

So what if just saying his name made her smile? That didn't mean she'd gotten all dressed up for *him*. So what if the way he'd held Ruby close the other night at Bethany's bedside had melted her from the inside out. That didn't mean she'd given him one thought as she swiped on the thin coat of mascara. And so what if the way he'd looked at her when he'd dropped her off had nearly made her feelingless toes tingle and caused her to almost lean in again. That had nothing to do with the fact that she'd swept her hair off her neck and chosen her favorite teardrop earrings.

"All right, then." Violet nodded, obviously patronizing Kayla. "We're ready to go when you are."

"You guys go ahead. I'll drive over separately. I promised I'd take Ruby out for ice cream afterward."

She avoided Vi's too-knowing look as Nate came up next to his wife, slipping an arm around her waist. "Is she beautiful enough yet?" His teasing eyes went to Kayla. "I guess she'll do. Come on, slow poke."

Vi grinned at her husband over her shoulder. "She wants to drive separately. Which means you get me all to yourself."

"I like that idea." Nate nuzzled his wife's neck from behind, and Kayla made a loud groaning noise.

Except, it did her heart good to see the two of them smiling and laughing together. Even if she didn't understand how they did it—how they went on each day, knowing what they had lost.

Was it because they had each other that they were able to endure it? Because if one fell, the other could pick them up, like their wedding verse said?

She pictured Cam comforting her when she'd cried. Pictured the way her hand had gone to his when the hospital had called about Bethany. Pictured the way they'd shared their deepest secrets and toughest challenges with each other.

And then she shoved those pictures away and grabbed her keys. Before she left the room, she pulled the barrette out of her hair and the earrings out of her ears. There was no time to wash off her makeup, but at least she didn't look like she was trying to impress anyone.

She headed for the door without another glance in the mirror.

By the time she got to the elementary school, the auditorium was packed. Kayla let her eyes roam the space, trying to figure out where there was room for a wheelchair.

"Kayla! Over here." Cam hurried to her side, and she couldn't command herself to ignore the flare of pleasure that went through her at the knowledge that he'd been watching for her.

She followed him to a side row, where an open space had been left for wheelchairs. "Don't you want to sit closer to the stage?"

He shook his head. "Ruby picked out these spots just for us."

As they settled in, Kayla felt a small shiver work through her.

Cam glanced at her. "Cold?"

Sure, they could go with that as the reason, not his nearness. "I forgot my blanket in the car." Which was true. She generally put it over her legs whenever she had to get from a parking lot into a building, but she'd been so focused on getting inside before the play began that she'd forgotten all about it.

"Here." He shrugged out of his jacket.

"Oh, I don't need—"

But he'd already laid it across her lap, and the house lights dimmed as the stage lights came up.

"Thank you," she whispered, tucking her hands under it and letting them soak up the warmth of his body heat that the jacket retained.

Cam nudged her as students in costume filed onto the stage, and she took a moment to pick out Ruby, adorable in her sheep costume. Then she let herself peek at Cam, who was beaming as he snapped pictures with his phone.

They both leaned forward as Ruby crawled to the front of the stage. She stood staring out at the crowd, and Kayla had a piercing moment of fear. What if Ruby had forgotten what she was supposed to do? But then she said, clear and loud and very sheep-like, "Baa. Christmas is a time of cheer. Baa."

The audience laughed, and even from her seat near the back, Kayla could see the smile on Ruby's face. Cam turned to her with a proud grin.

And that was it.

Her heart was done for.

For the rest of the play, she had to work hard not to notice every time he shifted in his seat, sending his spicy scent drifting her way. Had to concentrate on not noticing just how close they were sitting. Had to pretend she didn't want to slide closer.

She shifted her wheelchair subtly away from him. The best thing she could do was ignore these feelings and trust they'd go away.

When the play was done and the cast was taking their bows, she and Cam and the rest of their friends scattered through the auditorium let out a deafening cheer for Ruby.

"She did good." Cam's smile was lopsided and proud and oh-so-perfect as he stood.

"She really did." After that performance, Ruby would get the lead in next year's play for sure. Kayla couldn't wait to see it—if she was still in Hope Springs, that was.

But she was having a harder and harder time imagining being anywhere else.

"Excuse me," a woman's voice said behind them, and Cam turned to look over Kayla's shoulder.

"You're Ruby's uncle, right? Cameron?"

For some reason, that made Kayla laugh, but she covered it up with a cough as Cam said, "Yes."

"I thought so." She stepped around Kayla as if she wasn't there. "My daughter is in Ruby's class, and I volunteer in there a few times a week. From the way she talks, I was pretty sure you'd be a superhero."

Kayla's fake cough grew louder, and Cam eyed her, but she could tell he was fighting off a laugh too.

"Nope. Just a regular uncle."

"I was thinking maybe you'd like to get together for coffee sometime. I know how tough it is to be a single parent. Maybe we could—"

"That's very kind. But I have a partner in crime already." Cam smiled at Kayla, and her heart sped right toward her throat. He only meant partner as in someone who helped with Ruby, right? Not *romantic* partner?

"Did you see me? Did you see me?" Ruby rocketed right into the middle of the group, nearly knocking the other woman off her feet.

"Oh, I'm sorry." Cam gave a deep bow. "I was expecting Ruby. Not a *movie star*."

Ruby's giggle turned into a squeal as Cam scooped her up and twirled her in a circle.

Kayla's heart beat faster as she watched them. Did she want to be Cam's partner? For more than helping with Ruby?

She knew the right answer was no.

And yet, with each passing minute, she became less and less certain that it should be.

As Cam set Ruby down, the little girl dove into Kayla's arms.

"You are officially the best actor I've ever seen." Kayla squeezed her tight, noticing with a tiny bit of satisfaction that she wasn't necessarily proud of, that the other woman had begun to back away.

Kayla's friends gathered around them, all offering congratulations to Ruby. Kayla rejoiced to see the girl bask in the attention. She knew Ruby still wished her mom was here—they all wished that—but at least the night hadn't been completely ruined for her.

"So—" Cam turned to Kayla. "I believe there was a promise of ice cream."

Chapter 38

W alking on air. Wasn't that the saying? Cam was certain it applied to him tonight as he escorted Kayla and Ruby toward the school doors. The play had been perfect. Ruby had been a hit. And Kayla had been . . . stunning.

If it weren't for the fact that he hadn't wanted to miss a minute of Ruby's performance, he wouldn't have been able to keep his eyes off her. And now that the play was over, he didn't bother trying to resist.

But the moment they stepped outside, his attention was stolen by the scene in front of him. It had been starting to flurry when they'd arrived, but now the air was thick with swirling flakes, and a good inch of snow already blanketed the sidewalk.

He stopped and held out a hand, observing as a few large flakes landed on it and immediately melted. Fascinating.

"What are you doing, Uncle Cam?" Ruby's voice made him realize that both she and Kayla had continued down the sidewalk.

"Sorry." He gave them a sheepish grin. "I haven't seen a lot of snow in my life."

"And what do you think of it?" Kayla was watching him with a curious expression on her face.

"It's sort of magical, isn't it?" The way it danced in the air, the way it sparkled under the lights, the way it covered everything over, making the whole scene look clean and new and pristine.

"The first snowfall always reminds me of that verse," Kayla said. "'Wash me, and I will be whiter than snow.' Though I admit I'm not a big fan of driving in it." She bit her lip as she peered toward the road.

"Tell you what." Cam turned to Ruby. "How do you feel about hot cocoa instead of ice cream? Seems a little more fitting. And we can have it at our house so Kayla doesn't have to drive as far."

Ruby eyed him. "Can I have marshmallows in my cocoa?"

He nodded.

"And whipped cream?"

He laughed and nodded again. The girl may have gotten her negotiating skills from him.

"Then we have a deal." Ruby shook his hand as Kayla's laugh sparkled in the night air, only making the scene more magical.

Then they continued to their vehicles, Cam rushing to get Ruby buckled in so they could pull up behind Kayla and wait for her. He was slightly worried about her trying to maneuver her wheelchair in the snow—though he should know better by now. By the time they reached her, she was already in the car and disassembling her wheelchair. When she was done, he waved for her to pull out ahead of them, then followed her to Bethany's house.

He'd no sooner pulled into the driveway than Ruby shot out of the car and straight into the snowy yard, dropping onto her back and doing some form of lying-down jumping jacks.

Cam moved to Kayla's car and waited for her to assemble her wheelchair, then locked his hands on the backrest.

Kayla studied him. "What are you doing?"

He shrugged. "It's slippery out here."

She looked for half a second like she was going to argue but instead offered a quiet, "Thank you."

"You're welcome." He waited until she'd transferred into the chair and lifted her feet onto the footrests before he let go.

"Come on guys, make snow angels with me," Ruby called. She was standing over the one she'd just made, clumps of snow clinging to her hair. She took two giant steps away from it and plopped down again, starting a new one.

"I'm good, thanks." The snow was pretty and all, but that didn't mean he wanted to play in it. Besides, there was no way Kayla could . . .

"What, are you afraid of a little snow?" Kayla rolled her chair to the edge of the yard, then leaned forward and stuck one mittened hand into the snow.

"What are you—" But before he could finish the question, she'd lowered her body to the ground.

"What does it look like I'm doing?" Kayla shot him a grin as she scooted a few feet farther into the yard, then lay back. An irresistible giggle escaped as she slid her arms through the powder above her head and then down to her sides. After a moment, she sat up and wrapped her hands around both of her legs, then pushed them back and forth through the snow. Cam shook his head—this woman never failed to surprise and amaze him. Not that he should be surprised by anything she could do anymore. Or by his growing feelings for her.

"Come on, Uncle Cam," Ruby called. "You have to try it."

Cam eyed the snow, eyed Ruby flailing her arms wildly to make yet another angel, eyed Kayla, smiling up at him, snow sparkling in her hair.

With a shrug, he took two steps into the snow and dropped to the ground next to Kayla. "Oh, that's cold." He shivered as the powder worked its way down his collar.

But as he slid his arms and legs through the snow, jumping jack–style, the way Ruby had, he couldn't help laughing. It was as fun as it had looked. After a moment, he sat up to examine his handiwork. Not too bad.

"Now what?" he asked.

"Now you get up and jump away from it so you don't wreck it." Ruby demonstrated on her own angel, and Cam followed her lead.

"Hey, Cam," Kayla called from the spot where she was still sitting in her own angel. Her voice was strange, almost shy.

"Yeah?"

She blinked up at him, looking uncertain. "Do you think you could lift me out of my angel so I don't wreck it by scooting?"

His heart filled. He knew how much she hated asking anyone to do anything for her, so it was no small thing that she'd been willing to ask him for help.

"Of course." He moved to her side, careful not to step in her angel. She scooted to the very edge of it, and he bent over to slide one arm under her legs and the other behind her back. Then he lifted, pulling her in close to him as he stood. Her arm went around his neck, and he could feel her hand brushing the snow off, sending sparks down his spine.

"Thanks." He let himself bring his eyes to hers.

"You're welcome." Her voice was barely a whisper, and his eyes went to her lips. He'd been waiting all week for another chance to kiss her. Was this it?

"Can we have cocoa now?" Ruby popped up at his side.

Apparently not the time for a kiss.

"Yeah." But Cam didn't take his eyes off Kayla's as he brought her to her wheelchair and set her down.

Maybe after they had their cocoa and put Ruby to bed, they'd have some time alone. The prospect warmed him all the way down to his frozen toes.

"That cocoa may have been better than the Chocolate Chicken's." Kayla emptied her mug and gave a satisfied sigh. She couldn't remember a time she'd ever felt cozier than this. When they'd come inside from making snow angels, Cam had insisted that she change out of her cold, wet leggings and had dug out a pair of Bethany's sweatpants for her. They were a little big for her atrophied legs, but they were warm and dry—and they reminded her yet again of how thoughtful Cam could be. She wasn't sure how it had taken her so long to see it. Or maybe he'd only come by that thoughtful streak recently—she'd certainly noticed the way his whole personality had softened over the past six weeks as he'd taken care of Ruby. It seemed that taking on parental duties had brought out the best in him.

She grabbed the three empty mugs and balanced them on her legs to bring them to the counter, then spent way more time than necessary loading them into the dishwasher. She needed a moment to separate herself from Cam and Ruby—to remind herself, yet again, that though they felt like a family sometimes, they weren't. To stop wondering what it would be like to actually raise a family with Cam.

She didn't want that. Didn't need it.

It would be too easy to lose her independence if she gave herself over to a relationship. Look at the way she'd asked Cam to help her out of her snow angel before. That wasn't like her at all. Even if she'd enjoyed being in his arms, it wasn't worth the price.

"Okay, movie star, time for bed," Cam announced.

"Will you help tuck me in again?" Ruby blinked at Kayla with those sweet, big eyes, so much like her uncle's—who was also gazing at her, looking hopeful.

She glanced out the window, where the flakes swirled faster. "I'm sorry, sweetie. I think I'd better go. I'm not sure how the roads will be." That, and if she kept looking into those eyes—either of them—she'd be unable to resist the pull they had on her heart.

Simultaneously, both Ruby's and Cam's faces fell. Cam recovered first. "At least say you'll come over Christmas morning. I know Santa would want you to watch Ruby open her presents."

"Please, please, please come," Ruby threw in.

There was no way to say no to that. "All right. I'll come. But only if you two will come to Christmas dinner at Nate and Vi's."

"It's a deal." Ruby held out her hand, and Kayla shook it, allowing herself one quick look at Cam, who was grinning as widely as Ruby.

As she wheeled out the door and into the night, Kayla realized—her parents would be at Nate and Vi's for Christmas. And her mom would jump to conclusions if she found out Kayla had invited a man.

She'd just have to hope Mom assumed that Nate or Vi had invited him.

Chapter 39

"Hey, Kayla."

Kayla jumped at the sound of her brother's voice in the dim living room, lit only by the colored lights of the Christmas tree.

"Nate. You scared the daylights out of me. What are you doing, sitting here in the dark?"

"Praying. How was the ice cream?"

She wheeled toward him, skirting the path around the furniture she knew by heart by now. "We ended up having hot cocoa and making snow angels."

"Sounds fun." Nate's voice was warm, but the shadows on his face traced out faint lines she'd never noticed before. "I never asked. Did you make a decision about the mission trip?"

Kayla bit her lip. The decision had been weighing on her, but she couldn't bring herself to respond one way or the other. The conversation she'd had with Cam the other day had led her to believe that maybe God could still work through her, in spite of her own doubts. But on the other hand . . .

"Have you ever felt like you've lost yourself?" she asked her brother.

Nate let out a soft breath. "You know I have, Kayla. For years. Why? Do you feel like that?"

She shrugged. "I don't know. Sometimes. I can't figure out what God is doing right now, you know? I was telling Cam a couple weeks ago about how God works everything for our good. But I just can't find the good in Bethany being in a coma or in Ruby being without her mother. Or in you and Vi losing the baby . . ." She trailed off. She hadn't meant to bring her brother's sorrow into this. A sigh dragged from her lungs. "I don't know, I guess it all makes me wonder if God . . ." The thought was so awful, she wasn't sure she could say it out loud.

"Cares?" Nate filled in.

Kayla nodded miserably. "I'm sorry. I'm not the one going through loss. I shouldn't have brought it up. You and Vi are handling it so well and—"

Nate's sharp laugh stopped her. "Kayla, there's not a day that goes by that I don't feel like I'm falling apart on the inside. And I know Vi feels that way too. To think that our baby is . . ." He looked away, swallowing.

Kayla gaped at him. "You do? She does? But you both seem so . . . steadfast."

Nate brought his gaze back to her. "That's God's doing, not ours. I've been where you are, Kayla, remember? Wondering how God could let something so terrible happen to someone I love. I know how much it hurts. I know the questions that are going through your head."

Kayla sniffed, a tear sneaking from her eye. "This is so stupid. I already went through my doubting phase. I should be past this by now."

Nate laughed. "Wouldn't that be nice? One time in your life that you question God and then you're good forever. But you're human Kayla. And sinful—sorry to break it to you."

She swatted at him, even as she hung on his words.

"I'm just saying, things come along in this world, things we can't understand and don't think are fair, and we start to wonder again if

God really is in control. If he really does care about us. Sadly, doubt isn't one of those one-time things."

"So what do I do about it?" Kayla could hear the desperation in her own voice, but she didn't care. She needed to know how to get back to that place of faith she'd grown so comfortable in. "I keep trying so hard to hold on tighter, but I just can't."

"No, you can't." Nate leaned toward her. "But God can. He's holding onto you. Not the other way around. Even when it doesn't feel like it, he's there."

Kayla let out a long breath, nodding slowly. She still didn't feel one hundred percent better. But it was a relief, at least, to know she wasn't the only one who struggled with this stuff. And she knew Nate was right—God was holding onto her, even if she couldn't feel it right now.

"Thanks, Nate. You're a good brother, did I ever tell you that?"

Nate chuckled. "Not often enough." He cleared his throat. "And speaking of being a good brother, is there anything I should know about you and Cam?"

"No. Like what?"

"Like are the two of you seeing each other, or . . ."

"No." Kayla tried not to sound defensive.

"Oh." Nate shrugged. "I thought you liked him."

"I do." Well, she hadn't meant to blurt that out. Especially not to her brother.

"So what's the issue?"

"That *is* the issue," she said impatiently.

"I may be kind of dense about these things," Nate said. "But that doesn't sound like an issue."

Kayla huffed at him. "You know I don't have any intention of ever getting married or anything. I can't give up my independence for anyone. Not even him."

"And you think he'd ask you to give up your independence?"

Kayla shook her head. "He wouldn't have to. It just happens. Look at you."

"Me?" Nate gave her a truly baffled look. "What about me?"

"Well, you're not as independent as you were before you got married, are you?"

Nate snorted. "I think you're forgetting that before I got married I was in prison."

"Okay. Bad example. But don't you ever feel like you've given up part of yourself to be with Vi?"

Nate looked at her as if she was off her rocker. "I don't feel like I gave up part of myself. I feel like I found part of myself that I didn't know was missing."

Kayla gave him a dubious look, pushing away thoughts of all the times she'd been with Cam and Ruby and felt like everything in her was complete.

Nate pushed to his feet. "I'm going to go find Vi." He squeezed her shoulder. "Don't let fear hold you back if you think this guy might be worth it. But if he's not the right one, don't settle for anything less."

He disappeared from the room, leaving Kayla to sit in the dark.

She closed her eyes, sat still, and let a little whisper of a prayer work its way from her soul.

Chapter 40

*C*am couldn't remember the last time he had enjoyed Christmas so much.

And it was only nine thirty in the morning.

But as Ruby opened her last present, a feeling of such complete contentment washed over him that he wasn't quite sure what to do with it. Except smile as wide as his mouth allowed.

As Ruby pulled the wrapping paper off, Cam glanced at Kayla, whose smile was also larger than life.

Ruby's deafening squeal pulled his attention back to the gift unwrapping.

"A *real* dollhouse. I love it." She bounced to her feet, then sprang into his arms for a hug. "Thank you, Uncle Cam." The moment she'd pulled out of his arms, she was wrapping her arms around Kayla. "Thank you, Kayla."

Cam's heart pushed against his chest as he watched the two of them.

"Don't you mean, 'Thank you, Santa'?" Cam wasn't going to be the one to blow the charade.

Ruby giggled. "I know Santa's not real. Mommy told me last year. I just played along for you."

"Oh, in that case, maybe you can help me with something." Cam pointed to a wrapped box that remained under the tree. "Can you be a little elf and deliver that to Kayla?"

"What? Cam—" Kayla's eyes met his in surprise, as Ruby skipped to the tree.

"Be careful with it." He winced as Ruby bobbled the box.

Thankfully, she managed to get it to Kayla without dropping it.

She gazed at him for a few more moments, then dropped her eyes to the box and tore the paper off—almost with more enthusiasm than Ruby had. She pulled the cover off the box.

"Oh." She stared at it for a moment, then reached into the box and pulled out a snow globe with a horse and carriage passing in front of a church. Cam tried to work out if that had been a good *oh* or a bad *oh*.

"It's like the carriage we rode." Ruby bounced on her toes. "Remember?"

Cam held his breath. He'd debated getting the snow globe. For him, that carriage ride had been the start of something. Something he dearly hoped could become more. But for her, it might only bring back memories of her brother and sister-in-law's loss.

But when she lifted her eyes to his, they were warm and open. "This is beautiful. Thank you."

He nodded. "Should we get to church?"

"Not so fast." Kayla gestured for Ruby to come closer, then whispered something in the girl's ear. Ruby giggled, then skipped toward the front door and rummaged through a plastic bag Kayla had dropped off there when she'd come in.

"What's going on?" he demanded.

But Kayla blinked at him demurely. "What, you're the only one who can have surprises?"

"This?" Ruby held up a wrapped box.

"Yep. Go ahead and give it to him."

"What? Me?"

"You're the only him here," Kayla pointed out with a laugh.

"Yeah, but you didn't have to—"

"Neither did you. Just open it."

He took the box Ruby passed him and shook it. It was light and didn't rattle. "Not breakable."

Kayla let out one of her adorable snorts. "Good thing."

He knocked on it. "Not alive."

He lifted it to his nose and smelled it. "Not food."

Ruby giggled, and Kayla shot him a look. "We're going to be late for church."

"All right. I'll open it already. If you want to ruin the surprise." He tore off the wrapping paper in world-record time, then lifted the lid off the box.

A laugh burst from him as he spotted the t-shirt—it was exactly the same as his old one.

"It's to replace the one I got frosting on," Kayla said. "I didn't want you to be without your favorite shirt."

Cam lifted it out of the box and held it up to himself. Oh yeah, this was going to be his new favorite shirt, simply by virtue of who had given it to him.

"Thank you." He set the t-shirt aside, looking forward to lounging in it later. But for now they had to get going to church.

By the time Ruby had gone to the bathroom one last time and found her shoes and gotten bundled, they had only ten minutes before the service began. Thankfully, the house was only five minutes from Hope Church.

As he followed Kayla and Ruby from the house, Cam's eyes fell on the yard, where their snow angels had been partially obscured by a fresh snowfall.

That feeling of contentment filled him again as he thought of Kayla's comment the other night, about sins being washed as white as snow. Standing out here on Christmas morning, he couldn't deny that truth—a truth that bathed him in peace.

It was the kind of peace he hoped would never go away.

He opened Kayla's car door—it was Christmas and she was just going to have to deal with the fact that he was a gentleman—then skirted around her vehicle toward his own car.

His hand was on his door handle when the sound of tires crunching on the driveway grabbed his attention. Kayla couldn't possibly have disassembled her wheelchair and pulled out already.

But it wasn't a car pulling out of the driveway—a vehicle he didn't recognize was pulling in. An Audi. Funny, that was the same car he'd rented more than once when traveling with . . .

Danielle.

His breath left him in a rush as he spotted her behind the wheel.

What was she doing here? In Hope Springs? On Christmas?

He glanced at Kayla, who had paused in the process of transferring into her car, then strode toward Danielle's vehicle.

She opened the car door, gingerly placing a ridiculous open-toed shoe onto the unshoveled driveway. As she stood, her eyes went past him to first Kayla, then Ruby, then the house. She made a face. "I can see the appeal of this place." Sarcasm clung to her, thicker than the snow on the driveway.

"What are you doing here, Danielle?"

"Can we go inside? It's freezing out here."

He considered asking whether she had considered that it was winter here when she'd chosen her strappy shoes and gauzy blouse but kept his mouth shut.

"We were actually on our way to church."

Her nose wrinkled harder. "You don't go to church."

"I used to. And I've started going again."

Danielle lifted an eyebrow at him. "I flew all the way from LA to see you. On Christmas. And you're just going to ignore me?"

Cam sighed. He wanted to say yes. To say that she shouldn't have come. Because they were over. But maybe he owed her more than that. Maybe he owed her an in-person conversation, at least.

"All right." He scrubbed a hand over his head, that peaceful feeling he'd been basking in sliding away as he turned toward his car. He hated the idea of letting his niece down.

"Ruby, I think we're going to have to skip church today."

Ruby bounced toward them, giving Danielle a curious look. "Why? It's Christmas. Everybody goes to church on Christmas."

Danielle peered down her nose at Ruby. "Not everybody."

"I can take Ruby, Cam."

Cam closed his eyes for a millisecond. What must Kayla be thinking was going on right now?

He glanced toward her car to find that she'd wheeled halfway down the driveway.

"It's no problem," she added quietly. "You can catch up with us at Nate and Vi's." Her eyes flicked to Danielle, and she offered a genuine smile. "And you're welcome to come too."

Danielle gave her a fake smile in return but didn't say anything.

"But I want you to go to church too, Uncle Cam." Ruby crossed her arms and stuck her lip out in a pout.

"I know. I'm sorry, Ruby. I have some things to talk about with Danielle, and—"

"Who is Danielle?" Ruby demanded.

"She's my—" Cam stammered. What was he supposed to call her now? Ex-girlfriend, he supposed.

"I'm Cameron's fiancée," Danielle cut in.

Cam froze at the look on Kayla's face. "What? No. Danielle, we're not—"

"You're right," Danielle simpered. "You haven't put the ring on my finger yet. But as soon as I get you home, you can ask me properly."

Cam spluttered. There were no words. Why couldn't he come up with any words? And why was she acting like nothing had changed? Like they hadn't broken up three weeks ago?

They hadn't talked once in that time. And now she was saying they were still getting married?

"Danielle," he finally forced out. "You know we talked and—"

She wrapped a hand around his elbow. "Seriously, Cameron, I'm freezing. We need to go inside." She turned to Kayla. "It was nice meeting you. Thanks for taking Ruby off our hands for a bit."

Her hand on Cam's elbow tightened as she took a step toward the house. "It's slippery. Don't let me fall." She didn't glance back once at Kayla and Ruby.

But Cam did. "You're sure you're okay taking Ruby?" He tried to meet Kayla's eyes, but she refused to look at him.

"Of course." Her voice rang with false cheer. "We'll see you later."

"Kayla." There had to be a way to make this better, right here and now.

She waved him off. "We're going to be late for church. I'll bring Ruby to Nate and Vi's afterward." She opened the back door of her car for Ruby, then started to transfer into the driver's seat.

As he opened the door to the house for Danielle, Cam told himself to make this conversation quick so he could meet up with Kayla as soon as possible and explain everything.

Assuming she'd give him a chance.

Kayla stared at the words of the hymn on the screen at the front of church. But she couldn't make her mouth form them. Not if she wanted to hold back the tears that had threatened from the moment that gorgeous woman had introduced herself as Cam's fiancée.

She'd been over it a thousand times in her head. And no matter how many times she looked at it, she couldn't be upset with Cam. He'd never once led her on. Sure, they'd spent a lot of time together—but that had been to take care of Ruby, nothing more, she could see that now. Anything else she'd read into it was her own fault.

Even that almost-kiss at Dan and Jade's had been her doing, not his. No wonder he'd pulled away.

Where he'd meant friendship, she'd imagined more.

She was a complete idiot—and she felt it acutely.

The worst part was, she'd never wanted a relationship in the first place. So there was no reason to feel so crushed now that she knew there was no possibility of one. If anything, she should be relieved.

She let her eyes slip to Ruby, singing next to her, and to Vi on Ruby's other side, swaying to the music Nate led. Looked farther down the row to Sophie and Spencer with their kids and Isabel and Tyler with theirs. In front of them to Ethan and Ariana with Joy, and Jared and Peyton with Ella, and Jade wrangling Matthias while passing Hope a coloring book as Dan smiled at them from his seat at the front of the church.

She directed her attention back to the song. Just because having a family made all of them happy didn't mean she needed a family to feel complete. She had always been independent—always would be, if she had anything to say about it. Then she'd never have to worry about losing herself.

Except that, with Cam, it hadn't felt so much like she was losing herself as like she was becoming *more* herself.

She swallowed hard and ignored the thought as Dan stood to deliver the sermon. That was where her focus needed to be. On God's Word, on the reason he sent Jesus into the world that first Christmas. So she could share that message with the people of Malawi.

She'd done some more soul searching and praying after her conversation with Nate the other night and finally sent in her acceptance yesterday, though she'd decided to wait until after Christmas to tell everyone.

Peace settled over her as she considered the opportunity she'd been given to watch God at work. To witness how he could use even her fragile faith to do the work of his kingdom. The peace was tempered only by the ache that rose every time she thought of leaving Hope Springs for six months. Of leaving Nate and Vi. And Ruby. And Cam.

Cam is already out of your reach.

She allowed herself one more moment of grief, then pushed it aside. No reason to let herself wallow in her heartbreak.

No, it wasn't a heartbreak.

More like a heart scratch.

And she'd be over it in no time at all.

Chapter 41

*C*am paced the living room. He'd stopped noticing how small it was weeks ago, but he was painfully aware of it now, as he concentrated on the path between the still-leaning Christmas tree and the couch where Danielle sat gingerly, as if afraid she'd catch a contagious disease if she settled in.

"So, this is the place I couldn't tear you away from." She scanned the room, disdain clear on her face.

"What are you doing here, Danielle?" he asked again.

"I can't come to visit my fiancé for Christmas?"

He stopped and stared at her. "You know we broke up, Danielle."

She met his stare head-on. "And you know you only broke up with me as a negotiating tool. So I'm here to negotiate."

A disbelieving laugh escaped before he could think better of it. "It wasn't a negotiating tactic, Danielle."

She frowned at him, clearly doubting he was in his right mind. "Then what was it, Cameron? You haven't been yourself since you came here." She stood and crossed to his side, grabbing his arms and wrapping them around her waist. "Frankly, I'm worried. But I know that once we get you home, everything will be back to normal."

He sighed, disentangling his arms from around her and stepping away to look out the window. The word *home* sounded strange on her lips. Like it didn't belong to California anymore. "It won't, Danielle. Believe it or not, I'm more myself now than I've ever been."

She frowned at him. "That doesn't even make sense."

He shrugged. It wasn't like he could explain it either. But that didn't change the fact that he knew it was true. "I know. And I'm sorry. But I just don't see things working between us."

"You're being ridiculous. The Cameron I know wouldn't be so . . . I don't know, whatever you are right now. He would realize that we both want the same things. That's what makes us right for each other."

"Then maybe I'm not the Cameron you know," he said softly. "I'm sorry, Danielle. I really am. But those things I thought I wanted . . . they're not enough anymore."

"All right." Danielle crossed her arms in front of her as if getting ready to square off against an executive. "What do you want then?"

Cam hesitated. "I want a family. I want to spend time with them, the way my parents did with me, before they . . ."

Danielle's expression grew tighter. "A family is not on the table, Cameron. You know that."

"Yeah, I do. That's part of why I know we're not right for each other. Because I already have a family."

Danielle's eyes widened. "What, the girl? That's temporary. Mary said your sister woke up, so you can't use her as an excuse anymore."

Cam blinked at her. He'd never known Danielle to speak to his secretary. "Bethany has started to track people's movements with her eyes. But she's a long way from being able to care for Ruby. The doctors don't know if she'll ever get there."

Danielle stared at him, and he tried not to think about how, if it were Kayla he'd just said that to, she'd already have her arms around him.

"So, what, you're going to stay here and play daddy forever?"

Cam lifted his shoulders. "I don't know. Maybe." Honestly, the possibility didn't sound so bad.

"In case you've forgotten, you have a responsibility to my family. To my father. I haven't told him about our . . . issues . . . yet. I wanted to give you time to come to your senses. But if you're not going to . . ."

"I'm prepared for the consequences," Cam said calmly. "Your father can keep me on for the good work I do for him. Or he can let me go. Either way, I can't stay with you just to keep my job. It wouldn't be fair to you."

Danielle huffed out a breath. "What's not fair is that you're walking away from all of our plans. Our future. I already booked the Starlight, you know. Do you have any idea how humiliating it would be to call and cancel?"

Cam almost retorted that she should have thought of that when she booked a wedding venue before they were even engaged. But that wasn't fair. He'd given her every reason to believe he was going to marry her. He'd given himself every reason too . . . until it had been time to go through with asking her.

She whirled on him suddenly. "Does this have to do with that woman out there?" She gestured to the window, and Cam's eyes followed her hand, until he realized that she meant the woman who had been out there earlier.

"Kayla?" He swallowed. "She's been helping me with Ruby. Honestly, I don't know how I would have done any of this"—he gestured around the room—"without her. But I promise you that I was never unfaithful to you. Kayla and I were only friends."

"Were?" Danielle looked at him shrewdly. Ah, the pitfalls of having a lawyer for an ex-girlfriend.

He made himself meet her gaze. "I don't know what we are now. Or what I want us to be. But I do know that whatever does or doesn't happen with Kayla in the future, you and I don't belong together. You deserve someone who wants what you want and loves you exactly as you are. And so do I."

Danielle watched him for a moment, then looked away. "I thought I had found that person." She spun and strode down the hallway. He was going to ask where she was going, until he heard the click of the bathroom door closing.

He rested his head against the front window, staring at nothing. How was it that he'd managed to make two women look utterly betrayed in one day?

"Ruby seems like a sweet little girl." Kayla's mother pulled the garlic bread out of the oven. It was just the two of them in the kitchen as Vi tried to wrangle the rest of the guests to wash their hands and have a seat.

"She is." Kayla finished slicing the lasagna. "I admit she's stolen my heart."

"According to Vi, she's not the only one." Mom kept her focus on the bread she was slicing, but Kayla saw her gaze slide her direction for a moment.

"Vi doesn't know what she's talking about," she muttered, shooing Nate and Vi's dog away as he begged for a piece of lasagna.

"No?" Mom found a basket and started arranging the bread in it. "So you don't have any interest in Ruby's uncle?"

"He's engaged," Kayla said flatly, maneuvering her wheelchair to the refrigerator to pull out the Parmesan cheese.

Though she avoided looking at Mom, she could feel Mom watching her. "Since when?"

Kayla shrugged. "Always, I guess. I met his fiancée this morning." She didn't even have to struggle to get the words out. Which only proved that she was over it already.

"Oh sweetie, I'm so sorry he did that to you."

But Kayla shook her head. "He didn't do anything wrong, Mom. I may have misinterpreted some things, but honestly, he's never said he wanted anything more than friendship. Sometimes not even that." She laughed a little, thinking back on their earliest encounters. She was pretty sure he would have been content if she'd gone and dived into the lake. But somehow, over time, they'd started to . . .

Become friends. That was all.

"Kayla—" Mom's voice was soft.

"Really, Mom. It's fine. I'm not upset about it. Anyway, I'm not going to be here much longer."

"You're not?"

"Nope." She grabbed a spatula and slid it into the lasagna pan. "I accepted the mission trip. I'm going to Africa." She grinned as the realization sank in—she was really doing this.

Mom studied her. "You're not going as a way to run away, are you? Because that's not—"

"That's not why. I decided the other day. Before any of this. I just realized . . . It's not about me. I mean, I've really been struggling to deal with Nate and Vi losing the baby. . . . And then I was talking to Cam—" She ignored Mom's look. She couldn't help it if so much of her life recently had involved him. "And I found that God helped me speak to Cam's doubts even in the midst of my own. And I was overwhelmed that I serve a God who is that powerful. And I just . . . I want to let him work through me. I want to do the work he has prepared for me. You know?"

She let herself glance at Mom, taken aback by the tears shimmering in her eyes. She'd rarely seen her mom cry, even after the accident. "I do know." Mom leaned down and kissed Kayla on top of the head. "I'm so proud of you."

Kayla ducked her head before she could get teary too. "I'm a little scared," she let herself admit.

"I'd be worried if you weren't," Mom said with a laugh. "It's a big thing you're doing. But you'll have all of us here praying for you."

Vi poked her head into the kitchen. "How's the food coming?"

"All set." Mom smiled as Vi gave them a thumbs-up, then disappeared again.

"Come on." Mom squeezed Kayla's shoulder. "Let's get this food to the starving masses."

"Right behind you." Kayla placed a large cutting board across her lap, then reached for the pan of lasagna and rested it on the board, making sure it was secure before rolling toward the dining room.

She'd only made it a couple of pushes when the doorbell rang.

"Who else are we expecting?" she heard Nate call to Vi.

"Grace and Levi, but not until later." Vi looked up as Kayla entered the room with the lasagna and set it on the table.

Vi raised her voice, calling, "Come in."

They all watched the door, but it didn't swing open. Vi frowned, pausing in pouring juice into the kids' cups. "You want to get that, Kayla?"

Kayla wheeled to the front door, pulling it open. "You guys know you don't have to ring the—"

She broke off as her words were swallowed by her confusion. "Cam?" She peered behind him, but he appeared to be alone. "Where's your fiancée?"

"She's not my— Can we talk?"

"Cam!" Nate's shout carried from the dining room. "Come on in. We're about to eat."

Cam nodded but gave her a questioning look. "After lunch?"

Kayla rolled back from the door to let him in. "There's nothing to talk about. Come on, everyone's waiting to pray."

"Kayla, I want to explain." Cam's voice was low as he stopped in the doorway.

"Honestly, Cam." She made herself meet his eyes. "You don't owe me any explanations. Everything's fine." She didn't give him a chance to argue more as she wheeled toward the table.

She heard his sigh as he followed her.

Nate had grabbed another chair and was in the process of sliding it into place next to Ruby. Cam thanked him and sat, then leaned over to wrap an arm around his niece, pressing his face against her hair. As he straightened, he tickled her side, making Ruby let out a high-pitched giggle. Everyone around the table laughed, but Kayla found she had to look away to blink a few times.

When everyone had settled in, Dan began his prayer. "Savior of the world," his soothing voice rang out. "Though you are God from all eternity, you humbled yourself to come into this world as a man that first Christmas. You put yourself—the very maker of the law—under the law to keep it perfectly for our sake. You experienced all the hurts and the hardships and the griefs of your people out of your great love for us. Help us as we celebrate Christmas to remember that your story doesn't end in the stable—it ends at the cross, where you took upon yourself the sins of us all, so that we now have the promise of eternal life with you in heaven. In the name of our newborn King, Amen."

Kayla had to swallow before she could join in the chorus of "Amens." Something in the prayer had loosened the knot in her soul just a little further. Sometimes she forgot that Jesus knew what it was like to be a human. That he had gone through the same hurts and sorrows as she did. That he had done it out of love for her.

When she lifted her head, she found Cam's eyes on her, concern clear in them. She tried to ignore him, to focus on dishing food onto her plate and scooping it into her mouth and keeping up a conversation with Jade.

By the time the meal was done, she needed an escape. She picked up a stack of dirty dishes, placing them on the cutting board she'd set on her lap again. Maybe while she was in the kitchen, Cam would go home. Or at least follow Dan to the living room to continue the conversation they'd been having about football.

She stalled as long as she could unloading the dishes but eventually had to return to the dining room. Where she found Cam collecting his own stack of plates.

Silently, she grabbed the empty lasagna pan and wheeled back toward the kitchen. A moment later, Cam was there too, but fortunately Vi was right behind him with her own stack of dishes. Kayla silently begged her sister-in-law to stay right where she was.

"I asked Ruby what she thought of her presents," Vi said brightly, "and she said they were perfect. You two make a good team."

Kayla forced herself not to look at Cam, instead shooting Vi a warning look. She hadn't yet had a chance to talk to her sister-in-law alone and tell her about Cam's fiancée, and she could only imagine what Vi might say next.

But Cam beat her to it. "Yeah, we do. Kayla, could we talk now?"

Vi's eyes swiveled from Cam to her. Kayla could read the questions in them, but she shook her head.

"It's not necessary. Truly."

"Why don't you guys use the nursery?" Vi said. "It's probably the only place you're going to get some privacy. I'll keep an eye on Ruby."

"Thank you." Cam gave Vi a warm smile.

But Kayla shook her head again. "I'm going to help clean up. I—"

"Kayla." Vi gave her a stern look. "I've got plenty of help." As if to prove her point, Jade, Leah, and Sophie entered the room carrying more dishes.

"Please, Kayla." Cam's voice was soft, but not so soft that the other women didn't look from him to her curiously.

Fine. It was better than standing here and trying to explain to everyone what was going on.

"I'll be right back," she muttered to Vi. Then she made herself follow Cam out of the kitchen.

Chapter 42

For the second time today, Cam found himself pacing a tiny room, this one a heartbreaking reminder of what Kayla's brother and sister-in-law had lost—and of Kayla's grief over that loss.

And he had only made things worse by hurting her more.

He gripped the back of his neck, trying to figure out where to start. "I owe you an apology."

Kayla rolled away from the crib she'd been running her hands over. "You don't, Cameron."

Cameron? Since when did she call him by his full name? "Call me Cam. And yes I do. I should have told you sooner. I don't know why I didn't, actually." It hadn't been intentional . . . at least, he didn't think it had. It was just that his life in California had seemed so separated from his life here that Danielle had never really come up. And his relationship with Kayla had developed so slowly, from those initial days when they couldn't stand each other to a partnership in doing what was best for Ruby to a genuine friendship. It hadn't been until after he'd broken up with Danielle that he'd considered there might be more.

Still, that didn't excuse him.

"That you have a fiancée?" Kayla shrugged as if it was no big deal. The kind of thing people forgot to mention all the time. "You don't owe me any explanations. I never thought— It's not like we're— I promise you that my only feelings are for Ruby."

"She's not my fiancée." On that account, at least, he could set the record straight. "We were never engaged. I mean—" If he was going to do this, he needed to be completely honest. "We were supposed to get engaged, but I was having doubts. I tried to ignore them. It was the next logical step. We had the same goals, the same aspirations, not to mention her dad is my boss and he was starting to talk partnership."

Kayla looked away from him. "I get it, Cam. She was perfect for you."

"No." Cam said it more forcefully than he meant to, but he needed her to understand this. "I tried to make myself think so. But I knew she wasn't. I was supposed to propose at this big party—she had it all planned out, but she wanted to play it off like it was a big surprise. That was the night you called to tell me about Bethany, and . . . well, it never happened."

Kayla ogled him. "*That's* what I interrupted? Your proposal?"

Cam laughed. "Yeah." He moved closer so he could look into her eyes. "And it may be the best interruption that's ever happened to me. I was trying to convince myself to go through with something I knew wasn't right, because it had been part of my plan for so long. One more step on my road to a perfect life. And then you called and threw all my plans out the window when you convinced me I needed to be here for Ruby, and—"

"You could have finished your proposal first," Kayla exclaimed.

But Cam shook his head. "That's what I'm saying. I'm glad I didn't. Because I came here, and I met Ruby. And I met you. And somehow the two of you changed my life."

He saw Kayla's neck bob as she swallowed. "But Danielle—"

"I broke up with her weeks ago. When I realized that I couldn't go through with marrying someone I didn't love just because it was supposed to be part of my plan. The funny thing is—" He bent to gather her hands in his. "I didn't even realize I was starting to have feelings for you until after that."

"Cam . . ."

But he wasn't done. "I want to go out with you, Kayla. Or stay in with you. It doesn't matter. I just want to be with you. I know we haven't known each other for long, and for a lot of that time, you couldn't stand me . . ."

He paused as she laughed, then squeezed her hands tighter. "But I want to get to know you better. I want to spend more time with you—and not just to take care of Ruby. Unless your feelings really are only for her . . ." In which case, he would feel like a supreme idiot. But at least a supreme idiot who had taken a chance and gone for what he really cared about. Maybe for the first time in his life.

"Cam . . ." Kayla pulled her hands out of his, and his heart fell. It was what he deserved, but he'd still hoped . . .

"I've decided to go to Malawi."

Malawi? It took him a moment to catch up. Where had Malawi come into the conversation? And then he remembered . . . she'd been accepted to the mission trip. When Emma had offered her a job, he'd been sure she'd take the job over the trip—it's what he would have done. And she hadn't mentioned it in so long that he'd kind of forgotten about it.

"I hope this isn't because of Danielle. Because I promise . . ."

But Kayla was shaking her head. "It's not." She bit her lip, as if trying to decide whether to say anything else. "It's because of you."

His shoulders dropped. He couldn't blame her. But . . .

Maybe that meant it wasn't too late to convince her to change her mind.

"Truly, Kayla, I'm so sorry. If I could go back and do things differently . . ."

She was laughing gently, and he stopped. He hadn't thought there was anything particularly funny about his apology.

"It's not because of this, Cam. I started thinking about going after we went shopping last week."

"You're going so you don't have to shop with me anymore?"

She laughed harder this time. "No, you goofball. I'm going because of our conversation that day."

Cam stared at her. She had lost him. "I don't remember saying anything particularly wise that day."

She snorted. "It wasn't you, Cam. It was God. I mean, not like he said something. But he showed me that he could use even weak little me, with all my failings and doubts, to share his Word. *That* was how I knew I wanted to go on this trip. To see him at work in me and through me."

"Oh." He still couldn't say that he understood completely. But he *could* see how much it meant to her. "When do you leave?"

"January 2."

"Okay." He swallowed back the urge to ask her not to go. "That gives us a week. And then we can write, call, text. It's only six months, right?" Although right now, that seemed like an eternity.

Kayla shook her head. "I don't know if that's a good idea, Cam. I don't think I'll be anywhere that I can communicate regularly. And by the time I get back, you could be in California."

"But—" He was not letting this go without a fight. If he'd recently figured out what he didn't want, he'd also figured out what he did. And it was all right here—in her.

"I'm sorry, Cam. I just— I don't know what I want right now. I thought I did, before I met you. But now . . . Can we just leave things as they are? Be friends?"

He swallowed painfully. "Of course we can."

"Thank you." She squeezed his hand quickly, then pulled away. He kept himself from catching hold of her arm and begging her to reconsider. If this was what she wanted, then this was what he would do.

"Come on. We should get back out there." She bobbed her head toward the door. "Ruby is probably wearing Vi out." Sadness hung on her smile. "Man, I'm going to miss her." She hesitated, her eyes on his, and he held his breath.

But then she turned and wheeled out of the room. And he had no choice but to follow.

Chapter 43

She couldn't do this. Kayla sat in her car in the driveway of Cam and Ruby's house.

She was supposed to leave tomorrow, and she'd spent the past week rushing like mad to get everything ready. But she'd promised Ruby at church on Sunday that she'd come for one last meal with them.

But for the life of her, she couldn't figure out how she was supposed to say goodbye.

She drew in a slow breath. She could do this. She assembled her wheelchair and transferred into it, then grabbed a small bag off the back seat and made her way to the front door.

Ruby had it open before she could even ring the bell.

"What's in there?" Ruby instantly pointed at the bag on Kayla's lap.

"It's a surprise." Kayla popped her front wheels up and through the doorway. "It sure smells good in here."

"Uncle Cam is cooking."

Kayla eyed Ruby, trying to tell if this was one of her silly jokes. But the girl wasn't giggling.

"Seriously?"

"Yep. It's fabitas."

"Fajitas," Cam called from the kitchen.

No matter how hard she tried, Kayla couldn't keep her heart from speeding up whenever she heard his voice.

"Dinner is served." He appeared suddenly in the living room, and Kayla's heart decided it needed to accelerate to marathon speeds. He was wearing jeans and the t-shirt she'd given him. And a semi-sad smile.

"But I want to know what surprise Kayla has in her bag."

"Surprises are always better if you have to wait." Kayla tucked the bag next to the front table, which held a new vase—this one with real flowers—she noticed. "I'll show you after dinner."

Ruby took two seconds to pout, then grinned and flounced toward the kitchen.

Kayla gasped as she wheeled into the room after Ruby. The table had been set with a tablecloth and candles and place cards written in Ruby's sprawling handwriting.

"Oh wow. This is beautiful." She gave Ruby a hug. "Did you do this?"

Ruby nodded. "Welllll. I made the name tags. But Uncle Cam lit the candles. But he said I can blow them out later. Unless you want to."

Kayla laughed. Oh, how was she going to say goodbye to this little joy-bringer? "That's okay. I think you should do it."

Cam carried a steaming dish of chicken and peppers to the table, and Kayla inhaled. "Hey, it doesn't even smell like feet."

Cam's laugh was rich and full and it wrapped right around her. She had to stop soaking up all this wonderfulness—it was going to make it too hard to leave.

Kayla slid her wheelchair into the spot marked for her, noting with relief that Ruby had placed herself next to Kayla. But the relief dissipated as Cam took the seat across from her—now she'd have a perfect view of his eyes. Of the way the candlelight reflected in them, making them look warmer and brighter than she'd seen them before.

Cam offered her another smile, then folded his hands in front of him. "Would you like to pray? Or should I?"

The question sent joy right through Kayla. But there was no way she was going to be able to get through a prayer without breaking down in tears.

"Can I do it?" Ruby bounced in her seat.

"That sounds nice." Kayla bowed her head.

"Dear Jesus," Ruby began. "Thank you that Mommy can talk to me with her eyes now." Kayla nodded in silent agreement. She'd rushed to the hospital the other day when Cam had texted that Bethany had begun to blink for yes and no. It had brought tears to Kayla's eyes—and Cam's too, she was pretty sure—when Bethany had blinked "yes" when the nurse asked if she recognized Ruby.

"And thank you that Kayla came over tonight," Ruby continued. "And that Uncle Cam cooked fabitas that smell good. Please keep Kayla safe on her trip. I'm going to miss her because she is my best friend. But I know we can still be best friends even if she's far away. And I hope she gets to tell lots of people about you. Amen."

"Amen." Kayla managed to choke out. She sat blinking at her lap but it was no use. She had to quickly wipe at her eyes before she could take the fajitas Cam passed her way.

As they ate, Ruby filled Kayla in on all the things she'd missed as she'd been busy packing and making arrangements over the past week. Apparently, Ruby had started to work on jumping her horse. And Cam had signed her up for swimming lessons. And at school she'd auditioned for the spring play and gotten the part she wanted.

As Ruby continued her cheerful chatter, Kayla tried not to dwell on the fact that she'd miss all of these things. Ruby and Cam had become such a part of her life over the past two months that she was having a hard time imagining her life without them. But they'd all be fine. She knew they would.

Her eyes went to Cam. He was watching her with that same tender expression he'd worn when he'd told her that he wanted to be with her.

She'd relived that conversation a hundred times a day over the past week. But she couldn't see any other way it could have turned out. She was leaving for six months. And even when she got home, she didn't know what was next for her. She couldn't go to Africa with the need to keep up a long-distance relationship hanging over her head. Maybe when she got back . . .

But by then he'd likely be in California—he could even be in a new relationship.

The thought made the fajitas turn in her stomach. She made herself finish what was left on her plate anyway. Cam had gone to a lot of effort to make this meal. And truth be told, it was delicious.

The moment they'd cleared the table, Ruby was at Kayla's side. "Can we have our surprises now?"

"Ruby," Cam warned, but Kayla laughed.

"I think we've waited long enough to make them special." She wheeled to the living room and picked up the bag, reaching inside it. "Let's see, I think there's one in here for Ruby, isn't there?" She pretended to feel around. "Yep. There it is."

She pulled out the box she'd wrapped this morning.

"Unicorn wrapping paper," Ruby squealed right before she tore it to pieces. She barely paused to throw it aside as she opened the box. "Oh wow! I love it! I love it! I love it!" She pulled out the plush giraffe and squeezed it to her. "I'm going to name it Kayla."

"I'm honored." Kayla reached back into the bag and passed Ruby another wrapped box. "This one is for your mom. But if you want to open it for her, I bet she wouldn't mind. You can give it to her next time you visit."

Ruby tugged the wrapping paper off the box and opened it. "It's a book."

"*Little Women.* It's the book I've been reading her. I thought maybe someday she could read it to you."

"Thank you, Kayla. What else?" Ruby looked toward the bag.

Kayla laughed. "I'm afraid that's it."

"And a good thing too." Cam stepped forward. "It's time for you to get ready for bed, Rubes." He held up a finger, as if anticipating Ruby's objection. "No arguing. You go back to school tomorrow."

"I wasn't going to argue," Ruby said. "I was going to negotiate."

"Negotiate?" Kayla laughed. "Where did you learn that?"

"From Uncle Cam," Ruby said proudly, then turned to Cam. "How about I get to stay up five extra minutes tonight and then I'll go to bed five minutes early tomorrow."

Cam shook his head. "Nice try."

"Can Kayla at least help put me to bed?"

"Of course. If she wants to." Cam looked to her.

"You know I do."

"All right. Your negotiations worked," Cam said to Ruby. "You got what you wanted all along. Now go get ready."

Ruby made a face but scampered off toward the bathroom.

Silence fell between them, and Kayla searched for a way to fill it. But all the things she wanted to say were things she shouldn't say. Like how much she'd miss him. And how much the last two months had meant to her. And how much she wished he'd still be here when she got back . . .

"You're all packed?" Cam rescued her from her dangerous thoughts.

Kayla nodded. "About three times over. I'm so afraid I'm going to forget something that I keep unpacking to recheck. I even made Vi go through it with me."

"What time does your flight leave?"

She groaned. "Four a.m." Which meant she should get home and get some sleep since she'd have to be awake by two.

Silence fell between them again, and Kayla studied her fingernails. She had one more gift—but that one she wasn't going to give him until she was on her way out of the house.

"You're going to do great there, you know."

She shook her head. "I'm trying to trust that. But to be honest, I'm pretty nervous. Hope Springs is the farthest I've ever been from home on my own . . ." What in the living world was she doing traveling halfway around the world?

"Kayla, I know you. And I know how strong you are. You're going to go over there and you're going to share the Gospel, and it's going to be amazing. Somehow you always know exactly what to say."

Kayla swiped at her eyes. "Thank you, Cam." She hoped he knew she meant for everything. "You're not so bad at knowing what to say yourself."

"I'm ready," Ruby called from down the hallway.

Cam gestured for Kayla to lead the way to Ruby's room, and she tried to give him a brave smile. But the whole time they read a story and Ruby said her prayers and Cam tucked the blankets tight around her, saying he was making her into a fajita, Kayla had to fight back the burning in her throat.

When she wheeled to Ruby's bed and Ruby threw her arms around her, she gave up holding it back.

"Don't be sad, Kayla." Ruby patted her cheeks. "I'm going to pray for you every day."

Kayla nodded and gave the girl one more squeeze. "And I'll pray for you every day too."

"And Mommy and Uncle Cam?"

Kayla let go of the girl and retucked the blankets around her. "You better believe it."

"See you when you get home." Ruby yawned and snuggled deeper into her blankets. "I love you."

Kayla managed a shaky breath. "I love you too, Ruby. Sweet dreams."

She wheeled out of the room before her few tears turned into a torrent.

In the living room, she ran her hands over her cheeks. She must look like an absolute mess right now. "Sorry." She gave Cam a rueful smile. "I know it's not forever, but I'm going to miss her so much."

"I know."

"I should—" She fumbled. What had she been about to say? Cam's eyes had captured hers, making her forget everything but how warm and inviting they were.

With supreme effort, she looked toward the door. Yes, that was what she'd been about to say. "I should go."

"Do you have to? We could watch a movie or something." Cam's voice held just the slightest note of pleading, nearly weakening her resolve.

But staying would only make saying goodbye harder. "I have to get up to go to the airport in a few hours."

Cam nodded and gave her another sad smile, as if he'd known all along that would be her answer.

"Here." She picked up her coat and dug in the pocket, pulling out a small, wrapped box. "This is for you. But don't open it until after I leave."

"What is it?"

She laughed. "For someone who likes surprises, you sure don't seem to understand how they work."

He stepped forward and reached toward her. But instead of taking the box, his hands wrapped around hers. She stared at them for a moment, letting the tingles from his touch travel up her arm, then met his eyes.

"Kayla," he whispered. And then he was leaning down toward her and she was stretching up toward him, and their lips were meeting.

The kiss only lasted a moment, but it was enough for Kayla's heart to break and mend a thousand times. Everything about it was right and wonderful and . . . fleeting.

Cam straightened and unwrapped his hands from hers, bringing the gift with him. "Thank you."

Kayla nodded wordlessly, then rolled her chair to the front door and pulled it open. It took every ounce of effort she possessed to say the words she'd been dreading.

"Goodbye, Cam."

She made herself roll out the door and down the sidewalk, made herself get in the car, made herself turn it on and back out of the driveway. Made herself acknowledge, as she drove away, that it might be the last time she ever saw him.

Chapter 44

Sam stood outside the hospital, staring up at the gray sky. It seemed like the past three weeks had been a string of one gray day after another, as if Kayla had taken the sunshine with her out of the country.

He reached into his coat pocket, wrapping his fingers around the compass she'd given him before she left—engraved with the words, "Be strong and courageous," just as Dad's had been.

He was going to need courage to do this.

He tried to conjure up what Kayla would say, if she were here with him. Probably something wise, like how he couldn't do this on his own—how he could only do it through Christ in him.

All right then, Lord, he prayed in his head. *I know you've forgiven me.* The beautiful, shocking truth of that message had worked its way into his heart over the past weeks, reawakening parts of his soul that he'd closed off for far too long. *Now please help me forgive Bethany, as you have called me to do.*

With a nod and a quick breath, he made his way into the hospital and up to Bethany's room, his steps resolute.

But when he entered her room, he faltered. He hadn't anticipated that she might be sleeping. It gave him a startling flash of all those weeks she'd lain in bed, completely motionless, and they hadn't known if she'd ever wake up. But this wasn't the motionless sleep of a coma, and after a moment, as if she sensed him there, her eyes fluttered open.

"Cam?" Her speech was halting—she'd only started to talk a week or so ago, and she struggled with finding the words she wanted—but she pushed herself up against the pillows, so that she was almost sitting. "Where's Ruby?"

"Still at school. Listen, Bethany. I have something I need to say, and I don't want you to interrupt me because, frankly, I'm not sure I'm going to be able to get through it." His words came out too fast, but he couldn't slow them down.

Bethany blinked at him, and he wasn't entirely sure she was understanding what he said. The doctors said she would likely continue to be easily confused for quite a while yet.

He gulped in a breath. "I have been so mad at you for so long. I've held onto that anger so long because I thought it was a righteous anger. I thought you didn't deserve to be forgiven for what happened to our family. I thought I'd go through my whole life holding it against you." He had to stop and just breathe for a second.

But he wasn't going to quit, now that he'd started. "I was wrong," he said simply. He studied her, watching him, studied his own heart, beating steady and sure. "I forgive you." He blew out a breath. There. He'd said it. And, more than that, he'd meant it.

"Okay," Bethany said, as if he'd told her the nurses were bringing her a bowl of Jell-O.

Cam blinked at her. And then realized it didn't matter. He hadn't forgiven her for her sake. Hadn't done it to hear how thankful she was or to get an apology from her. He'd forgiven her because as someone who knew forgiveness, he could no longer withhold it.

"Okay," he agreed. "Do you want to go back to sleep?"

She shook her head. "Stay. . . . Please."

Cam nodded and plunked into the chair next to her bed. "Do you need anything?"

She shook her head. "I miss . . . that woman."

Cam tipped his head, trying to figure out who she could mean. "One of the nurses?"

Bethany shook her head, frowning as if concentrating. "With the . . . book."

"With the— Oh." His heart squeezed. "Kayla. Yeah. Me too."

"She has a nice voice."

"Yeah, she does." Oh, how he missed hearing her voice.

"You're . . ." Bethany searched his face. "In love?"

Cam started to shake his head but then stopped himself. "Maybe I am," he said slowly, wondering how Bethany had figured it out before he had. "But it doesn't matter. She's in Africa. For six months."

"Write to her," Bethany said simply, not even pausing to search for the words this time.

"I don't know if I should. I told her I was fine with just being friends."

Bethany's lips tipped into a smile. "Friends . . . write."

"Yeah." Cam grinned. He supposed they did.

Chapter 45

"*Mail* for you," Jasmine, one of the other missionaries, singsonged, dropping an envelope into Kayla's lap as she sat reading her Bible on a blanket under the shade of an acacia tree.

"Thank you." Kayla put a finger in her Bible to hold her page and smiled up at Jasmine. Though the woman was a good seven or eight years younger than Kayla, she'd become a close friend over the past twelve weeks.

"It's from Cam again," Jasmine pointed out—unnecessarily, since Kayla's eyes had picked out his handwriting the moment the envelope had landed in her lap.

"Yep."

"Well, are you going to read it?" Jasmine prompted.

"Yep. As soon as you give me some privacy," Kayla quipped.

Jasmine laughed and waved as she made her way back toward the small thatch-roofed building that housed the mission. "Don't get so caught up in it that you miss dinner again," she called over her shoulder.

Kayla laughed as she tore into the envelope. When she'd received Cam's first letter a month after she'd arrived here, she hadn't known what to do with it. She'd been missing him, thinking about him every day. And yet, she'd been afraid that opening his letter would only make things harder. She'd left it tucked into her Bible for a whole week before she'd worked up the nerve to open it.

And when she had . . . it had felt like Cam was sitting right there next to her, talking to her, making her laugh. Just like he had in Hope Springs.

In the weeks since then, she'd begun to look forward to his letters more than she cared to admit. He sent news and pictures of Ruby, who apparently was quite a swimmer and had stolen the show in her play. And he shared updates on Bethany's recovery—and even an occasional message from her, which was so good to hear.

She'd debated writing back—what if it only encouraged him to think there was more between them than there could be—but in the end, her desire to say hi to Ruby had won out. Or at least she had told herself that was the reason she'd picked up her pen.

As she let her eyes fall on his letter now, her heart took up the familiar song at the sight of his words on the page.

Dear Kayla,

Your last letter made me laugh because it was the very thing I had been thinking about and was planning to tell you. But you phrased it better than I ever could have: "Faith doesn't mean understanding everything God does. Faith means believing everything God says." That's . . . deep. And also so simple, when you think about it.

Kayla nodded and lifted her head to scan the horizon. The sun was just lowering over the distant hills. She'd seen more heartbreak and suffering here than she ever had at home. And yet, she'd also seen more joy and hope and trust as well. It was at the funeral of a young mother, as the pastor had read the familiar words of Psalm 23, that it had occurred to Kayla: She didn't have to know *why* God had allowed this woman to die to believe that he had saved her and that she would dwell in the house of the Lord forever. Just like she didn't need to know why God had allowed her accident or Bethany's coma or the death of Nate and Vi's baby to believe that in all of those things he was with them.

She dropped her eyes back to the paper.

Ruby was excited to hear about the play you're planning to do with the schoolchildren. She says if you need a sheep, she could come and be one. And she volunteered me to bring her.

Kayla laughed. Oh, how she longed to see them.

Over the past week, Bethany has made huge strides. All she can talk about these days is going home. The doctors say that should be possible in a week or two if she keeps progressing like this.

Kayla drew in a breath. She was so happy for Bethany. And yet, she couldn't help the tiny swoop of disappointment. If Bethany was recovered enough to go home, then Cam wouldn't need to care for Ruby anymore. Which meant he wouldn't need to stay in Hope Springs.

She pushed the thought aside. Now was not the time for her to focus on her own selfish desires—now was the time to rejoice with Bethany.

Anyway, I hope you're doing well there. Ruby says she misses you, and so does Bethany. And . . . I miss you too.

With prayers for you always,
Cam

Kayla let herself read the letter again, then tucked it into her Bible and pulled herself back into her wheelchair. She'd better get dinner before the others ate it all.

As she filled a dish with nsima, the thick maize porridge they had with most meals, she tried to stop dwelling on the fact that by the time she returned to Hope Springs, Cam would likely be gone. It was no surprise—she'd known that even before she left. And it wasn't like she had any plans to remain in Hope Springs once she found a job . . .

wherever she found one. She let herself toy briefly with the idea of looking for one in LA. But she dismissed the thought quickly. For one, she'd never enjoyed big cities. And for two, that might be rather presumptuous, given that she'd told Cam she wanted to remain just friends and he hadn't pressed the issue once since then.

"I know that look." Jasmine elbowed her as she pulled up to the table. "It was a good letter, huh?"

Kayla shrugged. "It was fine."

"Mmm hmm." Skylar nodded on the other side of the table. "Fine. That's why you have stars in your eyes."

"Why I— I do not."

"Come on, Kayla. You have to admit that Cam is more than a friend. He writes every week—and every time you get a letter, you get all . . . in-love looking." Jasmine wiggled her eyebrows at Kayla.

"In-love looking?" Kayla scoffed at her friends. "That's not a thing. And even if it were, I do not get anything of the kind. Because I'm not in love with him." In *like* with him, yes. In wanting-to-spend-time-with-him, yes. In a talk-all-night-and-share-your-deepest-secrets kind of friendship, yes. But not in love.

Thank goodness.

"Don't worry, she'll figure it out sooner or later," Skylar stage-whispered to Jasmine, who nodded with a giggle.

Kayla ignored both of her friends and shoveled another bite of nsima into her mouth, trying hard not to let the word *love* linger in her heart.

Chapter 46

"We're going to need at least two more strings of lights," Cam called to Bethany as he looped the strand of lights in his hands over a tree branch at the edge of the patio he'd just finished installing in Nate and Vi's backyard. The July humidity clung to him, making sweat trickle down his neck.

He was also going to need a shower when he was done with this job.

He glanced at the time. It'd be cutting it close to finish the job and get home and back before the party tonight, but he was not going to miss this for anything.

"I'll make a quick run to the store," Bethany said, standing from the spot where she'd been planting a rosebush next to a statue Nate and Vi had placed as a memorial for their baby. "I'd better write it down." Though she'd made a remarkable recovery and often seemed almost her old self—the Bethany he'd known before she'd gotten involved with drugs—she still struggled with short-term memory issues. "You want to stay here, Rubes, or come with me?"

Ruby looked up from where she'd been playing in the dirt. "I'll come with you."

Cam watched mother and daughter walk hand-in-hand toward the front of the house, marveling again at how similar they were—both with long blonde hair swinging behind them and that cheerful, almost bouncy walk.

Over the past few months, as he'd gotten to know his sister again, he'd grown in love and respect for her—for the way she'd cleaned up after learning she was pregnant with Ruby, the way she'd left a situation where she knew she'd face constant temptation to make a home here, the way she'd worked so hard at rehab so she could get home to Ruby.

Her recovery had gone so well, in fact, that she'd been ready to take on full-time responsibility for Ruby a month and a half ago. Cam had gone so far as to pack his bags and load them in his trunk. But when it came down to it, he couldn't leave. Not when it felt like every beat of his heart belonged to Hope Springs.

To being with Ruby. And even with Bethany. And maybe, someday, with Kayla.

LA may have been where his house was. But Hope Springs was *home*.

He'd flown back to California only long enough to sell his house, wrap up a few loose ends at the office so he wouldn't leave George in the lurch, and apologize once more to Danielle—who was now seeing an artist and seemed genuinely happy.

And then he'd come back home, crashing with Ruby and Bethany until he'd closed on his own house two weeks ago. That didn't mean his relationship with Bethany was perfect—there were times he still had to fight off the old anger about what she'd done to their family—but he prayed day by day to let it go and cling instead to forgiveness. And each day it got a little easier.

The sound of the patio door sliding open drew his attention.

"Wow, this looks great." Vi stepped onto the patio and surveyed his work. "You're definitely good at this, Cam. If you give me some business cards, I'll put them out at the antique shop."

"Thanks." He brushed his hands on his pants, taking a moment to examine the warm brown and red tones of the pavers that formed the patio and complemented the outdoor fireplace he'd constructed. "I need to get a couple more strings of lights up, and then everything should be done."

"Great. We're going to be leaving for the airport in a few minutes."

"Remember, don't tell her."

"I haven't spilled the beans yet," Vi said. "And you haven't spilled mine, right?" She rubbed at her slightly protruding belly.

"Not a word." He'd been sorely tempted a few times to include Nate and Vi's good news in his letters, because he knew how happy it would make Kayla, but he'd held up his end of the bargain.

Vi smiled. "It's going to be so good to see her, isn't it?"

"It really will." Speaking of which—Cam turned to get back to work. Unless he wanted to see her in this smelly, dirt-covered state, he had to get this job done.

Why was she so nervous?

Kayla watched out the plane's window as the ground below quickly drew closer.

But it wasn't the landing that was sending butterflies through her nerves. It was being home. Which made no sense at all. As wonderful and transformative as the mission trip had been—and as much as she was going to miss the people she'd met—she couldn't wait to see her brother and sister-in-law. And Ruby and Bethany and all her friends.

And Cam.

Except, Cam wouldn't be here. He'd written six weeks ago to say he was all packed and ready to go back to California. Although he didn't say much about his life there—and she could never work up the courage to ask—she assumed it was going well. In his last few letters, he had seemed different somehow . . . happier maybe. Apparently

California life was agreeing with him. And now that she was home, he'd have no reason to keep writing to her.

Kayla pushed the gloomy thoughts away as she transferred into the narrow wheelchair the flight attendant had rolled to her seat. By the time she'd maneuvered off the plane and transferred into her own chair on the Jetway, Kayla's nerves had transformed into anticipation. She was *home*.

Months of pushing her wheelchair across rutted dirt paths and patches of thick grass had left her arms stronger than ever, and she quickly powered up the Jetway, through the airport, to the baggage claim area. Fortunately, it wasn't a busy airport, and Nate and Vi had said they'd be . . .

Right there.

The moment she spotted them walking toward her, she covered her mouth to keep the squeal back.

But as Vi bent to give her a hug, she couldn't keep from letting out a small squeak. "You didn't tell me." She touched a hand to Vi's rounded belly.

"It was kind of a surprise to us. And we wanted it to be a surprise to you too." Vi was laughing as she squeezed Kayla tight. "It's so good to see you."

Kayla squeezed back, then hugged her brother. "Seriously, you guys, how could you keep news this big from me?" She felt like Ruby, wanting to bounce in her chair.

"Oh, trust me, there's bigger news." Nate failed to hide a mischievous smile.

"What is it?" Kayla was still smiling from the first news.

But Vi hit her husband's arm, then matched his mischievous expression. "You'll have to wait and see."

"Oh, come on, you can't do that to me."

"Watch us." Nate grabbed her bag from the baggage claim, then led the way out of the building.

The entire way to the parking lot, Kayla continued to beg them to tell her whatever this other news might be—and she would have kept going all the way to Hope Springs, but a pleasant drowsiness fell over her almost the moment they pulled away from the airport. "I'm just going to close my eyes for a minute," she mumbled.

She woke up to Vi's gentle shaking.

Her eyes sprang open. "What? Oh." She looked out the window. They were parked in Nate and Vi's driveway. "Sorry. I think I fell asleep."

"Yeah." Vi laughed. "We thought you might want to wake up for your surprise."

"Surprise?" Kayla was instantly alert. "Now?"

Vi hit her with that mysterious smile again and got out of the car. Nate opened Kayla's door and slid her wheelchair into place for her to transfer.

As she did, she noticed all the cars parked on the street in front of the house. Way more than she'd ever seen there before aside from when . . .

Ah, so that was the surprise. A party.

Kayla lifted a hand to her hair. She didn't even want to know what it looked like after spending the past two days traveling. Oh well, she knew her friends would welcome her, messy hair and all.

She followed Nate and Vi to the front door, ignoring the prickle of disappointment that came from knowing that one person would be missing. Getting to see everyone else would more than make up for that.

"Welcome home." The cry was so loud and so warm and so welcoming, that Kayla let out a genuinely surprised laugh. And now her disappointment really was gone, as she gazed on the faces of all the people she'd grown to love during her time in Hope Springs. There were hugs all around and laughter and question on top of question about the trip.

When she'd finally greeted everyone and had been forced by Vi to go to the kitchen and fill a plate with food, Kayla looked around the crowded house. This was so wonderful, but her heart was aching to see Ruby—and to speak to Bethany in person. Maybe Vi hadn't thought to invite them. Which was fine. Her sister-in-law had done more than enough already. She could always go visit Ruby and Bethany tomorrow.

"Kayla, do you have a second?" Emma popped up at her side. "I was hoping we could talk."

"Of course." Kayla set her plate down and gave Emma her attention as the other woman leaned against the counter next to her.

"You know I started that new social interactions group before you left, right?"

Kayla nodded. As much as she'd loved the trip, she'd had her moments of wondering if she should have accepted the job after all. Especially since now she was going to have to start her job search from scratch.

"It hasn't exactly been going great," Emma said, with a wry laugh. "Actually, I'm not going to lie. It's been going pretty terribly. I've had two coordinators quit already. I think they didn't quite realize what they were getting into, and the group is . . . challenging. What I really need is someone who has some experience." She gave Kayla a pointed look, and this time Kayla didn't miss the cue.

She shook her head, laughing.

Emma raised an eyebrow. "Is that a no or a yes?"

"Sorry." Kayla touched Emma's hand. "It's a how-does-God-do-that. I spent most of the flight home making a list of all the possible places I could look for a job. I wanted to hit the ground running. And instead God ran a job right at me."

Emma smiled. "So a yes?"

Kayla bit her lip. It all felt so right. Hope Springs had seemed so much like home before she'd gone to Malawi that she couldn't imagine living anywhere else. But— "Can I pray about it, just to be sure?"

"Of course." Emma straightened and squeezed her shoulder. "Take all the time you need."

Kayla picked up her plate again, marveling at the way God worked things out sometimes.

"Where's Kayla? Where's Kayla?" The little voice Kayla would know anywhere came from the living room, and in an instant, Kayla had set her plate down and was wheeling past the others to sweep Ruby into a hug.

"I missed you." Ruby's arms threatened to cut off Kayla's airflow, but she didn't care. She'd hug the little girl all day if she could.

"I missed you too. I think you grew two feet while I was gone."

Ruby giggled. "Silly, I always had two feet."

"I think she means two feet *taller*, Ruby." A blonde woman came up behind Ruby, and Kayla recognized her instantly.

"Oh my goodness. Bethany. It's so good to see you on your feet. You look wonderful."

The woman gave her a shy smile. "It's nice to finally meet you. And be able to thank you."

Kayla waved off the gratitude, but the woman leaned down to hug her, sandwiching a giggling Ruby between them.

"I don't know what would have happened without you . . ." Bethany sniffed and wiped at her eyes as she stood, and Kayla had to swallow back her own emotions. Who would have thought that seeing Bethany's car go off the road that day would have changed her life so dramatically?

"Did you get to tell lots of people about Jesus?" Ruby asked as she unwrapped herself from around Kayla's neck.

"I sure did. It was . . ." But there were no words to describe what it felt like to see someone come to know their Savior. It was like watching a plant leave the shackles of its seed behind and soak up the sun.

"That's good. But now you're going to stay here forever, right? Just like—"

"Ruby!" Bethany's voice held a warning Kayla didn't understand, and the little girl clapped a hand over her mouth.

"Sorry, Mommy."

Bethany smiled at her daughter and wrapped an arm around her. "Come on, let's go get you some food."

Kayla stared after them, completely baffled as to what that had been about but also completely overjoyed to see Ruby reunited with her mother. After a moment, she realized she'd never eaten her food either and made her way to the kitchen after them.

She picked up her plate just in time to see Bethany pull her phone out of her pocket. Bethany grinned as she looked at the screen, then showed it to Ruby, who jumped up and down.

"Where are you?" Bethany said as she held the phone to her ear. "Ruby almost just gave you up."

She listened for a moment, her smile growing wider. Then she said, "Will do," and hung up.

She bent down and whispered something in Ruby's ear that made the girl giggle, then run to Kayla.

"Come with me." Ruby grabbed the plate of still untouched food out of Kayla's hands and set it on the table.

Kayla gave Bethany a curious look, but Bethany wore that same mischievous smile Nate and Vi had worn earlier.

"Where are we going?" she asked Ruby.

"Outside."

"Why?"

But Ruby shook her head. "I can't tell you."

"Why not?"

"It's a surprise." Ruby was bouncing her way toward the front door.

"Another surprise?" What could possibly be left to surprise her with?

But she followed Ruby to the door.

Ruby burst outside and gestured impatiently for Kayla to follow.

With a shrug, Kayla popped her wheels over the threshold and made her way toward the small ramp that lay over part of the steps leading off the porch.

Out of the corner of her eye, she thought she caught a glimpse of something moving near the driveway, and she turned her head.

Her hands lifted off her wheelchair to cover her mouth as a disbelieving, joyous laugh-cry made its way up from her core.

This couldn't be real. He couldn't really be standing there.

Cam.

Holding a bouquet of flowers and smiling that oh-so-perfect smile and bouncing on his toes the same way Ruby did.

Her eyes met his and she had two seconds to enjoy the warmth and the hope in them before he was striding toward her, his long legs carrying him so fast that she still hadn't quite registered what was going on when he leaned down and wrapped her in a tight hug.

"I missed you," he murmured into her hair.

All she could do was nod around the tightness in her throat as her hands rested on the firm muscles of his shoulders. He was solid and real and . . . *here.*

As he pulled back, he handed her the flowers.

She cradled them in her arms, but she was too busy trying to figure out what was going on to look at them. "What are you doing here?"

"Nate and Vi invited me," he said with a sly smile.

She hit him lightly with the flowers. "You know that's not what I mean. What are you doing *here*, in Hope Springs?"

Cam glanced past Kayla, to where Ruby stood in the doorway. "You want to tell her, Rubes?"

"Uncle Cam lives here," Ruby burst out, bouncing and clapping her hands in front of her.

"You— What? Since when?"

Cam looked to Ruby again, raising an eyebrow. "What's it been? Six weeks?"

"Six weeks?" Kayla squinted, trying to remember the exact date of the letter in which he'd said he was moving. "But in May you said you were going back to California."

Cam shrugged. "I couldn't do it. I realized my life is here now. With Ruby and Bethany and—" He looked up. "Ruby, why don't you go inside. If anyone is looking for us, we'll be inside in a little bit, okay?"

"Okey dokey." Ruby saluted him, then pulled the door closed behind her.

Kayla tried to sort out which question swirling around her brain to ask first. It wasn't easy, the way her heart was skipping around her chest and distracting her from all rational thought. Cam was here. Not in California. *Here.* "What about your job?"

"Come here." He jogged down the porch steps, gesturing for her to follow.

She hesitated. She honestly didn't know if she could handle any more surprises today. But the excitement in his eyes led her to roll down the ramp and follow him to the driveway.

He paused in front of some sort of work truck parked there. "Ta da."

Kayla blinked at the vehicle, uncomprehending. And then her eyes focused on the logo. "Moore Landscaping."

She gasped. "Cam! You did it? You started a landscaping company?"

He ducked his head but then lifted it with a smile. "I'm in the process. Your brother and Violet were technically my first clients. But it's a start. Bethany has been helping . . ."

"Cam, this is amazing. I'm so happy for you. Wait. You did some work here? Can I see it?"

He nodded, looking pleased. "It's the back patio." She followed him through the grass to the backyard, where the old, cracked concrete patio had been replaced by beautiful pavers in rich, warm tones. Strings of lights led from the house and across the patio, drawing her eyes to a stunning outdoor fireplace.

She rolled onto the patio, letting herself admire his handiwork.

"Wow, Cam. This is beautiful." Finally, she turned to him and asked the question that had been begging to be asked since Ruby had said he lived here now. "Why didn't you tell me about any of this?"

"I know how you like surprises." He grabbed a patio chair and pulled it up in front of her wheelchair, sitting close enough that their knees nearly brushed. "And also, I didn't want to freak you out."

She laughed. "Why would I be freaked out?"

"Because—" He reached for her hands and wrapped his around them. "I told you before you left that I was fine with remaining just friends. But the truth is, Kayla, I moved here because I want to be closer to Ruby and Bethany, yes. But I also wanted to be close to you. Because . . ." He cleared his throat. "Because I love you. And I'm sorry if that freaks you out, but there it is."

Kayla drew in a breath filled with the warm, delicious smell of him. "It doesn't freak me out," she said quietly.

"It doesn't?"

She shook her head, not sure herself why it didn't. But it came to her then, and she almost laughed with the wonder of it. "It doesn't. Because I love you too." It was a love that had been deepening for so long that she couldn't believe she hadn't realized it until now.

He lifted his eyes to hers, and she could read the joy and the hope in them. She didn't want him to look away—ever.

She leaned forward, wrapping her arms around his neck and drawing him closer. Her eyes fell closed as his soft breath brushed her lips. And then his lips were there, warm and caressing and . . . perfect. Her hands slid to his face as his slipped into her hair. It felt like she had been waiting for this kiss her whole life, she thought, as she pulled him closer. And also like it was always meant to be right now.

Chapter 47

*C*am's fingers slid happily through Kayla's hair as she snuggled closer to him on the couch in his living room as they watched *It's a Wonderful Life*. Even though Christmas was over a month away yet, Kayla had insisted that they had to watch it now, to get them in the Christmas spirit. Cam had readily assented. Any excuse to curl up with her was fine by him.

The four months since she'd returned from Malawi had been nearly perfect, and he'd soaked up every moment with her, finding it impossible sometimes to remember that he hadn't known her his entire life.

"I love you," he whispered, nuzzling his chin into her hair.

She tilted her head up to brush a kiss onto his lips. "I love you too."

They both jumped as her phone dinged with a text. Nate had called an hour ago to say that Vi had gone into labor but that they shouldn't come to the hospital yet since it would likely be a while. He was supposed to text them when it got closer.

Cam peered at the phone over Kayla's shoulder.

"Wait. Is that . . ."

Kayla squealed and nodded.

It was a picture of Vi holding a baby, all pink and swaddled in a blanket, a wild tuft of hair sticking up at the top of its head.

Another text came through seconds later. *Liliana Kay Benson. 7 lbs. 3 oz. 20 inches.*

Nate sent a picture of himself grinning as if he were about to burst.

"I'm so happy for them." Kayla nuzzled into Cam's arms for a second, then sat up. "Want to go meet my niece?"

"You know I do." Cam turned off the movie. "I hope we have a family like that someday."

Kayla's head whipped toward him. "You do?"

Cam froze. He'd been thinking that for months now—pretty much since the moment he'd first told her he loved her—but he hadn't meant to bring it up yet. He knew how much her independence meant to her, and he didn't want to rush her into anything. He'd been thinking maybe at Christmas, he'd ask her . . .

But he nodded. "Yeah, I do." He hesitated, then took her hands in his. "But I know you're not ready yet. So don't worry, I'm not going to pressure you or anything."

Kayla tilted her head at him. "You know I'm not ready?"

"I mean—" Cam fumbled. "Are you?"

"You'll have to ask me to find out." Kayla's voice took on a teasing tone, and her eyes sparkled.

"What? Now?"

She shrugged. "Or whenever you're ready. It doesn't have to be now."

Oh, it was going to be now. If she was ready, there was no way he was going to wait another day.

He jumped up from the couch and sprinted to his bedroom, to the box he had tucked into the nightstand.

"Cam?" Kayla's voice carried to him as he popped back into the hallway.

She gave him a relieved smile as he hurried toward her. "You really shouldn't disappear on a girl after saying something like that."

"Sorry. I had to get something." He clenched the box in his hands. It wasn't even a proper ring box. Just an old check box he'd found lying around Mom's house when he'd cleaned it out.

When he made it back to the couch, he hesitated, joy, nerves, and a wild, unbridled hope colliding so hard in his heart it made him dizzy.

Slowly, he reached for her hand, then lowered himself to one knee.

Kayla covered her mouth with her other hand. "You're really doing this now?"

He nodded, his smile feeling huge and yet wobbly at the same time. He blinked once. Looked away. Blinked again.

Kayla's hand came to his cheek, rubbing against the stubble there, and he realized he hadn't shaved today and was wearing jeans and a t-shirt. Not exactly the romantic proposal he had been imagining.

And yet . . .

He knew he wanted to do this right here, right now.

"Kayla." His voice came out raspy, and he brought his eyes to hers to find that she was blinking back tears.

Ah man. He was never going to get through this without falling apart.

But he drew in a slow breath. Cleared his throat. Squeezed her hand tighter, then let go and opened the check box, revealing a simple princess cut diamond ring. The stone was much smaller than what he could afford. And it hadn't cost him a thing. But he knew none of that would matter to Kayla.

She would understand the value of this ring.

"This was my mother's wedding ring." His voice cracked. For Pete's sake. He had to pull it together. But how could he, when the woman in front of him had come to mean everything to him? "And I would be honored if you would wear it. If you would spend the rest of this life at my side." He pulled the ring out of the box and held it out to her. And now, instead of tears, he could barely hold back the laugh. He was really doing this. And nothing had felt more right in his life. "Kayla Benson, will you marry me?"

Kayla's laugh mingled perfectly with the tears on her cheeks. Instead of answering, she leaned forward, slid her hands around his neck, and pressed her lips to his.

But when she pulled back, she gave him a serious look. "Are you sure about this? You know our marriage might not look like other people's. We might have to make adaptations or—"

Cam grabbed her hands tight in his. "Kayla, whatever we have to do, we'll do it. If we can't have children, we'll adopt or we'll spoil Ruby and Liliana or, I don't know, we'll figure it out. All I know is, whatever it takes to make you happy, I'll do it."

"I can have children, Cam."

He let out a breath. "Well, there you go, then. Now, are you going to answer my question?"

But that serious look still lingered in her eyes. "That doesn't mean there won't be other challenges."

"Of course it doesn't." He laced his fingers through hers. "Just like any marriage. And we'll work through them. Together. End of story."

She nodded, a grin slowly pulling up her lips, and he let himself breathe a little easier. "So are you going to answer the question now?" He didn't mean to be impatient, but . . .

Kayla laughed, her playful tone returning. "You want an answer right now?"

"I can wait if you're not ready to answer. Five minutes or so enough?"

Kayla shook her head, her laugh still bouncing in her eyes and filling his heart to bursting. "I'll answer you right now. Yes, Cameron Moore, I will marry you."

"Call me Cam," he murmured, slipping the ring onto her finger before bringing his lips to hers.

Epilogue

"You look like a princess." A wide-eyed Ruby entered the room at the back of Hope Church where Bethany was just finishing up weaving a white ribbon through Kayla's dark hair as she twisted it into a braided updo.

"Thank you." The truth was, in this dress, with its halter neckline and tulle skirt, she felt like a princess. And in a few minutes she'd be rolling down the aisle to her prince.

She slid her hands down the white fabric that billowed around her legs. She'd had the seamstress remove just enough of the tulle so that it wouldn't get in the way of her wheelchair wheels.

She took in Ruby's matching dress and the flowers braided into her hair. "And you look like the world's most beautiful flower girl."

Ruby smiled and twirled, letting her dress flare around her legs. "Uncle Cam says you're going to be my auntie after this. But I want you to be my friend."

Kayla laughed. "I'll be both, silly."

The sound of a baby crying from the other side of the room pulled their attention to the stroller in the corner. "The best-laid plans," Vi sighed, reaching into the stroller to pick up five-month-old Liliana. She'd laid the infant down twenty minutes ago with the hope that she'd sleep through the ceremony. "I'm so sorry, Kayla."

"Don't be ridiculous. You know I want Liliana to be part of this too. If you don't mind holding her during the ceremony, I think that'd be precious. Or you can give her to Mom if you'd rather."

The baby let out a lusty cry and turned her face toward Vi's dusty rose bridesmaid dress.

Vi groaned. "Do you really need to eat now, little one?" She checked the time, then gave Kayla a desperate glance. "There's no way I can be done feeding her in the next five minutes, but if I don't, she's going to scream through the whole ceremony."

"Vi, relax. You know that little girl means the world to us. We can wait a few minutes to start the ceremony." She turned to Ruby. "Can you go tell your uncle Cam that we need about fifteen minutes?"

Ruby gave a solemn nod, then skipped toward the door.

Kayla bit her lip. She was anxious to see her groom. Maybe she should go over there and explain things to him herself.

She was halfway to the door when it shot open and Cam burst through, looking like her very own prince in his white tux and blue tie that intensified his eyes. "What's this I hear about my bride keeping me waiting?"

"Cam," Bethany scolded. "You can't be in here. You're not supposed to see each other yet."

"Oh, trust me," Cam said, never taking his eyes off Kayla. "We're supposed to see each other. Right now. Come with me?" He nodded toward the door, and Kayla followed.

The moment they were in the hallway, he stopped and reached for her hands. "You are the most beautiful—" He swallowed. "I can't believe how fortunate I am." His eyes welled, and Kayla couldn't help it. A tear dripped onto her cheek.

"You're going to ruin my makeup," she scolded. "And you should know that I'm the fortunate one here. I was so sure that if I ever gave my heart to someone, I'd lose myself. But somehow, with you, I feel like I've found the part of me that makes me even more whole."

"I know exactly what you mean." He bent to give her a long, slow kiss.

They pulled apart as the door to the dressing room behind them opened and Nate strode out. He looked from Cam to Kayla. "What's going on out here?"

"Nothing, sir," Cam said in a mock serious voice. "I promise your sister and I were behaving ourselves."

"Glad to hear it." Nate clapped a hand to Cam's back. "Do you think I could talk to Kayla for a minute?"

"Yes, but only a minute." Cam stepped back into the dressing room. "She has an anxious groom waiting for her."

Kayla forced her eyes off her future husband as the door to the dressing room clicked shut. "What's up, big brother?"

Nate opened his mouth, shook his head, tried again. "I just wanted to say that I'm proud of you."

Kayla smiled and took his hand. "I'm proud of you too."

Nate gave her a surprised look. "I didn't do anything."

"No." She shoved him. "Just made that amazing, tiny little human in there." She pointed toward the women's dressing room.

Nate's eyes went all dreamy. "She's pretty incredible, isn't she?" He shook himself. "But we're not here to talk about me. This is your day. And I'm so happy for you. I've never seen anyone live life as fully as you do, Kayla. The things you've overcome. The way you let your faith shine." He cleared his throat. "Anyway, I hope Cam realizes what an amazing woman he's getting."

"Oh, don't worry, he does." Kayla laughed. "He tells me that way too often."

"Good. Because you deserve only the best."

Kayla shook her head. "I don't deserve anything. But I'm grateful God has given it to me anyway."

"I know how you feel." Nate looked up as the dressing room door opened. His expression morphed into a goofy grin, and Kayla didn't have to look to know it must be Vi and baby Liliana.

"We're ready," Vi said. "Finally."

A surge of adrenaline went through Kayla as Nate opened the guy's dressing room door, calling that it was time to get this show on the road.

Cam came out of the dressing room, lighting her up with a smile that said how sure he was about this. And just like that, she wasn't nervous anymore. Just so ready for this moment. To get married. Right now.

As the guys disappeared down the hallway to wait for them at the front of the church, Kayla's dad fell in step next to her wheelchair.

As the first strains of "Jesu, Joy of Man's Desiring" filtered into the lobby, Ruby stepped into the church, sprinkling flower petals every few feet as she made her way down the aisle. Kayla clasped her hands at her heart as Ruby walked, remembering all the times Ruby and Cam had felt like family. And now they really were.

God was so good.

"You ready for this?" Dad whispered as Bethany and then Vi, holding a wide-eyed baby Liliana, started down the aisle.

"So ready."

Dad nodded, not saying anything, but leaned down and gave her a quick hug that said everything.

She hugged him back and then they were on their way down the aisle and the only thing she noticed anymore was Cam, standing and waiting for her, his smile so big it almost made her heart burst.

When they reached his side, Cam shook her dad's hand, then escorted Kayla to the low, backless bench Spencer and Tyler had fashioned for them after Cam had said he wanted to be able to look into his bride's eyes as they said their vows. Kayla maneuvered her wheelchair in front of it, then with Cam's hand on her shoulder and

Bethany at her side to help sweep the dress under her, transferred to the bench. Bethany moved the wheelchair out of the way and then it was just her and Cam, sitting on the bench in front of Dan.

The ceremony was a blur of "yeses" and "I wills" and Dan's sermon on Genesis 2:24 worked its way right into Kayla's heart. She squeezed Cam's hand as Dan read the words: "That is why a man leaves his father and mother and is united to his wife, and they become one flesh."

Comfort settled in Kayla's soul as Cam met her eyes. She'd thought melding two people into one flesh meant that each of them had to lose part of themselves. But it turned out that becoming one with Cam made her more herself than she'd ever been before.

Before she knew it, Dan was introducing them as Mr. and Mrs. Moore, and Bethany was bringing her wheelchair to her. She reached to transfer back into it, then turned and looked at her husband, glowing at her side. She'd always insisted on doing everything herself. But he was now part of her.

"Will you lift me into the chair?" She bit her lip. They hadn't rehearsed this part.

Cam gave her a lopsided smile. "I would be honored." He stood and tucked an arm under her legs and one around her back, then lifted her into the air.

But instead of setting her into the wheelchair, he bent his head just enough to bring his lips to hers in a gentle kiss.

The congregation burst into applause as he lowered her into the wheelchair. As he started to straighten, she grabbed the front of his tux and pulled him back down to her for another kiss. The applause intensified, and Kayla couldn't stop smiling as she finally let go of Cam, and they made their way down the aisle, his hand on her shoulder.

The moment they reached the lobby, they were inundated with guests offering hugs and congratulations. Kayla soaked it all in, grateful for her family, her friends, this community that had welcomed them so readily.

When the last guest had left the building, Cam turned to her. "That was easier than I thought it would be."

Kayla couldn't help the giggle. "You thought marrying me would be hard?"

"Marrying you? No. Sitting up there in front of everyone and trying to express how I feel about you? Yeah."

"Well, you did a beautiful job."

"You made it easy." He leaned down for another kiss, then pulled away to look into her eyes. "What now?"

"Now, we go take pictures."

"And then?"

"And then have dinner and our reception."

"And after that?" Cam's eyes danced.

"After that we have our honeymoon."

"Mmm." He kissed her again. "And then?"

"And then—" Kayla nuzzled her face into his neck. "We go through the rest of our lives together."

"Well then." Cam stood and took her hand. "Let's get started. Right now."

Thanks for reading NOT UNTIL NOW! I hope you loved Cam and Kayla's story! Catch up with them and all your Hope Springs friends as Bethany gets her own story in NOT UNTIL THEN!

And be sure to sign up for my newsletter to get Ethan and Ariana's story, NOT UNTIL CHRISTMAS, as my free gift to you. Sign up at www.valeriembodden.com/gift.

A preview of Not Until Then

This wasn't happening.

Bethany scanned the checkout counter around her, as if her purse would magically appear on it.

All she wanted was one day of the year where she had it together. It didn't feel like too much to ask that it be today.

But apparently she was bound to make a mess even of her daughter's birthday.

"That will be $21.99." The cashier—an older woman with kind eyes—repeated.

"I . . . Uh . . ." She felt at her shoulder again—the spot where her purse should have been. In the rush to get everything ready for Ruby's party, she must have forgotten it.

She rubbed at her temple. She couldn't show up to her own daughter's tenth birthday party without a gift. Not when everyone else would have one—probably one they'd purchased weeks ago. It was bad enough she was buying it at the grocery store, but she didn't have much choice; it was on the way to Ruby's school and it was almost time to pick her up.

She blinked at the necklace—a figure of a horse and a girl face-to-face within a heart. She had two choices: grab it off the counter and run out the door—or put it back on the shelf. There was a time in her life when the first would have seemed viable. But not anymore. Not even for Ruby.

"I'm sorry. I forgot my wallet. I guess I'll have to put it back." The words weighed her whole body down.

"Do you want me to set it aside for you?" The cashier slid the necklace into her hand and set it next to the register, sympathy in her voice.

"That would be nice, thank you." Bethany knew the woman's name, she was sure of it, but she didn't have the energy to search her mind for it right now. "I probably won't be able to get it until tomorrow. I have to get to my daughter's birthday party. Maybe I can give her an 'I owe you.'" She tried for a weak smile. At least she didn't have to worry about crying. The aneurysm had stolen that ability from her right along with a good chunk of her short-term memory.

"Here." A man's voice spoke from behind her, and someone reached past her to hand the cashier a credit card. "I'll get it."

"I . . . Um . . ."

Before Bethany could stop her, the cashier had already taken the card and run it through the register.

"That's very kind of you," the older woman said, beaming into the space behind Bethany. "Oh, doesn't this feel like the beginning of a romance movie? You make sure to get his name, dear." The woman winked at Bethany.

Bethany opened her mouth as she turned to look at the man. His left arm was in a sling, and he wore a gray flannel shirt, but the thing that struck Bethany the most was his face—all hard lines and angles, not a trace of a smile.

Say something, Bethany's brain screamed. But the words wouldn't arrange themselves in a straight line in her head.

"Here you are, dear." The cashier passed Bethany a small bag and handed the card back to the man.

Bethany was halfway to the door before she finally managed to turn and blurt, "Thank you," the words sticking together like paste as they came off her lips.

She didn't wait to see whether the man would acknowledge her gratitude.

Outside, the wind grabbed at her hair, and she pulled the zipper on her sweatshirt up higher against the early April chill as she scanned the parking lot. Usually she took a picture of where she'd parked, but she'd been in too much of a hurry today.

There. She let herself breathe out as she spotted the boxy maroon four-door only two rows away. Finally, something was going her way. Maybe that meant Ruby's birthday wouldn't be a disaster after all. She should have just enough time to stop home and wrap the gift before she had to pick her daughter up from school and bring her over to the stables for the party.

As she strode toward the car, she reached into her pocket for her keys.

When her fingers didn't brush against metal in her jeans pocket, she checked her sweatshirt.

Then she checked all the pockets again.

Empty.

Which meant she'd left the keys in the car.

"Please tell me I forgot to lock it," she muttered to herself as she reached the vehicle. With a quick prayer, she tried the handle.

It lifted—but the door didn't budge.

She peered through the window, letting her head rest against the cold glass as she spotted the keys dangling from the ignition.

"Really? Today of all days?" She hadn't slept well last night; she was sure that was the explanation for her increased forgetfulness today. But knowing why it was happening didn't change the fact that she was going to ruin her daughter's birthday. Poor Ruby hadn't done anything to deserve a mother who could barely remember to make a meal, let alone plan a perfect birthday party.

Be grateful, she reminded herself. She was still here to celebrate Ruby's birthday. Two years ago, that hadn't been at all certain. The aneurysm may have made things more difficult, but it hadn't taken her life.

She closed her eyes and offered a quick prayer of thanks—as well as a plea for help out of yet another situation. Then she let out a long breath and opened her eyes. This wasn't the first time she'd locked her keys in her car. Which was why she'd given a spare set to her brother Cam and his wife Kayla. She hated the idea of calling them to come to her rescue—again. But for Ruby's sake, she'd do it.

She reached for her back pocket, just as she spotted her phone—in the car's cupholder.

She groaned and pounded her fist against the car window.

Something like this would never happen to any of the perfect moms of Ruby's classmates—whose names she would probably never manage to remember.

She shook her head. Feeling sorry for herself wasn't going to help.

Okay, what else could she do? She could go in the store and ask to use someone else's phone—except it wasn't like she could remember any phone numbers to call. She had to look up her own any time she needed it, for goodness' sake.

She had no choice but to call a locksmith. But first she'd better call the school to let them know she was going to be late getting Ruby—again.

She tried the car door handle one more time, jiggling it up and down. "Aargh." She smacked the window again.

"Everything okay?" A man with his left arm in a sling, his right draped in shopping bags, frowned at her from the middle of the aisle.

"Yeah. Fine."

He stared her down. "You're sure? Because it kind of looks like you locked your keys in your car."

"I did." She sighed so hard it hurt. "It's my daughter's birthday."

The man gave her a strange look.

Right. There was no reason for him to care.

"Anyway—" She gestured toward the store. "I have to go call a . . ." Ugh. The word had escaped as she'd been talking. "Someone to unlock it."

"That could take hours." The guy moved closer. "I can get it open for you." Tension radiated from the set of the guy's jaw, and Bethany was torn between an instinct to run away and the need to get into her car.

"You're not going to break the window, are you?" Although if that was the quickest way to get her to Ruby, maybe it would be worth it.

The man made a sound she thought might have been a laugh, though there was no trace of humor in it and his mouth remained flat. "Hang tight a second. I'll be right back." He unloaded his bags on the trunk of her car, then jogged back toward the store, his slinged arm jouncing awkwardly at his side.

Bethany squinted after him until he reached the door, the beginning of a headache twinging behind her eyes. She took a few deep, controlled breaths in an attempt to stave it off. Her head could pound as much as it wanted *after* Ruby's party. But she refused to spoil her daughter's birthday any more than she already had.

Minutes passed. Bethany squinted toward the store. Maybe she should call someone after all.

She was just eyeing the guy's bags, trying to figure out what to do with them so she could go inside and ask to use a phone, when he emerged from the store. He jogged across the parking lot, his stride powerful despite the long metal rod in his good hand.

"Sorry. Took some convincing to get the manager to let me borrow these." He held up the rod and a screwdriver.

"What are you going to do?" A vague uneasiness crept over her. She'd never seen this man before, as far as she remembered—which admittedly wasn't saying much. But what if he was a con artist or something?

"Trust me. I've done this a thousand times."

"You've broken into cars a thousand times?" She pressed a hand to her stomach. Now what kind of mess had she gotten herself into? They seemed to follow her around these days. Her doctor said it was because the aneurysm had affected the impulse control center in her brain. "Maybe I should—"

"It's okay. I'm a cop." The way he said it seemed sincere, but Bethany eyed him. She didn't see a badge or a gun.

"Off duty," he said as if detecting her suspicion. He wedged the screwdriver between the roof and the top of the car door. "From Milwaukee."

"Oh." But that would be easy enough to lie about, wouldn't it? It wasn't like there was a way for her to check. She peered around the parking lot. It wasn't exactly crowded, but there were a few people getting into and out of cars. She supposed if he tried anything, she could yell for help.

Besides, by now she had to be at least fifteen minutes late getting Ruby. She didn't have any choice but to trust this guy.

He grunted as he pulled down on the screwdriver, opening a small gap at the top of the door. Bethany winced. If he damaged her car . . .

"Pass me the rod." He pointed his chin toward the metal rod he'd leaned against the car. Bethany picked it up and held it out to him.

He glanced at it, then at the arm that hung in a sling. "That's not going to work. Here." He took half a step back, still pushing down on the screwdriver with his other arm. "Come over here and slide the rod through this opening."

"Me?" How was she supposed to know how to do this?

The man made an impatient sound, and she stepped closer, catching a whiff of something slightly warm and woodsy and spicy that made her think of curling up in front of the fire on a winter day. Angling her body in front of his, she slid the metal rod in through the opening he'd created.

"Good. Now, see the unlock button on the side of the door?"

Bethany shifted to get a better view, accidentally bumping against his chest. An odd sensation went through her at the contact, and she scooted out of the way. "I see it."

"Good. You want to press that with the end of the rod."

"I don't think I—"

"You can do it." The quiet assurance in his words tugged at her, even though he'd obviously only said it so she'd try. He didn't even know her.

She pressed her lips together and concentrated on guiding the end of the rod toward the button.

She missed twice, but on the third attempt, she landed right in the middle of it. She'd never heard a sound as beautiful as the click of the doors unlocking.

"Yes!" She let go of the metal rod and grabbed the door handle, pulling it open—barely acknowledging the clang of the rod against the ground as it tumbled out.

"Thank you so much!" She threw her arms around the man, who grunted and didn't return the gesture. It took her a moment to realize it was probably because the hug was completely inappropriate. Stupid impulse control.

"Sorry." She let go and stepped back, then bent to pick up the rod.

The man nodded tightly as he took it. "You're welcome." He gathered up his bags, then started toward the store.

"Do you want me to take that stuff back inside?" It was the least she could do, and he surely had places to go too.

"That's okay. You have your daughter's party."

Bethany gasped. How did he know about that? Had she told him? Probably.

She suddenly realized she'd never called the school to say she'd be late. She jumped into the car and started the engine. At the last second, she remembered to open her window and call out one more thank you.

The guy lifted a hand in acknowledgment and kept walking toward the store.

As she pulled out of the parking lot, Bethany gave him one last look in her rearview mirror.

"That's not the way I expected you to answer that prayer, Lord. But thank you."

James plopped his purchases onto the table of his sister's farmhouse. That had been the most bizarre trip to the store of his life. The forgetful woman with the blonde hair and dark eyes had refused to leave his thoughts all the way home.

Only because it had felt good to be able to help someone again.

You always have to be the hero, don't you? His ex-wife Melissa's voice cut straight through the good feeling. At least this time helping hadn't cost him anything—if only because he didn't have anything left to lose.

"I see you bought out the entire supply of junk food in Hope Springs." His sister Emma eyed the bags as she bustled into the room.

"If you didn't insist on stocking your refrigerator with all rabbit food, I wouldn't have to." He pulled a bag of potato chips out and carried it to the pantry, wedging it into place on a shelf between a jar of homemade spaghetti sauce and a package that said chia seeds, whatever those were.

"You know it's not fair that you can eat like that and stay in shape, right?"

"Could have something to do with the ten miles I run a day." He'd started running after Sadie . . . and never stopped.

"Just you wait. By the time you leave, you're going to appreciate that health food can be just as delicious as junk food."

He snorted. By the time he left. If it was up to him, he wouldn't be here at all. Not that he didn't want to spend time with his sister—it must have been at least three years since he'd visited—but he'd only been here two days, and already he was going crazy. His job had been the only thing keeping him sane for the past five years. But when his captain had told him it was either take some of the years' worth of vacation he had accumulated or ride the desk for the next six weeks while his shoulder recovered, it hadn't really been a choice at all.

"How's the shoulder?" Emma plucked a package of beef jerky out of his bag and carried it across the room.

He rescued it just as she opened the lid of the trash can. "It's fine. I should be working. Give me something to do around here, at least."

"You know you're supposed to be recovering from a gunshot wound, right?"

"It was a graze. I'm fine."

Emma hit him with a hard stare worthy of their mother. He only supposed he should be grateful Mom didn't know anything about what had happened. Unless—

"You didn't tell Mom, did you?" There was no need to worry her, after everything she'd already been through.

Emma watched him the same way he watched a suspect during an interrogation. They'd both gotten that ability from Dad.

Finally, she relented and looked away. "No. But James, things can't go on like this."

"Like what?" He crossed his arms. He was just doing his job. Same as Dad had taught him.

"Captain said you didn't wait for backup."

"He called you?" Captain Burke may have been as close as a father to him, but that didn't give him the right to go interfering in James's life.

"He was Dad's best friend, James. He's worried about you."

"Whatever. He shouldn't have called you."

"It was either me or Mom," Emma said. "And anyway, he just wants to make sure you get the help you need. So do I."

"I knew I should have gone to Mexico," he muttered. Not that there was anything he wanted to do in Mexico. Or anywhere else. All he wanted to do was work. And the captain had made even that impossible.

Emma raised her hands. "Sorry. I'll back off. But it's been five years, James. You can't keep punishing yourself forever. Sadie wouldn't want—"

"Don't." They were not going there.

Emma pulled a package of chocolate candies out of his bags and slid some cans over in the cupboard to fit it. "I'm just saying, I'm here to talk, if you want. Or we have a great pastor at our church. I'm sure he—"

"Is that what you call backing off?" He wasn't going to talk about it. Ever.

Emma gave him a look but kept her lips shut.

"Just give me something to do before I go crazy."

"With one good arm?" But then Emma's face lit up. "I know. We're hosting a birthday party in—" She glanced at the clock on the oven. "About fifteen minutes. I could use some help with the pony rides."

James's stomach hardened. A birthday party meant kids. And kids meant remembering. "I'll pass, thanks."

"James, you can't avoid—"

"I'll muck out the horses tomorrow. And anything else you need done. Leave me a list. I'm going to go read." He grabbed the bag of chips out of the cupboard, then sprinted up the stairs to the guest room Emma had prepared for him. He was going to have to call and talk the captain into shortening his leave. Because there was no way he was going to survive here for six weeks.

James tossed his book onto the bed and stood. He'd been reading for an hour, and he wasn't sure he'd retained a word of the story.

His conversation with Emma had stirred up too many of the memories he worked so hard to forget every day. He'd tried thinking about other things: work, the new condo in Florida he'd helped Mom move into last year, even the woman from the store.

That thought was the only one that had provided a measure of distraction. He couldn't deny that she'd been beautiful, if a bit scatterbrained.

And affectionate.

That hug had been . . . warm and spontaneous and sweet.

And completely inappropriate.

But still, it had threatened to poke a pinhole into the Kevlar that he kept wrapped securely around his heart. Fortunately, she'd come to her senses and let go before that could happen.

He glanced out the window, wondering again if perhaps the party Emma was hosting was for the woman's daughter. After all, the woman had said she was on the way to her daughter's birthday party. And she'd purchased a horse necklace.

Or, well, he supposed he had purchased it.

He didn't know what had come over him. Only that the woman had looked so broken at the thought of disappointing her daughter. And the necklace she'd held—Sadie would have gone wild for it. Aunt Emma's house had always been her favorite place, and she'd thrown her arms around him and planted a big, wet kiss on his cheek when he'd said the next time they came here she could have her first horse ride.

James ripped his eyes away from the practice ring, where Emma was helping a young girl onto a pony.

His throat burned.

What he needed was some water.

He trundled downstairs to the kitchen, opening the fridge and pushing Emma's stash of vegetables aside to reach for a bottle of water. A movement caught his eye as he closed the fridge, and he was instantly on alert, spinning to face the intruder.

"Oh!" The woman from the store jumped backwards, bobbling the cake in her hands.

James lunged toward her just in time to steady the wobbling platter. He ignored the sear of pain that shot through his shoulder. "Sorry. I didn't mean to scare you."

The woman nodded. Well, that answered the question of whether this was her daughter's birthday party.

Slowly, he took his hands off hers, making sure she wasn't going to drop the cake before withdrawing all the way.

"Did your daughter like the necklace?"

"I . . . Yes." The woman looked startled. "Sorry. Who are you?"

Nice one, James. "I'm James. Emma's brother."

"I didn't know Emma had a brother."

"Oh." There wasn't much else to say to that. He didn't suppose Emma went around talking about her brother to random clients. "Anyway." He held up the bottle of water. "I was just getting this."

"Okay." The woman stared at him for a moment, then glided out of the house with the cake in front of her.

James watched her blonde hair ripple behind her, then let out a breath. There was something about her that raised a whole lot of questions in his head. Like why had she seemed surprised when he'd asked about the necklace? And why hadn't she acknowledged that he'd come to her rescue—twice—at the store? Not that he wanted to be thanked or anything. But she'd hugged him there and now acted like she'd never seen him before.

He ignored the tiny spikes of warmth that went through him at the memory of the hug. It didn't matter how much she intrigued him; she had a kid. And even if he had been willing to risk his heart on a woman again, he'd never risk it on another child.

More Hope Springs Books

While the books in the Hope Springs series are linked, each is a complete romance featuring a different couple and can be read in any order. Wondering whose story is whose? Here's a helpful list:

Not Until Christmas (Ethan & Ariana)

Not Until Forever (Sophie & Spencer)

Not Until This Moment (Jared & Peyton)

Not Until You (Nate & Violet)

Not Until Us (Dan & Jade)

Not Until Christmas Morning (Leah & Austin)

Not Until This Day (Tyler & Isabel)

Not Until Someday (Grace & Levi)

Not Until Now (Cam & Kayla)

Not Until Then (Bethany & James)

Not Until The End (Emma & Owen)

And Don't Miss the River Falls Series

Featuring the Calvano family in the small town of River Falls, nestled in the Smoky Mountains of Tennessee.

Pieces of Forever (Joseph & Ava)

Songs of Home (Lydia & Liam)

Memories of the Heart (Simeon & Abigail)

Whispers of Truth (Benjamin & Abigail)

Want to know when my next book releases?

You can follow me on Amazon to be the first to know when my next book releases! Just visit amazon.com/author/valeriembodden and click the follow button.

Acknowledgements

At the risk of sounding like a broken record in the acknowledgements sections of my books, I have to say once again that none of this would be possible without the support of several amazing people and one amazing God. To God goes all the glory for this book—and every book I write. But this book, more than any other, has challenged me and stretched me. For so long, I felt like I was going in circles and not quite sure what this story needed to be. I still don't know exactly how it all came together in the end, but I am so grateful that it did—and all I can say is God is good! I thank him every day for the privilege of getting to write books that share his love. And what a love it is! A love so great that he forgives us not seven times, not seventy-seven, not seventy times seven, but endlessly. He takes all our sins away and makes us "whiter than snow." And for that, I give my greatest thanks.

I also thank God for giving me an incredibly supportive husband who reminded me through all those days when I didn't know where this story was going—and when I may have whined a little too much about that—that God has given me this incredible blessing of getting to do what I love (and even on the hardest days, I love it) and to share God's love through it. So thank you, Josh, for giving me chocolate and flowers (isn't he the sweetest?) and making me laugh and listening to me talk about people who only existed in my mind for so long. And thank you also for sharing in the adventure of this life with me. I know that neither of us imagined in that flurry of "yeses" and "I wills" on our wedding day that the journey would be quite so winding—or quite so amazing!

And as long as I'm thanking God, I have to thank him for the four wonderful children he has blessed me with. I think there's a little touch of each of them in Ruby—from her mismatched clothes and spunky attitude to her heart-melting hugs and childlike faith. What a rich source of inspiration you four are—and what a blessing that I get to encourage you each day to use your very unique gifts to God's glory.

At the time of writing these acknowledgements, I haven't had a chance to see my parents, sister, in-laws, or extended family much in the past year—and yet, they have all continued to support and encourage me on this journey, and for that I thank each of them.

And to my incredible advance reader team: Every time I finish a book, I get so excited to send it out to you. But as soon as I hit send, that excitement turns to fear as I wait to hear what you think of the story. Thankfully, you never keep me waiting long! And you are so generous in your support, feedback, and encouragement! You are a major part of this journey, and I thank you from the bottom of my heart for always being there. A special thanks to: KAM0846, Trista Heuer, Vickie, Debra Payne, Patty Bohuslav, Lincoln Clark, S. Golinger, Gary Richards, Bonny D. Rambarran, Jeanne Olynick, Terri C., C. Beck, Teresa, Michelle M., Diana Austin, Trudy, Nancy Fudge, Melanie A. Tate, VSW, Lindy, Mary S., Rhondia Cannon, Teresa Martin, Tonya C., Ellie McClure, Maxine Barber, Daphne Goodman, Sherry L. Deatrick, Paula Hurdle, Becky Collins, Darla Knutzen, Jenny M., Sandy H., Kelly Wickham, Vickie Escalante, Ann Diener, Lynn Sell, Jaime Fipp, Ilona, Becky C., Jan Truhler, Jenny Kilgallen, Sarah Rooney, Chinye, Shelia Garrison, and Connie Gandy.

And I know I've said this before, but I hope you don't get tired of hearing it: Thank you to you, for spending your time in Hope Springs. I hope your visit has been delightful and that you leave filled with a reminder of the true hope that is found only in our Lord and Savior, Jesus Christ.

About the Author

Valerie M. Bodden has three great loves: Jesus, her family, and books. And chocolate (okay, four great loves). She is living out her happily ever after with her high-school-sweetheart-turned-husband and their four children. Her life wouldn't make a terribly exciting book, as it has a happy beginning and middle, and someday when she goes to her heavenly home, it will have a happy end.

She was born and raised in Wisconsin but recently moved with her family to Texas, where they're all getting used to the heat (she doesn't miss the snow even a little bit, though the rest of the family does) and saying y'all instead of you guys.

Valerie writes emotion-filled Christian fiction that weaves real-life problems, real-life people, and real-life faith. Her characters may (okay, will) experience some heartache along the way, but she will always give them a happy ending.

Feel free to stop by www.valeriembodden.com to say hi. She loves visitors! And while you're there, you can sign up for your free story.

Made in United States
Orlando, FL
24 April 2024